WINTHROP MANOR

WINTHROP MANOR

*A Novel of Great Love
During the Great War*

MARY CHRISTIAN PAYNE

Sign up for the newsletter to get news, updates
and new release info from Mary Christian Payne:

www.TCKPublishing.com/mary

Published by TCK Publishing

www.TCKPublishing.com

Get discounts and special deals on books at

www.tckpublishing.com/bookdeals

To Jim
The Only Dream I Ever Had That Never Died in The Face of Reality

1

❧❦

In early May 1914, James "Win" Bradley, Viscount Winterdale cantered his magnificent stallion, Black Orchid, along a lane that passed in front of a small cottage owned by a gentleman named Roderick Chambers. The cottage sat outside of Winthrop-on-Hart, a little village in Hampshire, England. The quaint hamlet, surrounded by rolling countryside, rested in a lovely valley near the river Hart, from which the village took its name. Though his Christian name was James, no one in his memory had ever used that name when speaking to him. His more distant acquaintances called him Winterdale, and closer friends, along with family, always knew him as Win.

It was a spectacular day, with the bluest sky and trees that were filling with young leaves, turning the surroundings into a green, misty veil. Win was feeling on top of the world—it was wonderful to be young, free, and unencumbered. As his horse ran rapidly 'round a curve in the road, he spotted a woman standing in front of the cottage he had seen from a distance. She appeared to be a fetching young lady who was pruning roses on an arch over the gate leading to the cottage. She wore a simple, ankle-length frock printed with violets and a wide-brimmed sunhat adorned with lavender ribbon.

Win glanced towards her, and she looked up, her attention no doubt drawn by the sound of hoof-beats. Pulling on the reins, he came to an abrupt halt. He dismounted. The young lady removed her gardening gloves and moved rather timidly towards the white-picket fence. Win secured Black

Orchid to the hitching post outside the gate, and he began to stride in the girl's direction. He studied her closely as they approached each other. Drawing nearer, he was astounded to find that he had apparently stumbled upon a young lady who appeared to be uniquely impressive, in the midst of what was primarily sheep-herding country. Her hair was chestnut -coloured, and it reached her shoulders. She had as fine a complexion as he had ever seen, with a definite pale-pink luminosity on her high cheekbones. Win was particularly taken with her eyes. They were vivid blue, topped with straight, dark brows and matching long lashes. She was taller than average, with a minuscule silhouette and a tiny waistline, which contributed to an overall impression of willowy delicacy.

"What a splendid stallion," she exclaimed, leaning against the fence, her curls stirring a bit in the breeze.

He wasn't surprised to note that her voice was as lovely as her other attributes. She reached up and brushed a strand of hair from her eyes.

"What is his name?" she asked.

"Black Orchid. I've just brought him over from Ireland. I plan to race him at Ascot in June. He holds an outstanding pedigree." Win paused. Reaching across the fence, he took hold of her hand.

"Forgive me. I should introduce myself," he said, smiling broadly. "My name is James Bradley. Actually, my given name is James. But I've always been known as either Winterdale or Win. My father is the Earl of Winthrop, and I am officially known as The Viscount Winterdale. My acquaintances call me Winterdale, but my close friends and family refer to me as Win. Please, feel free to address me as Win. I thought I was acquainted with most everyone in this area, but I don't recall ever meeting you. Are you new to the region?"

"Yes, Win, I'm rather new to this area," she answered, displaying a sweet, dimpled smile. "My name is Josephine Chambers. My uncle owns this cottage. His name is Roderick Chambers. Since your father is the earl of Winthrop, does your family have a conectioi with the nearby village, Winthrop-on-Hart?"

"Yes, as a matter of fact, it takes its name from our home, Winthrop Manor, a holding just outside Winthrop-on-Hart. The village was a coach stopover during Henry VIII's reign. It's said he was a guest at Winthrop Manor many times."

She placed her hand over her heart, drawing in a deep breath. "Oh, how truly grand," she said. "Of course, I'm well aware of England's marvellous history, but having spent the majority of my life in London, I've not had the occasion to view a home such as yours. I would think you'd be overcome by its yesteryear surroundings."

As she spoke, Win noticed a certain shyness revealing itself. A soft blush coloured her face. He also detected a habit of listening intently when he spoke to her. Her eyes opened wide, and she obviously concentrated on every word he spoke. Clearly, she was genuinely interested in what he was telling her. He suspected she was unaware that her lack of sophistication added immensely to her charm. He would have wagered she hadn't been introduced to society and was probably unfamiliar with the world of nobility.

Miss Josephine Chambers vastly intrigued Win. After twenty-four years as an elite gentleman among the gentry, he was weary of aristocratic ladies, to whom he felt obligated to pay homage, especially when the London Season came 'round. London then became an enormous marriage market. The Season, as every member of the nobility knew, consisted of endless balls, debutante parties, punting on the Thames, tennis matches, and countless nights of frivolous nonsense, during which each young lady tried to outdo the others with jewels, diamond tiaras, and superb gowns, all designed to attract a titled husband. Josephine gave the impression she was unaware of young ladies who counted the number of gentleman they might charm until settling upon the one who offered the most magnificent manor house and most distinguished title. She probably didn't know that such a goal was the aim of most gentlewomen who participated in the Season. Nor did he believe she'd ever learned the art of attempting to deceive a suitor, by batting her eyelashes and whispering perfectly rehearsed lines on warm summer nights in country house gardens amidst roses and lilacs. Apparently, she was a simple girl with simple ways.

How delightful, thought Win. *She seems so shy and innocent.* "Josephine... I think you have a very pretty name. Where were you raised, since you aren't from this region?"

"I lived in Nottinghill, London, before moving here. My father was quite a well-respected architect. He designed some magnificent structures and had a world-wide reputation. My parents were on their way to New York City when they were lost on the Titanic. He was to meet with a gentleman regarding a plan to construct a large building there. Both Mother and Father died after the ship collided with the iceberg. Needless to say, my life changed enormously following their deaths."

"I imagine so," Win exclaimed. "What a disastrous tragedy. That wasn't such a terribly long time ago. When did the ship go down? Wasn't it April of 1912? That was only a bit over two years ago! I'm so sorry to hear of the wretched loss you sustained." He *did* feel true sadness upon hearing that an enormous catastrophe had happened to her at such a young age.

"Thank you, Win. That's very charitable of you. I appreciate your kind words. I was devastated, of course. To be honest, if such a horrid thing had to be, I'm grateful they perished together. They loved each other so dearly. I cannot imagine one of them having to continue living without the other."

"Have you brothers or sisters?" Win asked.

"Yes, one brother. His name is Andrew. He's just graduated Oxford and will be a barrister. I have no doubt he'll do very well. He has found employment in London. I came to live with my Uncle Roderick after my parents' death. I stayed in the City and continued my studies with my governess until our house was sold. It's awfully different, living in the country, but I *do* like it. However, it still seems quite new." She was silent for a moment. "So, Win, do you spent a lot of your time in the country, or do you find yourself bored here?"

"I spend a fair amount of time here. I'm the eldest son, so I'm expected to take over the reins at Winthrop Manor someday. There's a lot to learn about overseeing such a large holding. Nevertheless, I *do* enjoy a trip to London on occasion. My family owns a townhouse in Mayfair. I find that a few days there is enough. I actually prefer the countryside. I'm not terribly taken with City life. I've learned most London ladies in your age range are seeking a wealthy husband with a title."

"Oh, goodness. I can't imagine." She frowned. "I do think your home sounds lovely. Nevertheless, I wouldn't marry you just because you live in an old, historic mansion."

Win roared with laughter. "Josephine, that was a delightful comment. I don't recall mentioning marriage, but your outlook is superb. It does appear that London graced you with sound sense and poise."

She blushed more profoundly. "If I have sense and poise, it's due to my upbringing. My parents were keen on keeping a proper balance in one's life. Money was not their primary interest."

"Have you participated in a London Season?" he asked.

"Oh, no. That isn't for me. I have no title, and, to be honest, I find the entire affaire rather ridiculous. I think it's a silly bit of nonsense," she answered. "London becomes a place I don't care to be during The Season. You described it perfectly. All the girls *are* seeking wealthy husbands. What possible difference can such a thing make? Love is all that should matter, as far as I'm concerned." She paused, clearly in deep thought. Before Win had a chance to respond, she continued. "At any rate, eighteen years is far too young to set up housekeeping and begin to produce children."

"You truly are quite naive, Josephine." He chuckled. "Love has very little to do with marriages among the aristocracy. I'm twenty-four years now, and my parents are beginning to badger me about finding a bride, but that's a subject upon which I intend to hold firm. I'd prefer a marriage like that which your parents appear to have enjoyed."

"Yes, they had a wonderful marriage. I agree with your outlook," she responded. "After all, living day in and day out with another person would surely be terrible if no love existed between them."

"I shall hold out as long as possible, but sooner or later, there will be no more arguing about the matter," answered Win. "I'll have to satisfy their wishes and take responsibility as heir to Winthrop Manor. I can only hope that between now and then, I'll be fortunate enough to find a special young lady to be by my side forever. Most of the women I've met during past Seasons have been so impressed with family names. It's nearly unbearable to spend much time with them. As I said, they're primarily seeking a wealthy, titled gentleman. The thought of spending my life with that sort of creature is appalling. However, as the eldest son, it will be my duty to carry on the family name."

What an extremely attractive young lady, Win thought. She was absolutely adorable. Still, in addition to the myriad of other reasons she would never be considered suitable for him, she appeared to be decidedly too young. His parents would never approve of her. Not because of her age, but because she was not of the aristocracy.

"Elisabeth, my sister, will definitely be doing the Season next year. Though I want her to have a splendid time, I don't wish to see her become engaged at an early age. I've never spoken with her about my feelings, but I intend to. She generally sets great store by my opinions."

Josephine smiled. "I'm sure the Season is a most enjoyable time for some young ladies. However, as I said, I wasn't brought up to participate in such fanciful activities. To be sincere, the entire ordeal sounds perfectly wretched to me," she said, frowning.

Win found her honesty refreshing. There was absolutely not one iota of artifice associated with her. This was exactly the sort of lady he hoped to meet one day. Yet, he had to keep reminding himself that she definitely would never meet the standards his parents had set long ago.

2

⁂

The next day, Win arrived again at the Chambers' cottage. This time, there was nobody outside, so he tethered Black Orchid to the post and walked over to the white picketed fence. Then he opened the gate and walked to the front door. He rapped, using the ornamental brass knocker, and the door immediately opened.

"Good day," greeted Win. "My name is Lord Winterdale—Win—and I met your niece here outside your cottage yesterday."

Josephine's uncle nodded. "Yes, Josephine told me about you. It's a pleasure to meet you, my lord."

"Please, call me Win. May I come in?" Win craned his neck to see over the older man's shoulder. "Is Miss Josephine at home?"

"Yes, certainly," answered Roderick with a laugh. "I believe she's in her bedchamber."

"Josephine," he called up the stairway. "We have a visitor. Lord Winterdale—er, *Win* is here to see you. Come downstairs and join us."

Josephine peeked out of the upstairs window in her room and saw Win's horse tied to the post. Looking into the mirror, she pinched her cheeks and bit her lips to give them a little colour. After running a brush through her curls, she dabbed a bit of cologne on her wrists and behind her ears. She was dressed in a rose-coloured lawn dress with long sleeves and a collar trimmed in lace. It was certainly more stylish than that which she'd worn the previous day while gardening. She'd been sitting on a window seat, reading a Jane

Austen novel. The book had caused her to dream of romance among the landed gentry. It brought to mind Lord Winterdale, when, suddenly, her uncle had announced that the gentleman himself was waiting downstairs.

She laid her book on a small table beside the four-poster bed and made her way down the straight flight of stairs to the hallway. There stood Win, dressed in his equestrian attire, gloves and crop in his hands. Her uncle took the items from him, laying them on a chair in the foyer. Win was so astoundingly attractive that Josephine had to take a deep breath before she was able to speak. The day before, she'd been on one side of the fence, and he had been on the other. This time, they were only a few feet apart. He took her hand and kissed it. His hair was tousled, as it had been the previous day, but because she was closer to him now she was able to clearly see the deep-blue colour of his eyes, and the long, dark lashes enhancing them. Everything about him was faultless, even his perfectly shaped mouth. He carried himself with pride, appearing to be one of those men who never had a wrinkle on his collar or cuff. *Every young lady in the county must be mad for him*, she thought.

"I'm so pleased to see you again, Miss Josephine. I made this impetuous stop in hopes of finding you at home."

Josephine could feel her colour rising. "Thank you, Win. It's lovely to see you again, too," she answered.

"I've come to invite you—and your uncle and brother, of course—to Winthrop Manor for a dinner party. I checked my calendar and believe the last Saturday evening in July would be a perfect time for you to pay a visit to Winthrop Manor. That's the twenty-fifth. My parents were delighted to hear I'd met new neighbours, and my sister was thrilled to learn of another young lady in the vicinity. My parents think Oliver, my brother, will be happy to hear of the dinner gathering. They believe he'll attend. Everyone was saddened to hear about the loss of your parents. I've taken the liberty of inviting a chum of mine from Oxford. He now lives in a quaint village known as Cloverhill, not far from Winthrop-on-Hart. He's the village physician over there. I've a suspicion Elisabeth has more than a slight interest in him. However, it wouldn't be appropriate for her to invite him to Winthrop Manor without others present. It should be a rather charming party. My family is most anxious to meet you."

"What do you think, Uncle? Could we attend this dinner party?" Josephine longed to say yes, but she had no idea how her uncle would feel about such a thing. Win's invitation came as quite a surprise.

"I don't see any harm in going," Uncle Roderick said. "Of course, we'll need to take a trip to London before then—you'll need a new gown for such an occasion—but there should be plenty of time for that."

"Yes…the last weekend in July allows time for such a journey. I do hope you find this satisfactory. I wish it could be scheduled earlier, but I'll be awfully busy training for Ascot until then," Win told them.

"Perfect in every way," answered Uncle Roderick.

"I'm very honoured by your invitation, Win," Josephine said. "I didn't have in mind we'd be privileged enough to be invited to dine at your historic home. May I ask what the proper attire for such an occasion will be?"

"Generally, for a small dinner party, we would dress formally. Not terribly ostentatious, though. Simple evening wear. I feel certain that Mother and Elisabeth will wear floor-length frocks, but tiara's and jewels would be over-doing it."

Josephine breathed a sigh of relief, for she owned neither a tiara nor jewels. She *did* have her mother's lovely pearls and a diamond hairpin. Uncle Roderick would need a new suit of evening wear. Josephine was grateful, for he seldom spent money on himself.

"I'm so glad to hear you'll be available," Win continued. "I look forward to it immensely. It should be a jolly time for all of us."

"It's so nice of you to think of us. It's been ever so long since I've attended a dinner party. Elisabeth and I are the exact same age. I hope we'll find a lot in common," exclaimed Josephine. "I suppose she'll be taking part in the 1915 Season, since by then she'll have turned eighteen. Is that correct?"

"Yes. That's the plan. Perhaps you'll change your mind by then and choose to participate, as well."

"Ah, but you forget, my lord. I would need a sponsor who's a member of the aristocracy. I truly don't believe I would fit in at all, and I'm not of the gentry. As I said yesterday," she continued, "I'm not at all certain I wish to participate in such lengthy and fanciful affaires. I'm beginning to realise that I'm very much a country girl."

"Yes, but a very poised and polished one," he answered. Turning to her uncle, Win said, "Roderick, I've included a widowed lady in your age range, who lives in a cottage near our home. Her name is Lucille Kenslow. I hope you have no objection."

"No. Certainly not. It will give me an opportunity to brush off my manners. It's been quite some time since I've been a lady's escort. There was a period when I was quite the man about town, back in my university days, but since moving to the country, I've undoubtedly lost my touch. I was married for many years, but I lost my wife to illness several years ago."

"I believe you'll like Lucy." Win smiled as he patted Uncle Roderick on the shoulder. "Well, I need to spend a considerable amount of time with Black Orchid today, so I'd better be on my way. However, I'll be happy to stop for a visit again sometime soon."

"That would be lovely," Josephine replied. Then she turned to her uncle. "When will we be taking our journey to London?"

"Today is Wednesday. I'll arrange for a trip beginning Friday. We'll undoubtedly spend several days. Perhaps even a week."

Josephine was astonished. *A week in London will cost a pretty penny.* Roderick was known to be very careful about where he spent his assets and how much he spent. The bewilderment must have shown on her face, for he chuckled.

"The time has come for you to join other young ladies your age in becoming a fashionable lass," he told her. "The time always arrives when young ladies wish to be belles of the ball."

"I scarcely think I'll ever be that." Josephine's cheeks grew warm. "Nevertheless, a few new garments would be very enlivening."

"I believe you have yourself underrated, Miss Josephine," said Win. "You'll be the belle of many balls, I can assure you."

3

After Win left, Josephine turned to Uncle Roderick. "Oh, Uncle. How exciting! I never dreamed we'd be invited for something so special. Do you think I'll fit in with this sort of group?"

"Absolutely, Josephine. Why ever wouldn't you? You're a remarkably fetching young lady. We can't have you spending the rest of your days clipping roses and reading Jane Austen. You've reached the age where more exciting things lie in store for you."

"Is that why you're willing to make the journey to London?" she asked, following her uncle as he went into their neat but tiny kitchen.

"Yes, certainly. You'll soon turn eighteen, my dear. Your parent's left quite a large sum of money in trust for you, and also for Andrew. It will be soon be yours." Uncle Roderick poured them each a cup of tea. "I want to see you have the best life has to offer. I know what your parents' wishes were. You've a level head on your shoulders, and you belong in elite society. The money is there for you to have whatever you desire."

Josephine accepted the china teacup from her uncle, and the two of them sat at the little kitchen table.

"Oh, my, how grand!" she said. "My life is going to change a great deal, isn't it?"

"Yes, undoubtedly. But it's important for you to continue making wise choices. You've been raised properly and taught all of the etiquette one needs to take a place among the best people in society. Just remember you have a sweet, naive way about you. Don't lose it, Josephine. Be yourself. You needn't try to change into somebody else."

Josephine added a couple sugar cubes to her tea and stirred the steaming liquid. "No, never, Uncle." She shook her head. "I have no intention of reinventing myself. My fondest dream is to have a small, quaint cottage with a thatched roof and a charming garden. I have no desire to find myself in a position where I oversee a great house like Winthrop Manor. I don't wish for a title. I'd like to meet a very special man and fall in love. Then all I want is a simple, quiet life."

"My dearest Josephine. Your dream is a realistic one. Nevertheless, there's the possibility of other options. I have a suspicion Lord Winterdale has more than a passing interest in you. What would you do if that were the case?" He raised an inquiring brow and took a sip of his tea.

"Uncle! Lord Winterdale and me? I can't conceive of such a thing. I'm sure his parents have much loftier goals for him. I can't picture myself as part of his world. Of course, he's extremely attractive and seems very kind." She sighed, thinking about just how very handsome he was. "What lady wouldn't find him desirable? But marriages must be more than love matches in his world. One's cultural upbringing matters greatly. I haven't the faintest knowledge required to oversee a great house like Winthrop Manor."

"You've never even seen it. Make your decisions based upon reality. You may find yourself very comfortable and at ease in his home."

Josephine gave a very unladylike snort. "That, dear uncle, is a dream, I fear. The elite classes are very susceptible to inflexibility and are prone to look down upon others who weren't raised in their aristocratic world. I think I'll find myself ill at ease in such a setting, where I suspect few if any other women would accept me. Even when I was younger, it was obvious who was raised in an aristocratic setting and who wasn't. The gentry are prone to look down upon those of us who've had refined but simple upbringings."

"Well, let's attend the dinner at Winthrop Manor, and see how you feel after that. You have every attribute a member of the gentry would be seeking. I should feel proud to show you off in any setting. I suspect the same is true of Lord Winterdale. At any rate, we're speculating about a future that may never become reality. First and foremost, I want you to marry for love. You're well-placed, financially, and will want for nothing. You needn't seek a husband on the basis of a need for security."

Josephine nodded. "I'm very happy to hear that, Uncle, for I cannot imagine marrying a man I didn't love with all of my heart, and he must feel the same way about me." Now that she knew she needn't worry about money, she felt much better about her future. Regardless of what happened, she needn't rush into anything.

"You'll have to excuse me now, Josephine." Uncle Roderick pushed back his chair and got to his feet. "I'm going to write a letter to Andrew and tell him of our invitation. I think it would be wonderful if he could find time to make a short journey home. We see him so seldom."

Josephine finished her tea, then stood to clean up their dirty cups. "Yes, do try to persuade him to pay us a visit. I would love to have him by my side when we visit Winthrop Manor."

"I'll do my best. In the meantime, you must decide which garments you're going to take with you on our journey to London."

"Tell Andrew he can meet us in London and make the journey back to Winthrop-on-Hart with us," Josephine said.

On Friday evening, Josephine and her uncle found themselves ensconced in a splendid, two-bedroom suite at the Savoy Hotel in London. Josephine had never been exposed to such luxury. The baths were marble with mahogany-encased tubs, and the walls were covered with white silk fabric. The down mattresses were covered in linen sheets and pale-green silk comforters, which matched the draperies that fell to the floor in lovely puddles of shimmering silk.

Josephine felt as though she'd been transported to another land. She couldn't imagine Uncle Roderick having been willing to pay the exorbitant price for such overwhelming luxury. She'd not enquired as to where they'd be staying, for she was all but certain his answer would be the name of a small, out-of-the-way hotel in a not-very-upscale neighbourhood. When he gave the name of the Savoy Hotel to the taxicab driver, she'd had to stifle a gasp. Never having been inside that spectacular London hotel, she certainly had heard a lot about it. Andrew had once told her of having taken tea there with a favourite young lady he'd wished to impress.

After they unpacked their rather unsophisticated belongings, they made their way to the River Room, where Josephine ate the best dinner she'd ever consumed in her life. She ordered Beef Wellington, and Uncle Roderick had Lobster Newberg, nearly causing Josephine to topple her off the chair.

"Uncle, I've never known you to spend so freely before. I'm completely astounded. Andrew will never believe we're partaking of such grandeur," Josephine exclaimed.

"I thought it time for you to begin to learn about the finer things in life. I've chosen to subsist on a very simple budget, but that doesn't mean I don't have the means to live differently. I've spent very little of the money I've earned through the years. Believe it or not, I have a great amount invested. I own thousands of acres around Winthrop-on-Hart."

Josephine sat up straight in her chair, eyes wide in surprise. "Surely, you cannot be serious? I had no idea, Uncle. You've always been so frugal."

Suddenly, Josephine felt a tap on her shoulder. She turned to see her beloved brother Andrew leaning over to give her a kiss on the cheek.

"Andrew! You darling. How did you know where we were? I'm so thrilled to see you. It's been forever. Are you staying long?"

"Slow down, baby sister. Uncle wrote and told me your plans. Surely you didn't think I'd miss out on something so grand?" Andrew pulled out a chair and joined them at the table. "I assume you're here in London to find a gown, Josephine. I'm here on the same mission. I've outgrown my evening attire, so it's time to refurbish my wardrobe. I'll be searching for employment soon, so I've a need for suits, shirts, ties, and the like. This occasion at the neighbour's near the village sounds rather upscale. How did you meet the son of an earl, Josephine?"

"I was clipping my roses when he came riding by on a spectacular horse. He's recently had it sent from Ireland, with plans to run him at the Ascot races in June. We chatted, and the next thing I knew, he was inviting Uncle and me, and you, if you're able to make the journey, to a lovely dinner party at his parents' home, Winthrop Manor."

"What a bit of luck! Will there be other guests?"

"Oh, yes. His sister, Elisabeth, a brother, Oliver, a widowed neighbor lady, and a chum of his from school who is now a physician. I don't know if he's included anybody else. It sounds divine." Josephine glanced at her brother. "Would you like to order something? Are you hungry?"

Andrew nodded toward her plate. "That looks delicious, but I've already eaten. However, a good cup of coffee would be nice." He smiled. "So what is the required dress for this function?"

"Formal, but not too flamboyant. I'm sure you know, after three years at Oxford." She looked to her uncle. "Uncle Roderick, do you think you could go find our server and ask for a cup of coffee for Andrew?"

Uncle Roderick nodded and excused himself.

"I have a good idea about what's required," Andrew said in response to Josephine's inquiry.

Uncle Roderick returned a few seconds later and resumed his seat. "Your coffee will be here momentarily. I ordered an entire pot, just in case."

Andrew nodded. "Thank you." He grinned at his uncle. "Roderick, you're looking fine. Are you here on a shopping expedition, too?"

"Yes, I haven't anything suitable to wear. Of course, I'm also here to keep a keen eye on our Josephine. This will be her first formal gown. I know she'll look spectacular, but I'm going to make certain she chooses correctly."

"I rang your office and was surprised to hear you were at the Savoy," Andrew said. "I expected a much more down-market hotel. What's become of you?"

Roderick laughed. "Oh, in my younger days, I was well-versed in the best of everything. However, I was always a country boy at heart. Thelma adored the English countryside, so we made our home there. It's been a good life, and a profitable one."

"Profitable?" echoed Andrew. "For some reason, I've never thought of it in those terms."

"I've invested in a great amount of land over the years. Thousands of acres, in fact. Now, land costs have increased enormously. I suspect someday there will be a building boom in many of the rural areas. My land should be of enormous value when that time arrives. It's already increased many times over."

Their server arrived, carrying a large tray that held a coffee carafe and three large mugs. She set the carafe and mugs on the table, and then she filled each cup three-quarters of the way full. "There's cream and sugar," she said, nodding toward the sterling silver set on the table. "Will there be anything else?"

Roderick looked around the table before addressing the woman. "No, I think we're fine for now. Thank you."

The server nodded and walked away.

Andrew picked up the conversation again. "I had no idea you had accumulated so much wealth, Uncle. You've always lived so thriftily."

"Yes. I explained all of this to Josephine. I have, indeed, been prudent when it came to finances. Then, of course, your parents left that substantial estate for the two of you. Josephine will get her portion when she turns twenty-on, as you did, Andrew. So the time has come when you'll both be taking control of your own money. I believe I've taught both of you to be properly cautious with your funds." Uncle Roderick paused and took a sip of his coffee. He nodded at Andrew. "Naturally, I expect that you'll want to live an up-scale life, but I truly do hope you won't be too extravagant. Your trust has grown into a fortune. It can be of more value if you're sensible. Invest wisely, and find a suitable wife who understands your motivations. Live in a fine style, Andrew, but always keep in mind that emergency's do occur in life. I want you to be prepared in case of dire need."

"I understand what you're saying. My father taught me well, and so have you. You needn't have concern. I know the value of a pound. I'm also very much in favour of charity."

"Yes, I am, too." Josephine nodded. She chewed and swallowed another bite of the delicious, tender beef, then said. "So many people aren't as fortunate as we are."

"Yes, I've known young men at Oxford who haven't a clue as to how much it costs to live. I don't ever intend to become one of those people. Josephine," Andrew said, pointing at her with his teaspoon, "you have to have the same vigilance."

"I agree, but I had no idea that we were in such an exceptional financial situation. Don't worry, I have no intentions of squandering my inheritance on foolishness. I've never been one to fritter away money. Just because I've now learned that I'm worth substantially more than I ever dreamed, that doesn't mean I intend to forget its importance. You needn't worry about me. I have a very levelheaded side when it comes to finances. Uncle knows my dreams. They're really quite modest. A charming cottage surrounded with flowers in a lovely wooded setting. I assume I'll marry someday, but I'm in no hurry for that step. Finding a gentleman who shares my dreams probably won't be easy, especially if he should learn that I'm in a healthy financial position. There are a lot of men who can't be trusted. I'm well aware of that."

"Good for you, sister. Promise me that when that day comes, you'll talk everything over with me. I want to make certain you find the love you deserve."

4

⁓

Roderick and Josephine were up early. They met Andrew in the dining room of the elaborate hotel, where they enjoyed a splendid breakfast. Then they went their separate ways. Andrew was interested in clothing he needed for himself, while Roderick and Josephine were on a mission to find the perfect gown for the Lord and Lady Winthrops' dinner party.

Since it was the end of the era of the elaborate fashion etiquette that placed the late Edwardian women in a different world to the rest of the twentieth century, Roderick and Josephine encountered many new designs. They discovered that the 1913 hemlines were beginning a slow rise, showing a little of the ankle. Josephine was somewhat shocked by such a change. Yet, over and over, the shop associate's assured her that she would be in proper style if she selected such a frock. Another change was that the waistlines were raised, creating a column-like empire line to the gown, which they called *directoire*, made famous by a French designer named Paul Poiret. Nearly all of the evening dresses consisted of gowns constructed of soft fabrics, such as chiffon or fine silk, and they all had open necklines and short sleeves.

Josephine found precisely the dress she was dreaming of at a small boutique near Harrods's. Its colour was pale pink, and it was layered with soft organza over silk. Its description matched that of the new look, with short, puffed sleeves and an empire waistline, but there was also beautiful pleating on the bodice, decorated with lovely lace. The moment she saw it, she knew it was the gown for her. The sales associate recommended matching silk slippers and white gloves. She had not been presented to the king and queen and had no wish to do so, but because she was very near age eighteen, she would wear her hair in an up-do.

Grecian styling had been introduced, which took the hair to the back of the head. It had been a usual style in 1913, but Josephine had never tried it. Many women had begun to have what were known as permanent waves, but Josephine had no need for artificial curls. Her own hair was abundant and absolutely natural with lavish curls, chestnut in colour with lovely streaks of lighter and darker strands, which, Josephine knew, many other women would have given a fortune to have possessed.

After she'd found her perfect frock for the party, Uncle Roderick also urged her to purchase some other lovely day dresses, cashmere chemises, and a new coat, as well as several pair of suitable shoes for the arrival of winter.

Then the two found their way to the menswear department at Harrods's, where Roderick was outfitted in proper evening wear for the Winthrops' party. Josephine convinced her uncle that it was time for him to add to his daytime wardrobe, and since he now had men who did the actual labor on his land, he had no need for the rather seedy apparel that comprised his wardrobe. He chose a multitude of shirts, a gray cashmere suit, and several Norfolk jackets for hunting and leisure. Naturally, shoes, gloves, and hats were added. When the day was over, they were both enormously worn out. Their feet hurt, and both were tired from trying on clothing all day.

Arriving back at the hotel, they were happy to see they hadn't missed afternoon tea. They went to their rooms, had a wash, and then returned to the lobby. A sumptuous tea was being served. They'd eaten nothing since breakfast, so they filled their plates with a selection of freshly prepared finger sandwiches, including cucumber, egg mayonnaise with cress, smoked salmon with cream cheese, and coronation chicken. There were also warm scones with clotted cream and curd, and a variety of cakes and pastries. Naturally, they had their choice of a wonderful range of teas. The feast ended with a selection of delicious sweets, including pain au chocolate, peanut butter fudge, sugar plums, and truffles.

Josephine couldn't remember ever being so filled with such delicacies.

Andrew came in while they were enjoying the high tea, and he sat down on a soft, comfortable sofa. They invited him to join them. He answered by telling them that he would sit a moment but had enjoyed a hearty luncheon with a chum from school. Their merchandise was being delivered, after necessary alterations, so Roderick and Josephine described, as best they could, the purchases they'd made. Andrew, too, had added several suits, shirts, and ties, as well as the obligatory evening wear. They discussed attending the theater that evening, but each was too tired to think of going out again.

Later in the evening, they developed an appetite again and rang room service for sandwiches. Then they took to their chambers for a much-needed lie-down.

Josephine fell asleep and dreamed about her lovely, new gown, the Winthrops' dinner, and Win.

It was a dream-filled week. Although Josephine and Andrew had made London their home all of the years their parents had lived, they were both older and appreciated it so much more. They visited places they'd seen before but viewed them through new eyes. Josephine, in particular, appreciated the antiquity of the city. She didn't even remember having visited Westminster Cathedral, although she had, and they even took journeys to such places as Hampton Court, the incredible estate that Henry VIII had built for his second wife, Ann Boleyn. They hired a car and driver, exploring charming villages in the Cotswold Hills, lunched at the ancient Lygon Arms Hotel, and continued on to Bath, Salisbury, and ancient, mysterious Stonehenge. They even discovered small villages they'd never heard of before. Josephine vowed to return to Awre-With-Blakeley, a wonderfully pleasant hamlet that contained an old church dating to before the year 1000.

Their last night in London, they attended *The Girl on the Film*, which had opened its London production at the Gaiety Theater on April fifth. Each of them had forgotten how much they enjoyed live drama. Andrew made the return trip to Hampshire with them. He'd completed his classes and would begin his new employment soon. Of course, that meant a return to London. He had been fortunate in having been offered an apprenticeship reading law with one of the City's top solicitor's firms.

5

⚚

When the train arrived at the Winthrop-on-Hart station, it felt good to be back in familiar territory. Their train pulled into the small station, and Josephine turned to her brother.

"How strange it is that a person adapts so quickly to unfamiliar surroundings. Here I am, having spent the majority of my life in London, yet home is now the village and countryside surrounding Uncle Roderick's farm."

"Yes. I know," replied Andrew. "I feel the same way. I, too, have grown to love the English countryside. If my Oxford degree wasn't in law, I'd be sorely tempted to spend the rest of my days in this area. However, employment opportunities would be nearly impossible to find."

"You might, at least, give it a try, Andrew." Roderick spoke up. "If I remember correctly, your chum Tom Drew, the physician, thought he would have to settle in London. Yet, he was able to find an elderly physician who was ready to sell his practice in Winthrop-on-Hart. You never know unless you try."

"I just may do that, Uncle," Andrew answered, as he helped to gather their valises and various boxes of purchases. "However, it seems a bit rude to accept an offer, as I've done, and then turn around and tell them I don't want it."

Although automobiles were being manufactured in various parts of the world, for the most part, horses and carriages were still the prevalent mode of transportation for short distances. Trains were the means most people used to journey from small villages with larger cities. Win owned a Rolls Royce and, of course, the family had a chauffeur. Uncle **Roderick** still depended on the horse and carriage, although he did have his new automobile. Still, it had been easier for her uncle to wire the stationmaster and request that a car and driver be made available for them. The automobile was waiting at the station. They were laden with much more baggage than they'd had upon leaving. The lovely gown, intended for the dinner party, lay carefully in a large box, protected by tissue-paper. Each of the men had their own purchases, too, but the hired driver assisted in getting everything organized in the vehicle. Josephine wondered if she would be seeing Win again before the anticipated dinner. He'd said he would be riding Black Orchid each day until Ascot, which took place during the first four days of June. It was now late May, so the event was rapidly approaching.

As it turned out, Josephine did not see Win again between the end of May and the start of the Ascot race the beginning of June. Although she kept busy, visiting with her brother and tending to her garden, she couldn't help but think about her handsome neighbor and wonder when she might set eyes on him next.

Win was, of course, not actually riding Black Orchid in the world-renowned race. He had a well-respected jockey doing the honours for him, as he sat in one of the enclosures, though not the Royal space. He did sit with several of the well-known owners of many other horses running that day. 1913 was a special year at Ascot, because it was the year that the Ascot Authority Act was initiated, which continued to manage the racecourse for many years thereafter.

Black Orchid did not perform well, but the excitement of owning a thoroughbred running in the most prestigious race in all of Great Britain was a thrill in itself.

Win normally would have stayed at Ascot for at least two nights, chatting with other owners, but he was in a most anxious mood to return to Winthrop Manor. His primary interest was stopping to see Josephine, whom he knew was supposed to have returned from London by then. He left Black Orchid in the stables at Ascot, to be transported back to Winthrop Manor the next day. Then he boarded the first train and headed for Winthrop-on-Hart. He slept on the train, and when he woke, he saw that the sun was up and the sky a lovely blue. The Rolls was waiting to carry him to the manor. He gathered his belongings and heartily greeted the family's carriage driver, David Carlisle.

"Not such good luck at the race, eh, my lord?"

"No, but it wasn't a great surprise. There were some incredible thoroughbreds in the running. It was a strange race. A man ran out onto the track, causing the horse in the lead to fall, and *Prince Palatine*, who also won last year's gold cup, won again."

As the auto moved along, the two continued to chat.

"I thought perhaps you'd stay a few extra days. We were surprised to receive your wire, saying you'd be returning this morn."

"Yes, I saw no reason to stay. I have tasks that need the be completed here, and I'm also thinking of making this a special day. The weather is so wonderful. I've not had a picnic in ever so long, and I intend to ask Vera if she could put together a nice basket for me." Vera Whitaker, their cook, made the most delicious chicken, and Win hoped she had some available to add to the picnic basket.

"Have you someone special to picnic with, sir?"

"Yes, as a matter of fact, I do. At least, I hope so. I intend to have a wash, change into a fresh shirt and britches, and then try to make arrangements."

"Don't tell me you've found a young lady in this vicinity whom you fancy?"

"Quite possibly, David." Win laughed. "We shall see."

The Rolls Royce turned into the gravelled drive leading to the manor Win would one day own. The house dated to the fifteenth century, although some parts were a good deal older. It had the common manor house arrangement, with the central hall edged by rooms in gabled wings at each end. The large window on the right lit a chapel. The hall had a three-story range in succession along the front, with more gables above it, so the overall effect was quite different from that of most medieval manor houses; instead of the usual long roof of the hall, the house presented a fascinating, serrated outline, emphasized by old-style lime wash on the walls. The house had been added to several times over the years, so it was immensely long and expansive.

Win was out of the car in a flash, and David followed with the luggage. Inside, Win's mother was standing at a round, Victorian table sorting through the day's post. When he stepped inside, she looked up. She set aside the envelopes and opened her arms to welcome him home.

"Win! How very good to see you. We were surprised to learn you would be returning so quickly."

Win embraced his mother. "Of course, you know the race results. Not good for my poor Black Orchid but still an exhilarating experience. I decided I'd rather be back here than spend another night at Ascot. I'm going in to visit with Mrs. Whitaker for a moment, and then go upstairs for a wash and change of clothing."

"What on Earth have you to discuss with Mrs. Whitaker?" His mother frowned.

"It's such a glorious day, Mother. I thought a picnic might be nice. I've met a young lady whom I rather fancy. She makes her home with her uncle, and he lives in our area. I intend to find out if she'd like to accompany me."

"Well, this is the first I've heard of a young lady. When and where did you meet?"

"Mother, this is not the first time we've discussed this." Win frowned. "If you recall, I told you about her and her uncle, and they're coming here for a dinner party next month. Surely, you haven't forgotten!"

"Ah, yes…" His mother nodded. "The neighbors you met while out riding that day. However, I certainly don't recall you saying anything at all about having developed an attraction for the girl. Is she from a fine family then?"

"She seems to be. Her parents went down with the Titanic last September, and her uncle, who lives near Winthrop-on-Hart, has taken guardianship of her and her brother, Andrew."

"Have they education? Has she been presented?"

"Oh, Mother, I don't know every detail about her." Win hedged. He had no intention of having this discussion with his mother right now. "We've only chatted a couple of times. No, she has not done the Presentation, as she just recently turned eighteen. I do know Andrew, her brother, has finished at Oxford. Her name is Josephine Chambers. She's a charming young lady."

"You know your father and I would much prefer that you choose a lady of fine breeding and first-rate manners. I hope she meets those requirements.

Your father and I will look forward to making this young lady's acquaintance. You must remember your heritage and the responsibilities that lay ahead of you. The lady you someday choose as a bride will also become a countess."

"Good god, Mother. I didn't say I intended to marry her. I find her enchanting and would like to know her better. You and Father will have an opportunity to meet her next month. I think we should keep the dinner party small but smart. I've invited Josephine, her brother Andrew, Elisabeth, of course, my friend's uncle, Roderick Chambers, Tom Drew, the young physician from Cloverhill who's a chum of mine from Oxford, and perhaps the widow Mrs. Kenslow from over on Lilac Lane. Those are all neighbors. It would be nice to know them better. What is your opinion?"

"I've no objection to your proposal. Have you chosen an exact date?"

"It's really entirely up to you, Mother, but I thought perhaps rather soon. Perhaps the last Saturday in July if you haven't anything else planned."

"It sounds fine as far as I'm concerned. I haven't anything on the calendar during that time. Of course, you'll want a full course, won't you, darling? Although these people are mostly strangers, I always like to make a nice impression."

"Yes, Mother. I've already mentioned the possibility of a social evening of this sort to Josephine and her uncle, telling them it wouldn't be ostentatiously formal. Of course, evening wear for the men and dinner gowns for the ladies. Does that suit you?"

"Yes. I see no reason for jewels and the like. I don't know these people, and I certainly don't wish for them to feel out of place."

"Thank you, Mother. I'm going to have a chat with Vera about today's picnic, but I'll also mention the dinner party."

Win turned and walked down the stairs to the first level, where the kitchen was located. Vera was standing at the sink with her back to him, polishing silver. She had been with their family for nearly fifty years, since she was eighteen years of age. Since the day of his birth, she had been devoted to him. She'd always referred to him as Jay, from the moment she'd first laid eyes upon him. When asked why she called him Jay instead of James or Jimmy or even Win, Vera forever said it was it was because there had been a young man in her neighbourhood, while growing up, whose name had been James, but everyone had adopted the name Jay for him.

Vera loved Oliver, Win's younger brother, too, but there had never been any question that Win, as the eldest son, was the apple of her eye. She often said she hoped to live long enough to see him married and settled with his own son, ensuring that the family line would continue at Winthrop Manor. Win thought the world of Vera, too. His earliest memories were filled with her sweet, plump face, asking if he would like a batch of biscuits, cookies, or a chocolate cake. While he had been at Oxford, she'd sent boxes of his favourite sugar cookies and wrote long, difficult to comprehend letters, since her grammar and English skills could have used improvement.

"Good morning, Mrs. Whitaker. You look like you're busy this fine day. Doesn't Radcliffe usually do that sort of thing?" Win asked, pointing to the silver coffee pot Vera was polishing. Radcliffe was the family's butler.

Mrs. Whitaker turned. "Oh, I do whatever strikes my fancy, Jay. You know that. This seemed like a pretty morning to tackle such a chore. I'm sorry your horse didn't take first at Ascot. I followed the race in the newspaper. Perhaps next year you'll have better luck. Can I prepare something for you to eat?"

"I really never thought I'd win at Ascot. It was pleasant to be there and to see the crowds of people dressed in their finery. Thank you for asking if I'm hungry, but no. I had something else in mind if I won't be interrupting your polishing task."

"Whatever you need or want, I'll be most happy to oblige. What can I do for you?" Vera asked.

"I've decided on a picnic, because it's truly such a spectacular day. I have a companion whom I intend to invite. Would it be a hardship to ask if you might prepare a basket for me? It would require the usual items. Finger sandwiches, possibly some fruit, perhaps various kinds of cheeses, a loaf of French Bread, and, naturally, a bottle of fine wine? A white Chardonnay, I should think. And if you happen to have any of your amazing chicken, you could add some of that, too."

"That would be no problem whatsoever. Perhaps also a sweet of some sort? I have some petit-fours left from yesterday's tea. Shall I include them?"

"Marvellous. You're a gem, Mrs. Whitaker."

"Will you be wanting this prepared at any certain time?" she asked.

"I'm going to have a wash and change of clothing. After that, I'll be ready to set out for what I hope will be a splendid picnic. Will that allow adequate time?"

"Certainly. The basket will be ready when you're prepared to leave. Can you tell me approximately the number of picnic guests? I'll have a better idea about how much to prepare."

"Oh, certainly. There will only be two of us. You will, of course, include plates, glasses, silverware, and napkins?"

"Jay, my dear, when have I ever prepared something of this sort without including proper utensils?" she responded.

"I know. I was only making an attempt to get a rise out of you," James replied, laughing.

"Well, you've failed, as always. Now, dash on out of here, and let me get on with the task you've assigned me." She took the cloth she was using to polish silver and swatted it at him.

"Thanks again. You're a marvel. Oh, and before I leave, I also want to mention that we've a small dinner party planned for the last Saturday in July. There should be eight people present, although I've not spoken with all of them yet. Nonetheless, I suspect everyone will be able to attend. I leave the bill of fare up to you. I do wish a full course menu, but it's not to be over-the-top fancy. I'm sure you can imagine what I have in mind."

"I understand completely. Now, hasten on your way," she answered, moving her hands in a shooing motion. "I certainly have spoiled you from day one, Master Jay. I wonder what you'd do without me?"

Win smiled. "I don't even want to think about that, Mrs. Whitaker. Someday, when I marry, Mother and Father will move to the dower house, and God only knows where Oliver will be off to, but you must promise you'll always be here to look after me."

"Never fear. You had better make certain you choose a proper wife. That will be my primary concern."

"Have no fear," he answered merrily. "I'll make certain to obtain your approval."

With that, Win trotted back up the stairway and continued to the third level, where his own suite was located. Entering the bathroom, he shed his clothing and ran a tub of water. He soaped his hair well, to rid himself of equine odor. When he emerged, he felt like a new man. He padded to the cupboard and extracted a pristine, starched white shirt and gray, casual trousers. When he'd completed dressing, he looked first-rate. He added a dab of men's cologne and combed his hair into its usual style, parted on one side and allowed to fall across the opposite eyebrow.

He moved back down the stairway to the kitchen. There, just as promised, was a lovely, wicker basket, filled with every delicacy he'd requested, including the cold chicken. He gave Mrs. Whitaker a quick kiss on the cheek, causing a blush to form on her chubby cheeks.

"You seem to be in fine fettle today, my handsome Jay. I do hope whoever you're sharing this picnic with deserves you."

"The question, Mrs. Whitaker, is whether or not I deserve her," he said. Would Josephine find him handsome? He certainly hoped so…

"There isn't a person in this land who wouldn't deserve you. I'll trust your good judgment."

He thanked her profusely once again and then called for David to bring the carriage 'round.

In no time at all, Win arrived at the Chambers Cottage. He asked David to wait while he rushed rather quickly to the front door, where he rapped twice. Josephine answered. Although it had been but a couple weeks since he'd last laid eyes upon her, she seemed to be even more appealing than the first time they'd met. Her hair was styled in an upsweep, with chestnut ringlets framing her face. Her cheeks were glowing, giving the appearance that she might have been out in the sunshine.

"Win!" she cried delightedly. "I didn't expect you. I thought you were still at Ascot. I read the newspapers, and I'm awfully sorry Black Orchid didn't do particularly well."

"Oh, that… It makes no difference. I wanted very much to get back to Hampshire."

"Really? I would have thought Royal Ascot terribly exciting."

"Yes, quite, but I had other things on my mind. I took an early train back from Ascot, and I've already been to my home and had a wash. Now, I'm fully prepared to ask if you'd like to accompany me on a picnic. It's such a splendid day. I've had our cook pack a sumptuous array of food for such an outing. I do hope you're able to say yes. I shall be very disappointed if you're unable to come with me."

"Oh, what a lovely idea. I don't believe I've ever had the pleasure of a picnic. That's amazing, isn't it? Picnics aren't so much a done thing in London. Not frequently, anyway. Nevertheless, what about attire? I'm not certain I have anything appropriate." Josephine glanced down at the dress she wore.

"What you're wearing at the moment is absolutely ideal."

She was clad in a white lawn dress. The gown had wrist-length sleeves and a high collar, and it was most becoming on her, especially with her hair swept up on the top of her head in its mass of ringlets.

"Are you certain it's appropriate? I truly do want to go. Shall I fetch a hat or a bonnet?" She glanced over her shoulder. "It will only take me a moment."

"Only if you're worried that the sun might burn your lovely skin. I think you'll be fine. I know of a spot with a very large, old elm. It will provide wonderful shade if the sun should grow brighter."

"I was outside earlier, tending my roses. The sun was heavenly. I think I'll pass on wearing a hat or bonnet. You've surprised me so. I never dreamed I'd be seeing you today, let alone accompanying you on a picnic."

"I'm absolutely delighted you're able to go. I took a great chance asking Mrs. Whitaker, our cook, to prepare the luncheon. I don't know what I'd have done if you hadn't been home or had made other arrangements this afternoon."

"I can't think of any arrangements I wouldn't have changed to accompany you today," Josephine answered.

"Well, then, we're remarkably fortunate, aren't we? Shouldn't we tell your uncle of your plans? Of course, Andrew is welcome to come along with us, too." Secretly, Win hoped Andrew wouldn't be available. His primary desire was to spend the afternoon with Josephine.

"Andrew has gone to look at some livestock with Uncle Roderick. I'll leave a note, so they know I haven't disappeared into thin air. Come into the house. I'll find some notepaper and an ink pen. It should only take a moment."

This was only the second time Win had been inside the Chambers' home. While Josephine went in search of paper and pen, Win took a look around. It was quite traditional, in the sense that a staircase went straight upwards from the front foyer, and a parlour was on the right of the entryway. To the left was a dining room. The floors were golden wood planks, and there was a fireplace in both the parlour and the dining room. While nothing about it resembled Winthrop Manor, it was an enchanting cottage and very homey. Josephine returned from the parlour, carrying a notepad and an ink pen. He watched as she wrote in lovely, feminine script, admiring her delicate fingers and oval-shaped nails.

"There. That's done. Is there anything else I should fetch?" she asked, as she set her note propped up on the foyer table.

"We have every possible thing. All I need is you."

She blushed and smiled sweetly at him. "What a lovely thing to say," she answered.

"I mean every word of it. Come. David is waiting with our carriage. I'll have him drive to the spot I have in mind, and we can tell him what time he should come back to collect us."

They exited the front doorway, making their way to the Rolls Royce. David opened the door for Josephine and Win, and he introduced her to his long-time driver. They drove straight to an even narrower dirt lane, and then continued on for about a mile. There were no houses to be seen in any direction. The landscape was magnificent. Large, rolling hills and cliffs lined one side of the lane, and the other was dotted with soft green grass and thickets of trees.

"Ah, here we are, David. It's been so long since we've visited this spot. I hoped we hadn't forgotten the location."

"No, my lord. I remember it well. You used to come here as a child with your brother, sister and parents on picnics. You're right, though. It has been a long spell."

David drove back down the narrow lane, and Win and Josephine were left to proceed with their picnic. opened the wicker basket, removing a sizable, red-and-white checkered blanket. He spread it under the enormous elm tree he'd remembered, although it was much larger now. The ground beneath it was quite level, particularly on the side where roots didn't create an uneven surface. Then Win took out plates, glassware, linen napkins, and utensils, leaving the marvelous cuisine prepared by Mrs. Whittaker in the basket until they were ready to eat. He also removed two crystal wineglasses and a bottle of French, white wine. He poured each of them a glass.

6

Josephine settled herself comfortably on the blanket, spreading her white lawn skirt over her legs. Win rolled up the sleeves on his white linen shirt and opened the collar. It wasn't a particularly hot day, but it was only eleven o'clock in the morning. A slight breeze moved the leaves on the trees from time to time. It simply couldn't have been a more splendid setting. Win leaned his back against the large tree trunk. He began to reminisce about the times he and his family had visited the locale when he was a small boy.

"Time goes so rapidly, doesn't it? It seems like yesterday that Oliver, Elisabeth, and I were chasing one another round this tree, playing hide and seek, while my parents prepared a picnic lunch. I even remember once making an attempt to climb one of the lower branches. But I fell, and my mother wasn't having any more of it. Fortunately, nothing was broken. Mother is the disciplinarian in our home. My father is quite reserved but has an even temperament. Mother makes most of the more important decisions." He smiled ruefully.

"Do you believe she would approve of me?" asked Josephine, as she sipped her wine. It was a bold question, but her concern about his parents' approval had been of paramount importance, almost from the moment they'd met.

"I can't see any reason why she wouldn't. Why do you ask?" He scowled.

"Because it's discernible that I'm not of the aristocracy. No matter how successful my father was or how well-known, let's be honest, Win. In the eyes of someone with a title, my family was in trade. I'm wise enough to know that people of the gentry consider those who are in trade to be utterly beneath them. I am well-acquainted with many young ladies who have attended fine ladies' boarding schools. I'm well aware of those who are and are not considered of superior birthright."

"I won't lie, Josephine. Yes, there are certainly those in the upper classes who harbour such attitudes. Hopefully, my family isn't among them. To be honest, we've never discussed the topic. This is the twentieth century. Things are changing. I'd be most surprised if my parents aren't completely charmed by you. I can't imagine who wouldn't be."

"That's kind of you. I'd like to believe it's true, but I have doubts. I suppose we'll find out when the dinner party you have planned comes 'round. Does it particularly matter, anyway?"

"Does what particularly matter?"

He tipped his head to one side. He honestly didn't seem to understand that without his parents' approval, any future relationship between him and her would be fraught with troubles.

"Whether your parents are charmed by me or consider me beneath you in class."

"It matters to me," he responded.

"Why"? Josephine felt a little shiver. She'd been somewhat apprehensive about asking such a question. Would he think she was fishing for compliments?

"Because I care a lot about you," he said in a straightforward manner.

It was the answer she had hoped for, but her naturally wary nature made her uncertain as to whether she was reading too much into his reply.

"Thank you. I care a lot about you, too, but we need to be realistic. We scarcely know each other, Win, and we truly do come from different worlds."

"Josephine, please do stop this talk about different worlds. Thus far, I've not felt the least bit of discomfort in what you label 'your world'. I hope you aren't uncomfortable with me. I don't see any evidence that you are. We're simply two people, not terribly far apart in age, who apparently share a very similar world-view. No matter what our lives have been like leading up to this moment. I'm normally a very indecisive person. Yet, when I see something I know is right for me, there's never any question in my mind. I truly believe I could search the world over and never find another lady like you."

"I don't know what to say. You're going to be an earl someday, overseeing a vast, magnificent estate. We're like chalk and cheese. I said that to my uncle just the other night. He was speculating on the possibility of a relationship between you and me. I cannot imagine ever being a part of your world."

"My world is not so very different from yours. The question isn't whether you can imagine living in my world. Could you imagine living without me in *your* world?"

His question stunned her. "To be honest, I've never given such an idea much thought. That would be so foreign to me. I've always been content with my way of life. I absolutely cannot abide phoniness or contrived behaviour. I haven't met your family, so I can't comment upon them, specifically. However, in general, most every person I've ever met, even briefly, who claims the upper realms of society as their heritage has behaved quite unnaturally. Affected, artificial behaviour. I've always been loath to spend even one second thinking about spending my life amongst such people. I realise I'm moving far ahead of myself, Win. You've said or done nothing to indicate a desire to have me spend my life with your sort. I am only trying to make clear to you my feelings about artificiality in general." Josephine surprised herself with her extremely open, forthright words.

"Do I personally assume an artificial or contrived air of superiority?" he asked.

"No, of course not. If you did, I can assure you I wouldn't be here today. From what I know of you, you're very down-to-earth and genuine. Please don't think I'm criticising you. It isn't you. It's the sort of people who make up the nobility or aristocracy or gentry—however you wish to phrase it."

While speaking to Win, Josephine couldn't keep from thinking that he seemed to be everything a lady could wish for. *He is so extraordinarily handsome,* she thought. *I love his dark hair, his blue eyes, and his tall, slender build.*

He also didn't attempt to camouflage the fact that he was sensible, kind, and honest. He'd undoubtedly make any woman a joyful bride. Still, he was twenty-four years and had already taken part in several Seasons, all to no avail. Apparently, he'd ceased attending parties and balls, and the only activity that attracted him was horse racing. Ascot was obviously his favourite. She was keenly aware that the race drew attention from the Royals and was a "must do" on the debutante calendar each year.

Win was the son of an earl. It would never do for Josephine to allow herself to think he might be attracted to her. He would *have* to marry within his class. She was very well-schooled regarding the conventions regarding the class structure in Great Britain. Her father had been successful, and neither she nor Andrew had ever wanted for anything, but she knew she would not be welcome in his world.

She felt a slight wave of gloominess come over her. The class system in England seemed very unfair. Even though two people might find themselves highly drawn to each other, those who were members of the aristocracy, such as Win's parents, would never tolerate their son marrying a commoner.

Josephine had always been told she was a habitually sunny, light-hearted young lady. Yet, the customs of her country caused her some irritation. *How silly*, she thought. *He may be handsome and debonair, but my life can never be entwined with his, simply because he was born into a different class than I was.*

"I completely understand what you're saying," Win said, interrupting her thoughts. "I also find it difficult to tolerate such behaviour. But what you don't seem to realise, my dear Josephine, is the fact that our similar views on this issue is one of the primary things I believe we have in common. All of my life, I've found myself in the midst of exactly the sort of people you describe. Not every single person assumes such attributes, but I freely admit that a large number do. That's precisely what I found so utterly refreshing about you from the moment we met. How else to say it except that you're very real, authentic, and unfeigned? I don't believe you've a pretentious bone in your body. That is an endearing and unusual attribute."

Josephine shifted on the blanket. "Your complimentary words are very nice to hear. Nevertheless, if your parents don't feel I live up to the expectations of the lady they anticipate their son spending his life with…?"

"Then I believe I'd have to try very hard to convince them they're wrong. If I found it impossible to do so, I'd be very inclined toward leaving the lifestyle you speak of and choosing a different path."

"Surely, you can't be serious? That would be mad," she uttered, gazing at him in shocked surprise.

"Not so very. What is the purpose of living if one isn't able to spend their life with the person whom they adore?"

"You may believe that now, but years later, when middle age arrives and the bloom is off the rose, how can you be certain you wouldn't regret such an enormous decision? It would literally mean relinquishing your birthright."

"Yes, because I know what sort of man I am. If I make up my mind, I don't change it. You haven't answered my question yet."

"Which question?" She frowned, unable to recall what he'd asked her.

"Whether you would be willing to allow your mind to follow in the same direction that mine already has?"

"Oh, Win. I don't know. You frighten me a little. I'm not certain I'm familiar with the feelings you speak about so blithely. You have some years on me. I've just turned eighteen. To be completely honest, I've never even been kissed."

Win set down his empty wineglass. "Come here, you lovely creature," he murmured, as he opened his arms wide. "Come see what your first kiss will be like."

In an instant, she found herself in his arms. Next, his soft, tender lips met hers, and the warm embrace intensified. Win held her more tightly, and the kiss became deeper. Her hair stirred a bit when a soft breeze moved through the leaves. It seemed that the birds were singing more vibrantly. Had her hearing become more intense? She felt as though she'd been transported to another place. All of the questions worrying her moments before had vanished when his lips met hers. She wished she could stay in his powerful, strong arms forever. The kiss ended, and she rested her head against his chest.

"Is this what it feels like to be in love?" she whispered.

"Yes, Josephine. It is for me, and from the way you responded to my kiss, I believe it is for you, too."

Once again, their lips met, only with more passion. He bent her back on the blanket, and they lay close together. Josephine had no more doubts. Her heart was racing. The feeling was tangible. *Oh, god,* she thought, *don't ever let this end.* Before the passion went any further, Win released her from his arms.

"We must cease this for the moment. It would be sinful for us to continue in this vein, although, I have to say I've never wanted a woman more in my life."

"Would that be so wicked, when we know that we love each other?" asked Josephine. She really had no idea about such things.

"Not so terribly wicked, my darling, but certainly immoral. I don't ever want to be accused of taking advantage of your youth and inexperience. The correct time will come, my sweet Josephine."

"When will that be?" she asked.

"I don't know the answer to that question yet. However, I suspect I shall very soon." He sat up and helped her to rise, as well.

"Oh, Win. I do find you so attractive, so good and kind. But do you understand that all I've really ever wanted out of life is my dream cottage with a breathtaking English garden and lots of pets?"

"That's a young girl's dream. You have no idea yet what you *really* want from life. I can promise you that your wishes will change considerably as you mature."

"You told me when we first met, on the day you rode by Uncle Roderick's cottage, that I had a very good head on my shoulders."

"Yes. You do. Nonetheless, you haven't experienced very much of life yet. A pretty cottage with a fine garden really is a young girl's fancy. Eventually, you'll wish for more. Don't you want children of your own and a husband?"

Josephine thought for a moment and then nodded. "I suppose so. I've really never thought much about it. As I told you, I'd never been kissed until you held me a moment ago."

"And you enjoyed it, didn't you?"

"Yes. I can't deny that. However, isn't it possible that's merely physical attraction? My mother taught me about such things."

"We'll leave it at that for now, Josephine." He smiled. "I believe, as we grow to know each other better, your feelings will also grow."

"Perhaps," she answered, looking down at the ground.

There was a pause in their conversation. In her heart, she would have loved to kiss him once more. Nonetheless, she was wise enough to know that it would be dangerous to allow feelings to override common sense. She looked up.

"Win, don't you think we had better eat the delicious lunch your cook has prepared? It would be horrible to waste it, and surely, her feelings would be hurt."

"Of course. I'd never do anything to hurt Mrs. Whitaker. She's been with our family forever. You'll meet her," he continued as he reached to unpack the various delicacies the cook had prepared. "Ah, she's provided a marvellous variety of food. Here, Josephine. Look. I hope you're hungry. There's enough here to feed an army."

"I *am* hungry, but good grief. I don't think there's any way we can consume all of that."

"Then we'll save what's left. You can take it back to your uncle and Andrew."

"That's a fine idea." She smiled.

They tucked into the food and finished the bottle of white wine. While eating, they chatted, but Josephine didn't allow the conversation to stray back into uncharted territory. After they finished their lunch, Win returned the leftovers to the basket. He reserved them in one container, so Josephine might take it back to her uncle's cottage.

"I see David with the car, driving toward us," said Win. "Time seems to have flown."

"Yes. It most certainly has. It's been a wonderful day, Win. I'll never forget it. After all, I received my very first kiss." She smiled, and her cheeks grew warm.

7

❧❧

Weeks passed, and Win made certain he and Josephine saw each other often. She always woke thinking about what to wear, since she expected he would be coming by the cottage after sunset. They went on outings to Winthrop-on-Hart, rode horseback together, played games in the Chambers' parlour, and chatted on the porch while fireflies flew about, night after night. Roderick thought Win was splendid, and he never failed to give permission for an activity the couple planned.

Josephine was thrilled to find that Andrew thought highly of Win, but she also sensed that he worried about her meeting the elder Winthrops. She suspected he thought her lack of a title would shadow the encounter. She had a feeling the Winthrops would not be any different from other aristocratic families she'd known. Josephine had never heard of such a family warmly welcoming someone with her heritage into their charmed circle.

One afternoon, she found Andrew in the parlor and decided to join him. She sat down, hoping to discuss any concerns her brother might have, thinking it best to clear the air.

"Andrew, I suspect you're worried about my growing relationship with Win. It must be apparent that I'm head-over-heels for the man. Surely, you can understand why. He's an extraordinary chap. I believe you think the world of him. Nevertheless, I also think you're of the opinion that I'm about to have my heart broken."

"Because you know as well as I do that the likelihood of his family accepting you is slim to none." Despite his words, Andrew's tone was gentle. "Aristocratic families just don't want a son marrying beneath himself. Particularly an eldest son. If he ever did so, there would be a scandal the likes of which you've never imagined."

Josephine shook her head. "No, Andrew. Win has assured me that his family will welcome me with open arms."

"I think you and Win are living in a fantasy world. That isn't the way things happen in real life. Not in Great Britain's present class system. Hopefully, someday, this nonsense will end. Until such time, we have to learn to deal with present reality."

"Don't you believe he cares for me? Do you think he's only trifling with me?"

Andrew shook his head. He leaned forward and took her hand. "I am certain he cares very much for you. Very much. I don't think he's trifling with you. However, feelings between a man and a woman are insignificant when it comes to a member of his class choosing a bride from a family like ours."

"What in blazes is the matter with our family? I know we're not titled. But I suspect our father had as much money as they do."

"That's quite possibly true, Josie." Andrew was the only person in the world she allowed to call her Josie. "But money isn't the only thing dividing you. I'm certain you know what I'm saying. I just don't want to see you hurt," he responded.

"I don't believe Win would ever hurt me," she answered. She stiffened her spine and squared her shoulders, certain of her feelings on that score.

"Not on purpose, no. However, I must to tell you, I've made a few subtle inquiries from people I've met in this area. Each person I've spoken to says that the Lord Winthrop is a splendid fellow. But the caveat is always that the Lady Winthrop is a shrew. Also, from what I've learned, the Lady Winthrop is the one who wears the pants in the family. If she doesn't find you suitable, the Lord Winthrop will stand with her."

"Who has told you this? They're probably insanely envious of the fact that Win and I have become very attached."

"No, Josie. These are people I know well. Chums of mine from Oxford. They also come from titled families. One is the son of a baronet. Another is the son of a duke. They wouldn't lie to me."

"Well, I don't give a whit. Win says his family will love me and welcome me with open arms."

"You haven't spoken to him about marriage, have you?"

"No, of course not. That would be highly improper, without my having met his family. Nonetheless, he's hinted at it. He doesn't show the least concern regarding my lack of a title. In fact, I spoke to him about that very thing. It was the day we went on the picnic. He said that if his parents didn't approve of me, he would leave them and allow his brother, Oliver, to inherit."

"That would be unheard of. Win is not thinking rationally. Love will do that to a man. All I'm asking is that you be cautious. Don't expect a miracle when we attend the dinner Win has planned. If his parents have any suspicion that your relationship is serious, I suspect they'll instruct him to end it immediately."

"All right, Andrew," Josephine answered with a sigh. "But I'm telling you, I am quite certain Win isn't the sort of person to have said the things he has to me if he were the least bit concerned about his parents' approval."

Andrew patted her on the shoulder. "All right, dear heart. I want so much for you to be happy. We'll leave it for now. Please, don't hesitate, though, to come to me with any concerns you have. Will you promise that?"

"Yes, Andrew, I promise that," she responded with a loving smile. She gave him a kiss on the cheek. "It will all work out though. I'm certain of it."

8

⚮

Win was once again on the Chambers' doorstep that very evening. She had invited him for dinner, and he had readily accepted. After a lovely meal, he asked if she would like to take a stroll outside.

"It's such a pretty night. The moon is very bright in the sky, and the stars are gorgeous. It's warm and breezy but not overly windy."

"Yes. Of course, Win. I'd love to. Do I need to fetch my wrap?" She turned, as if to go back up the stairway.

"No, I don't believe so. It's the end of June, after all. Come. I think you'll be fine."

They left the cottage, and Win gave her his arm. They walked down the cobblestone pathway and out to the gravel road. "Oh, it *is* a gorgeous night," he exclaimed. "Just look at the stars. There always seem to be more of them in the country. The City lights obscure them. Shall we walk down the lane to the gazebo behind your cottage? I've always loved gazebos. They remind me of the Victorian age."

Win took hold of her hand, and they strolled to the wooden structure, and for the first time, Win was free with his emotions, telling her how he'd never believed he would meet such an incomparable young lady. He actually told her he believed he had fallen over-the-moon in love with her. As they sat in the lovely, Victorian gazebo, he reached into his pocket and presented her with a velvet jeweler's box.

Josephine's heart felt as though it had reached an incredible speed. It was quite obvious what a box of such a size, obviously from a jeweler's, would contain. All of her life she'd dreamed of such a moment, but she had never in a million years thought Win would present her with an engagement ring before she had even met his family. Everything was moving so quickly. She knew that generally couples slowly grew to know each other before they reached the point she and Win had arrived at. Of course, there was absolutely no question in her mind as to whether or not she would say yes to the question she was sure he was going to ask. They had already generally agreed that sooner or later this time would arrive. Still, she found herself stunned when he presented the tiny, velvet box to her.

This was the moment every girl waited for. From the time she had been a young lady, only in her early teens, she had wondered what it would be like when it actually came to pass. Who would the man be? Would he be the handsome gentleman she'd always dreamed about? Would she be over-the-moon in love with him? Would she truly be ready to commit to spending the entire rest of her life with him? Interestingly, none of those questions now went through her mind. He was, indeed, all of those things and more. Nevertheless, the most important thing on her mind was that she was so completely in love with him, she could believe people actually *did* give their hearts away, as she was about to do with Win.

Even though she very well knew what to expect when she opened it, she knew she should act a bit coy.

"What in the world is this?" she exclaimed, composing her features into a puzzled expression. Her heart was beating very quickly.

"What do you suppose it is, my beautiful Josephine? Open it and see."

Josephine gingerly opened the box. Inside lay a magnificent ring, a large ruby completely surrounded by brilliant diamonds. Josephine was stunned. "Does this signify what I think it does?" she asked, her voice trembling.

"Indeed, it does, my pet. I'm asking you to be my wife. I don't want to rush you, and we can wait until you're a little older, if you wish, but I have no intention of letting you escape. I'll never find anyone like you again."

"But, Win, are you absolutely certain? I've not met your family yet. I still have grave apprehensions about what their feelings will be toward me. I don't believe it's even proper for me to accept such a gift, nor your proposal, without our having done this in a proper manner."

"Josephine, the only thing worrying me is whether or not you love me. If you do and we're both certain of our feelings, then please, darling, accept this ring, which will seal the fact that we intend to become man and wife."

"Oh, Win, of course, I love you. How could I not? You're every girl's dream of the perfect man. Nevertheless, I'm frightened."

He took her hand. "What's frightening you?"

"I've told you, over and over. Basically, I don't want to have my heart broken. And it will be if your family disapproves of me."

"How my parents feel is completely irrelevant to me. I do hope they welcome you warmly, as they should. However, if for some foolish reason they don't, it will have no influence upon my feelings. I love you. I am mad for you. Please, please,

let's put this talk of parental approval out of the conversation. This is my life, sweetheart. I'm going to live it with whomever I wish. You are the lady I wish to spend it with. Leave the rest of to me. Trust me, Josephine. I will never break your heart. That is a solemn promise. Make me the happiest man in all England, Josephine. Make me the happiest man in all the world. You know we're absolutely made for each other."

"Do you really believe that, Win? We come from such different backgrounds. I know you don't want to hear me say that again, but I can't help it. It frightens me."

"Josephine, only one thing matters. Do you or do you not love me?" He squeezed her hand and gazed intently into her eyes.

Josephine could no longer hold back her feelings. "Win, I *do* love you, too. So much. Of course, I want to be your bride." She paused. "All right. I'll trust you to know what's right. However, I have to add one caveat."

"What, my pet?" Win asked.

"I don't believe I should wear this ring until after I've met your parents the night of the dinner at Winthrop Manor.

"All right. But please keep it in a safe place. Plan to bring it with you the night of our dinner. After we've spoken to my parents, you can slip it on your finger. Do you agree?"

Josephine nodded. "Yes, my darling. We will do this as you wish."

Win took her into his arms again. They kissed long and hard. It was like nothing she'd ever encountered. She truly was head over heels in love.

9

❧❧

The last Saturday in July arrived. Josephine found herself much more nervous than she'd anticipated. Granted, Win was twenty-four years of age and quite mature enough to make his own decisions, but wasn't it simply proper etiquette to introduce the proposed groom's parents to the prospective bride?

Just as these thoughts were running through her mind, she heard hoofbeats come to a stop in front of Uncle Roderick's home. She peeked out the window in her bedchamber and saw that it was Win. After scurrying down the staircase and out the front door, she ran into his arms, just as he'd disengaged from the stirrup. He picked her up from the ground, spinning her 'round.

"Your timing is excellent, my precious Josephine." He laughed and kissed her cheek.

"Oh, Win, I'm so glad you've come. I've been in something of a dither."

"What's troubling you now, darling?"

"All of a sudden, it struck me that we're about to announce our engagement to your parents. I know we've discussed this a dozen times. Nevertheless, I'm really all undone."

"We *have* discussed this a dozen times or more. Please, leave this to me. I don't think they're going to be terribly surprised. I have mentioned you to my mother on numerous occasions and have told her something of your background."

45

"You know as well as I do that men are supposed to introduce their brides-to-be in a much more suitable manner."

"Yes. I know that. I *am* going to introduce you in a very suitable manner. I've told you not to wear the ring until we've announced that we want to marry. You're making too much of this, darling. I intend to make the announcement before the other guests have arrived. We will arrive early and have an opportunity to chat with my parents before they're tied up with other visitors. By the time dinner begins, they'll know we plan to marry. You can wear your ring then. We'll simply enjoy dinner, chat with the other guests, and I intend to formally announce our engagement to everyone then.

"You'll have ample opportunity to meet my sister and chat with my parents. If they voice any objections, I've told you what my reaction will be. If we haven't finished speaking with them by the time the others arrive, after I've taken you back to your uncle's cottage, and everyone else has departed, I will ask to speak with them privately again. Josephine, please believe me. It does not matter what their reaction is. Naturally, I hope they're overjoyed. They're probably expecting something of the sort. I've told you before that I've mentioned you to them often. However, if there is any dissension, I've told you and told you that you will come first."

"All right, but I'm very anxious. I'll make certain Andrew and Uncle Roderick know of our plans. Perhaps that will help to calm me." Changing the subject, Josephine asked, "What is that box you're holding?"

"It's a corsage. An orchid. I wasn't certain about the colour of your gown, so I bought white with a bit of pink streaking through the petals. Will that do?"

Josephine threw her arms around Win's neck, holding him tightly. "Oh, you dear man. No one has ever brought me flowers before, let alone an orchid. My gown is a pale pink. This will look absolutely splendid with it. Especially with the bit of rose streaking through the bloom. You gave me my first kiss. Now, you've brought me my first corsage."

"I wish I could say that you were *my* first kiss. Yet, if I did, you'd know I was lying. After all, I *am* twenty-four. Nevertheless, I can certainly say with no hesitation that you are my first love."

"It doesn't matter. I know that however many kisses you've had before, the one you gave me counted most."

He kissed her sweetly. "I'm glad I make you happy, my pet. I don't ever want you to be sad."

"I cannot imagine being any more beaming than I am at this moment. The day you entered my life, God was smiling down upon me."

"He was smiling on both of us. It was planned from the beginning. I strongly believe we were meant to be together."

"So do I. I knew it the moment I saw you. I feel so utterly blessed."

"How are you wearing your hair tonight? In an upsweep or with all of those delightful chestnut ringlets touching your shoulders?"

"I thought in an upsweep, unless you feel your parents would find that inappropriate because I've never been presented?"

"I can't imagine that. They'll be too mesmerised by your beauty to think of meaningless things like Presentations. Josephine, don't you realise how incredibly stunning you are?"

She blushed. "No one has ever told me that before. Who would have? Other than Andrew and Uncle Roderick, and they don't really count. Remember? You're my first love."

❧

At precisely six-thirty, Win arrived in the Rolls Royce with David in the driver's seat. Naturally, Win and Josephine would sit next to each other in the back. Win rapped gently on the front door of the Chambers' cottage, and Roderick answered the knock immediately. Win entered the foyer.

"Ah, welcome, my lord," said Roderick with a broad smile. "Won't you please come in?"

Win followed Roderick into the parlor and took a seat on the sofa.

"Miss Josephine will be down momentarily," Roderick said. "Is there anything I can get you while you wait? Perhaps a brandy?"

"Thank you, sir, but no. I suspect this is going to be a rather fine evening. There will be a fair amount of alcohol consumed," Win said, chuckling.

"I understand completely. Make yourself comfortable then. I'm sure Josephine won't keep you waiting. She is always charmingly prompt. I've always considered that a good trait in a feminine companion," he added.

"Quite," responded Win. "I can't think of a favourable trait that Josephine lacks. Is Andrew at home?"

"Yes, however, I understand they're both preparing themselves for what they refer to as your 'delightful dinner party'." Roderick smiled. "I believe both decided to take a short lie-down before moving ahead with dressing for the event. Of course, you must have known that Andrew was going to be able to be with you this evening?"

"Oh, yes. Josephine told me. I hope no one is disappointed with the magnitude of this affair. It's really not a grand, formal occasion."

"Perhaps not to you, Lord Winthrop, but to those who make this cottage their home, I believe it has assumed the quality of a first-rate gala."

Win laughed heartily. "Well, I must admit that I, too, find it a rather unique celebration. I hope I'm not speaking out of turn, but I suspect you've already heard the rumour that Miss Josephine and I intend to announce our engagement this evening."

"I can't deny that I've heard whispers confirming that suspicion. I couldn't help but notice the eye-catching ring I've recently seen on the third finger of her left hand. I overheard her telling of her happiness to Andrew. I suppose she's waiting to make the announcement to me, until it's official, and you both have your family's approval. Assuming I'm correct, let me be among the first to tell you of my absolute delight at such incredibly happy news. I've known Josephine from the time she entered the world, and she's always been blessed with the ability to take one's breath away. I must say, I consider you to be the most fortunate of gentlemen."

Win got to his feet. He extended his hand and shook Roderick's.

"I feel like a chap who has just won the gold cup at the Derby. I find her absolutely beyond reproach in every trait imaginable. Thank you for your good wishes. We both believe God meant for us to be together. However, she won't be wearing her ring tonight, not until after we've announced our engagement to my parents. I'm awfully glad that you'll be with us, too."

"Ah… Here comes the much-admired Miss Josephine now," Roderick announced. "Win and I have just been extolling your many virtues, my dear."

Josephine made her way gracefully down the staircase. She was an absolute vision of loveliness, and Win caught his breath when he saw how truly elegant she looked. The dress she'd selected was divine. Her naturally high-coloured cheeks were reminiscent of old, English roses of pale pink luminosity. He couldn't recall ever having seen such a captivating creature. He silently thanked the Lord for having placed her in his life at the exact moment He had. Win couldn't wait to see the look on his mother's and father's faces when they were given their first glimpse of the enchanting and alluring Josephine Chambers. She wore the corsage he had given to her, pinned at the back of her chignon, and it was absolutely true that it couldn't have looked more appealing with the pale-pink gown.

She reached out her hand, and he bent to kiss it.

"My dear," he whispered. "You look bewitchingly mesmerising. I feel as though I'm the most privileged man alive. You might have had any chap you set your cap for, and I'm the lucky fellow you decided to beguile with your charms."

Josephine laughed in a gentle manner. "My darling, Win. It is *you* who might have had your pick of any of the grand ladies of the aristocracy. Why, if you'd been willing to wait only a minuscule time, you might have had Princess Elizabeth."

"She doesn't hold a candle to you." He smiled. "I wouldn't trade you for all of the stars in heaven."

"Goodness. This amiable session of agreeable compliments must end. You'll have me thinking I actually deserve you. To be honest, I'm beside myself with foreboding at the knowledge that I'm about to meet your parents. If they only give a slight bit of kindness, you know, I'll be fine. Nevertheless, while you may think that the royal princess doesn't hold a candle to me, I can assure you that your mother and father will not agree with your assessment. I wonder if you've given any thought to what will take place if they refuse to give us their blessing?"

"Josephine, you know that I have. Why, should that implausible and menacing response occur, I shall marry you at once, with sorrow that they will have missed the joining together of two soul mates who are clearly meant only for each other. So stop your apprehension. They can't help but love you as much I do. Come. Do you have a wrap? It's quite a warm night, and I doubt you'll have need for one. Nor do I suspect rain. If that should happen, we have extra umbrellas at the manor."

"I only need my gloves and my reticule. Am I wearing too much lip rouge? I felt a little was needed to correspond with my gown, but I surely don't want your parents to think I resemble a tart."

Win laughed heartily. "Darling, my sister Elisabeth displays much more lip rouge than you're wearing. In my opinion, the colour is dreadful. It's a scarlet red. So does my mother, for that matter. You look enchanting. Stop this nonsense, and let's be on our way."

"What about Andrew?" she asked. Her expression clearly showed how much she wanted to be certain that her brother would be nearby.

"Andrew knows of our plans," Roderick replied. "He's coming along in a bit. Don't worry. He'll be there. David will return for Andrew, and I intend to accompany him. We will be right behind you, my dear."

Josephine showed her pleasure with a sweet, dimpled smile. "Very good. I need him," she murmured.

Roderick held the door for them. Josephine reached over and squeezed his hand. She loved him so dearly and was completely aware that he understood her anxiety. She prayed the evening would be picture-perfect. She was so glad that Roderick would be following them soon. They settled into the back of the automobile, and David maneuvered it down the lane. The night was lovely with the moon a nearly full orb in the sky above them. Josephine's anxiety eased as she enjoyed the splendour of such an ideal summer night. Could there ever be anything more heartwarming than sitting next to the man you adored, riding along a road that led to the manor house someday meant to be his?

She knew Win loved Winthrop Manor with all his heart, and she had no intention of ever disappointing him with the fear she harboured about living in his opulent mansion. Bearing full responsibility for every standard being met— standards set generations before hers—caused Josephine to be filled with enormous fright, but she'd grown especially good at hiding her fears.

She still secretly clung to her dreams of a thatched-roof cottage and a front garden filled with the prettiest flowers England had to offer. Win promised to build just such a folly, but she knew he considered her romantic wish to be something along the lines of the doll's house, which Marie Antoinette had Louis XVI build for her—a child's plaything. Josephine, on the other hand, would have much preferred to make her dream the actual home for she and Win and to preserve the manor for engaging dinner parties, fancy balls, and the like. Nonetheless, she also knew that such an aspiration was a flight of fancy. She loved Win so astoundingly that she would follow whatever was expected of the wife of a viscount and eventual earl. She herself would be styled as viscountess, which did not inspire her. She was fully aware that someday, when Win himself became an earl, after his father had passed on, she would become a countess. She knew that as time passed, she would adjust, just as her uncle had once predicted.

Most of the time, Josephine would be addressed as Lady Winthrop, which she didn't find quite as distasteful. Still, she found the entire British class system foolishness and would have preferred that they be known as simply Win and Josephine. She'd never in her life liked the idea that because of the accident of one's birth, he or she was considered to be superior to those who weren't as fortunate. However, she managed to put such unpleasant thoughts out of her head, settling back to enjoy the starry, mild night with her beloved Win by her side.

When the auto arrived at its destination, after nearly a half-hour drive, Josephine, who had managed to be totally relaxed and supremely happy, felt a surge of apprehension. They were at Winthrop Manor. She had heard of its history and the love her fiancé had for it from the moment they'd met. The fact was, she had even been aware of his home before then. While her parents were still living, they'd occasionally paid a visit to Winthrop-on-Hart to call on her father's brother. She remembered them telling both Josephine and Andrew about the magnificent and unique manor house situated near the village. It was known as Winthrop Manor, and they had promised to pay a visit, so the children could see it for themselves, but that had never come to pass. With everything else that had transpired, especially their ghastly deaths aboard the Titanic, Josephine had completely wiped her memory of those former promises.

It was painful to recall the happy times she'd shared with her parents, making plans for future outings and envisioning a happy future. They'd been a wonderful family. While her memories were scant, due to the inordinate amount of time the Chambers' spent abroad, leaving the children in care of the nanny, Josephine had always known she was dearly loved. Had her parents lived longer, Josephine knew that she and Andrew would have joined them on their travels, where her father, in particular, would have made certain she and her brother had a sound knowledge of Western European history. That subject had been his true passion. How he would have loved the thought of his daughter living in a house dating to the 1500s. It saddened her to think he would not be present to walk her down the aisle, but she was exceedingly pleased that either Uncle Roderick or her brother would be present to do the honours.

As the carriage wound its way up the curved drive, she could barely make out the outline of the structure. It had grown very dark, and they were still a considerable distance from the house. Still, she could see the extreme length of the home. As they grew closer, she was able to make out the jagged roofline, for which it was well known. The whitewashed limestone stood out in the dark of the night. There was no question that it was supremely picturesque, and stood, as it had for hundreds of years, as a sentinel, guarding the surrounding area like a lonely watchman.

"Do you see why I love the manor, darling?" Win asked.

"Yes, of course. It reminds me of a lookout, acting as custodian for all who approach. Those who live here must feel supremely safe and secure."

"That's a lovely way to express it. When a home has stood as Winthrop Manor has, for over four hundred years, it does present a feeling that no harm can come to anyone protected by its stone walls."

"I'm anxious to view the interior. I can't imagine what a large staff it must require to keep it as pristine as I know it must be."

"We do have a large staff. It will take you awhile to learn all of their names. Don't let it worry you, though. In time, everyone will become very familiar. We've always been exceptionally kind and generous with those who work here, and that's made a significant difference in our ability to retain those who have made their home with us for years."

"Are there any particular names I should familiarize myself with? I do so want to start out on the right foot."

"I would think for the moment the only ones whose names should be committed to memory are Radcliffe, the butler, who's been here since before I entered the world; Mrs. Whittaker, the cook, who prepared our picnic basket and whom I swear could be head chef at the Savoy; and Mrs. Morris, the head housekeeper, who is completely indispensable. There are many others, such as footmen, kitchen helpers, parlour maids, and, of course, outdoor staff—gardeners and the like. Oh, and there is my mother's lady's maid, Janice, and Father's valet, Mr. Robertson. Still, I doubt you'll meet them tonight."

"My goodness, Win. That list in itself is overwhelming. I can't imagine I'll ever remember them all."

"Don't let it concern you. You're only human. Nobody expects perfection. Once we're married, a lady's maid will be added to care for you."

"What does a lady's maid do? Mother never felt the need for one."

"Well, I expect you will. They make certain your wardrobe is in tip-top condition at all times, they'll do your hair, help you select proper gowns for an evening of entertainment, suggest which jewels are appropriate with particular frocks. All of that, and more besides."

"Win, I haven't any jewels to speak of. I do have my mother's pearls, and of course, my gorgeous engagement ring. Nonetheless, I haven't an enormous jewel case or anything of the sort."

He leaned down and kissed her on the cheek as the car came to a halt in front of the entrance to Winthrop Manor. "My pet, you shall have a jewel case, overflowing with fine pieces. Mother will make certain you have the appropriate pieces that have been in the family for generations. You can't even consider being married without a tiara."

"A tiara? I thought only royalty wore such things? Win, I'd feel like a fraud."

"No, darling. You'll simply be moving into the aristocracy, as much as I know you despise the word. You'll get used to all of it. Perhaps, in fact, you can bring a certain authenticity to the entire concept of the class system. Come now. We've arrived. Don't be intimidated. You'll be the most beautiful woman present. Please don't forget. You're my intended wife. That makes you remarkably special."

They stepped out of the carriage, and David gave her his hand. Win followed, holding out his arm, so she could put her own through his. They ascended the few steps that led to the front portico. Immediately, the butler, Radcliffe, opened the door.

"Ah, Radcliffe. It's my pleasure to bring Miss Josephine Chambers to Winthrop Manor."

Radcliffe extended his hand. "It's a distinct pleasure to meet you, Miss Chambers. My lord, I believe your parents are expecting your arrival."

"Good. Thank you, Radcliffe. We'll just go in to see them." Turning to Josephine, Win enquired, "Do you need to have a wash-up before we proceed to the drawing room?"

Win sounded so formal. It wasn't the way he normally spoke. "No, I think I'm just fine," she replied, not certain whether it was the done thing or not.

Win didn't act as though she had committed a faux pas, so she took the arm he offered, and they began a lengthy stroll down a hallway, which she assumed led to the drawing room. Just a few steps beyond, on the right, there was an enormous area with gleaming hardwood floors and a giant fireplace surrounded by an ornately carved mantle, inset with white marble. It was so large that a massive statue could have stood fully erect in its center. The room was decorated in pale blue, with an elegant Persian rug covering a significant portion of the flooring. The rug was primarily blue with other pastel colours, including rose, creme, pistachio green, and pale yellow woven into the pattern. An over-sized, white velvet sofa sat facing the fireplace, with blue, down-filled pillows scattered at each end. Blue Bergere chairs faced each other on either side of the sofa.

In various parts of the room, inviting areas for conversation were clustered about. Three or four chairs sat in circles, facing graceful, marble-topped tea tables. The only objects d'art were crystal. Biscuit barrels, vases, small animals, ashtrays, and royal commemorative items adorned each surface. Josephine loved the room. It was so entirely inviting, and the colours were literally scrumptious. There was a definite impression of cool coziness combined with a sense of upscale ambiance.

10

❧

As they made their entrance, Win's father, the Lord Winthrop, stood in Josephine's honour. The Lady Winthrop, Win's mother, remained seated. Lord Winthrop smiled graciously, stepping forward to his son and Josephine. Reaching toward her, he grasped her hands with his.

"Welcome to Winthrop Manor, Miss Chambers. Win has spoken of you with admiration. We're pleased to have you as a dinner guest."

"Thank you, my lord," Josephine replied. "I'm most honoured to be invited to your lovely home. This room is simply breathtaking." She couldn't help but feel a sense of unease.

"Thank you, my dear. We recently had it renovated. We were rather delighted with the outcome. That sort of task is immense. Nonetheless, when one is a member of the peerage, one's home must reflect such a position," added the Lady Winthrop. She did not seem quite as welcoming as did Win 's father.

Josephine wasn't certain about how to respond. She immediately felt the Lady Winthrop was underscoring the fact that the Winthrop family was far superior to the rest of society. She hated to feel the way she did, but her immediate sensation was one of aversion. She definitely felt antipathy toward the Lady Winthrop. The Lord Winthrop, on the other hand, appeared to be an affable, approachable gentleman.

"Please, sit down," Win's mother continued.

The Lord Winthrop rang a small buzzer embedded in the wall. Radcliffe appeared almost immediately.

"My lord, what may I bring you?" he asked.

"I assume the young people would like something to drink, Radcliffe."

"Miss Chambers, what would you care for?" Radcliffe enquired.

"Perhaps a glass of white wine," she replied. She was sitting very straight with her legs together and directed to her right, as her mother had taught her when she was quite small.

"What would you prefer, my lord Win?" Radcliffe asked.

"I believe scotch with a dash of soda," Win answered. He reached over and patted Josephine's hand.

The Lord and Lady Winthrop had to have noticed his affectionate gesture toward her. The Lady Winthrop scowled.

"Yes, my lord. I'll be back momentarily," answered Radcliffe. "Do you or my lady wish anything more"? He turned his attention toward the Lord and Lady Winthrop.

The Lord Winthrop turned to his wife. "My dear?"

"Yes, I'd like another glass of champagne." Her expression was still definitely rather sour.

"Bring one to me, as well, Radcliffe," added the Lord Winthrop.

"Yes, my lord," the butler responded as he disappeared down the hallway.

The moment Radcliffe left the room, Win's mother turned to him.

"Win," she said, "I need to speak with you for only a moment on a private matter concerning the household." She looked to Win's father. "Will you two please excuse us for a moment?"

Win and his mother walked to a more secluded portion of the room.

"What is it, Mother? You seem a bit distressed. Is something the matter here at Winthrop Manor?" Win asked, concerned by her odd behavior.

"I'm not absolutely certain, Win. However, I want to alert you to something I've recently noticed. Vera has been demonstrating some strange behaviour of late. On some occasions, she seems perfectly sane and sensible. On others, she shows confusion. I'm not quite certain what should be done."

Vera—Mrs. Whitaker—had been responsible for overseeing all kitchen duties for many decades. Win thought of her as a member of the family. He'd never given much thought to her age, but in doing so now, he realised she had to be approaching her late sixties or beyond.

"Have you spoken about this with father?" Win asked, anxious to return to Josephine's side but also concerned about a person he'd known since birth.

"Yes, of course. He feels I'm making too much of this. She is, indeed, growing older. Your father feels her forgetful and sometimes confused moments are nothing more than a sign of declining age. I'm not so certain."

"Why don't you have her see a physician?" Win suggested.

"I've thought about that. However, I don't want to give the impression that we are worried something may be amiss."

"Tom Drew is going to be here tonight for the dinner. He's a physician, you know. Find a time to have him speak privately with Vera. Send him to the kitchens to thank her for a lovely dinner presentation. Let him speak with her for a spell. He'll be able to form an impression, which may help in determining exactly what is going on."

"That's a grand idea, Win. Thank you, dear. I'll do just that. Now, let's rejoin your father and our guest."

Win sat down again beside Josephine, and Radcliffe returned with a silver tray, holding the desired refreshments. Each glass was distributed to its designated owner.

"So…tell us about yourself, Miss Chambers. Win has related the tragedy you suffered in April 1912. We assume that has to be what brought you to our area from London. Is that correct?" Win's father asked.

Josephine was comfortable with the Lord Winthrop. He seemed to be making a true effort to be kind to her and was especially showing interest in her life. After all of the anxiety she'd experienced waiting for this night to arrive, she was finding the Lord Winthrop was a true gentleman. He reminded her of Win. Her darling fiancé had definitely inherited his father's personality. Perhaps all of the things she had worried about with regard to differences in backgrounds had been unnecessary.

It was kind of him to be showing so much interest in her, and she was glad to be able to converse with Win's parents, as she had a genuine interest in knowing them well. After all, she had no mother and father of her own, and this couple would be her mother and father after she and Win married. "Yes, that's right, my lord. Do use my Christian name, please. Call me Josephine. You needn't feel a requirement to be formal with me."

"I don't believe we know you well enough for such familiarity," uttered the Lady Winthrop. Her mouth formed an unattractive line. "Perhaps in time…"

"Mother, I would very much like for you to make use of Josephine's given name. She's going to be a frequent guest at Winthrop Hall. There's no need for such stiffness," Win said, his obvious irritation colouring his voice.

"If that's your wish, Win, I'll comply, although it doesn't seem perfectly proper to me," she answered.

"My lady, there's no need for such inflexibility. Now, continue, Josephine. Tell us about coming to live with your uncle and about how you and Win became friendly," the Lord Winthrop went on.

"Well, as you know, my parents were passengers on the ill-fated Titanic," she continued. "Both went down with the ship. It was truly horrifying. My brother Andrew and I were immediately contacted. I was at home, in London, with my governess. Andrew was at Oxford. He arrived home only to learn that we had no parents, nor even any remains to bury. My father was a well-respected architect. He travelled all over the globe. Mother always accompanied him."

"How quaint," exclaimed the Lady Winthrop.

His mother's smug attitude was beginning to anger Win, who was ordinarily quite passive where his mother was concerned. The Lady Winthrop appeared to be making a special effort to show her superiority toward Josephine.

"Yes, as a matter of fact, I think it was more than quaint on the part of Josephine's parents," Win interrupted. "In my opinion, not enough couples place emphasis upon the time and attention necessary for a marriage to be truly special. I find it extraordinary to think how much they must have adored each other. What Josephine hasn't told you is that her mother was offered the opportunity to leave the crippled ship with other women and children, aboard a lifeboat, but she chose to stay by her husband's side, thus perishing with him. Yes, Mother, I suppose that *is* rather *quaint*." Win's voice dripped with sarcasm, but he didn't give a whit. His mother needed reminded of her manners.

The Lord Winthrop cleared his throat. "Indeed. Yes, that is quite remarkable. Ahem. So, I gather the decision was made to send you here to

Hampshire to live with your uncle?" Obviously, he was anxious to move away from Mother's rude statement.

"Yes, my lord. My parents had appointed him as our guardian when we were quite young. We've both always adored Uncle Roderick. At first, I missed London, but I've grown to love the countryside. Andrew was in his second year at Oxford when we lost our parents, so he returned to school. He's home with us now, but he studied the law. Next, he'll be reading with a well-thought-of barrister in London. I only learned that recently. I knew he was searching for the proper individual to become associated with. Now, apparently, he has signed a contract. He's older than I am and has received his full inheritance, so he's completely independent."

"Are you planning a Presentation?" asked Win's mother.

Again, Win thought, the question seemed somewhat rude and a bit out-of-place. She was very well-versed in matters of a social nature, and, as such, would have been certainly aware that for Josephine to be a debutante during the 1913 Season, or *any* Season, was highly unlikely. She may have come from a solid, middle-class upbringing, but she wasn't of the aristocracy.

"I'm not of the nobility, my lady. Surely, you're aware I wouldn't be included in the Season," Josephine answered in a remarkably poised manner.

"Oh, yes. Of course. I'm so used to young ladies your age making preparations for the Season. I quite forgot," murmured the Lady Winthrop.

Win had reached the limit of his endurance. His mother was being intolerable. She certainly wasn't going out of her way to be warm and welcoming to Josephine, as she would surely have been to other friends of the aristocracy. Win placed his arm 'round Josephine's waist, pulling her close to him on the sofa.

"Mother and Father, before we go any further with this conversation, I wish to make it clear that this is the lady I have chosen to be my wife. I love her intensely," he announced.

His mother's face paled, and his father looked as though he had received a devastating blow. Win had never before witnessed such an unpleasant reaction from his parents. Mother appeared astounded, and Father's facial expression was most awkward.

Win turned toward his father, who was sitting in the chair opposite Win's mother. "I meant what I said. Josephine and I are over-the-moon in love. We are absolutely certain we're perfectly suited in every way. We're going to proceed with plans for a wedding in the Winthrop Manor chapel."

His mother apparently couldn't help herself. "Am I expected to be exultant at this news? Well, I shan't be. Win, if you follow through with such folly, I'll not have any part in it. I'm immensely sorry, Josephine. I'm sure this is a terrible disappointment. Nonetheless, you are not an ignorant young lady. You should have known that nothing could ever come of an amorous relationship with a viscount. "

"To put it simply, Mother, Josephine has more elegance than any lady I've yet to meet during a Season. The whole rigmarole is foolishness, at best." Win spoke rather arrogantly.

His mother continued to sit with rigidity and a standoffish manner. "Win, you are the heir to Winthrop Manor. Whomever you marry will become a countess. No young lady with a lack of credentials will be accepted into the aristocracy. I think you should remember that the Presentation and Season separate the common people from those who meet nobility's standards."

"All that matters is our love. People always say a couple should have an heir and a spare. I understand Oliver will be here tonight. He'll undoubtedly bring this Season's latest debutante. You can honour him with his lifelong dream. Oliver is a true Winthrop highbrow. He's always had a streak of resentment because I'm the eldest and will inherit. I'm sure he can and will find a suitable elitist who will marry him, so she can become a countess. I'd be more than happy to live a simple, normal life. The most important thing in the world to me is Josephine. Therefore, announce to Oliver that he will be stepping ahead of me in the queue to become the earl."

"Now, son, calm down," his father said. "You know that what you are proposing is not even feasible. The rules governing inheritance of titles are quite well-defined. For centuries, the English people have followed the laws of primogeniture, as you are well-aware. I couldn't disinherit you from someday becoming the earl, and thus, the gentleman who will succeed me as the owner and individual who will take the reins at Winthrop Manor, even if that were my desire. Naturally, your mother and I are shocked by your news. We had no idea you were even seeing this young lady. Now you've brought her to Winthrop Manor for the first time and announced your intention to marry. She *is* a lovely young lady. Nonetheless, she is not a member of the aristocracy, and you should at the very least give us an opportunity to contemplate our feelings."

Josephine stood and excused herself, making her way to the powder room. Win accompanied her, filled with anger at his mother's appalling behaviour. If the dinner hadn't been scheduled to begin in less than an hour, Win would have announced that he and Josephine were leaving at once. However, her Uncle Roderick and Andrew had never visited Winthrop Manor before, and it would have been exceedingly rude not to have been present upon their arrival.

Josephine splashed water on her face and held a cold cloth to her eyes, which were swollen and red from tears she'd shed. Win retrieved her reticule from the drawing room, where his parents still sat, looking bewildered and out of sorts. It was obvious that his father was angry, and his mother, instead of looking regretful for the offensive comments she'd made, was making an attempt to coax his father into seeing her point of view.

"I've come to collect Josephine's reticule," said Win. "If it weren't for the guests who will be arriving, we would both leave at once. I've never been so ashamed of anybody in my life, Mother. Your despicable words wounded Josephine to the core. What should have been a joyous evening for her has become a downright nightmare. She is trying to repair the damage your exceedingly unkind words did to her lovely face. She'll succeed, and we'll act the roles of our lives throughout what should have been a pleasant event. I hope you realize I shall never forgive your odious behaviour."

"You needn't be concerned that there will be any more impolite words. Yes, it's true, your mother acted rude and impertinent. I don't intend for that lovely young lady to ever find herself abused in such a fashion again. Now, please give her our profound apologies, and let's continue with a nice dinner party," said Father.

Win's mother's face turned scarlet, but she made no attempt to argue. It was the first time in his memory that his father had made disparaging remarks about her to their children. Win turned and left the room, pleased with the outcome. He returned to Josephine. She quickly removed a small brush from her reticule, as well as a powder puff and some lip rouge. In less than five minutes, she looked lovely. Win put his arms 'round her, telling her briefly of the words he'd spoken to his parents.

"There will be no more discourteous behaviour. I understand it will be most difficult for you, but I pray you're able to forgive my mother's incorrigible words. We can continue with the blissful evening we anticipated. I love you, darling. I meant every word I said. Either you will be accepted as my intended wife, or I shall relocate. You look heavenly, and I want this to be a special evening for you."

"I'm fine, Win. Your mother was merely astonished at our announcement. Quite obviously, she isn't ready to lose her beloved son. No one on Earth would be good enough in her eyes. Let's forget this unpleasantness. I don't hold grudges, Win. I love you, too, and thank you immensely for standing up for me. Nevertheless, the painfulness is over. Let's proceed with our anticipated merriment."

Win kissed her warmly. "You're one in a million, my precious angel. Thank you for being so forgiving. My mother will find, in time, that you have more refinement and style than all of the titled young ladies in the aristocracy."

Josephine laughed. "A rather overdone statement, Win, but a lovely one. Come, let's rejoin your parents, and forget anything prior to this moment."

Hand in hand, they returned to the drawing room. Upon entrance, Win's father stood and walked to Josephine's side. Normally, he was not a terribly affectionate man. Nonetheless, he appeared to make a great effort, holding Josephine gently in his arms for a moment.

"Forgive my wife's behaviour. We were both somewhat taken aback by the news of your betrothal. Now that we've had time to adjust, we both are very happy for you and our son."

"Is that the truth, Mother?" asked Win. "Are you ready to accept Josephine as your daughter, and treat her with love and respect?"

"Yes. Of course, I'm very happy for both of you. I was momentarily shaken by your announcement, but now I've had a sufficient period to grow accustomed to your news. Naturally, I'm delighted." His mother's voice was without inflection. She spoke in what appeared to be a rehearsed monotone.

"That's fine, then," Win remarked. "Let's please make the other guests comfortable, and have an enjoyable evening."

"Absolutely, son. There's no question whatsoever about this being a splendid occasion. I intend to send Radcliffe to the cellars for several bottles of our finest champagne. This will be a remarkable celebration, as it should be. It's not every day that an elder son becomes engaged, let alone to a young lady as captivating as Josephine," the Lord Winthrop remarked.

"Quite" replied his mother in a soft voice. There was no evidence of joy radiating from her.

The Lord Winthrop stood and went in search of Radcliffe. The Lady Winthrop excused herself, saying she needed to visit the powder room.

"Our other guests should be here shortly," she added. "I also need to check on Elisabeth and make certain she's nearly ready to come downstairs. If either of you want or need anything else, feel free to summon Mrs. Morris or Radcliffe."

"Thank you, Mother. I think we're just fine for the moment," answered Win.

11

Josephine heard the rustling of taffeta. Elisabeth descended the staircase a few moments later. She made her way to the drawing room and immediately approached Josephine. She held out her hands, taking Josephine's into her own.

"How perfectly lovely to meet you. Mother has just told me your happy news." She kissed Josephine on both cheeks and then did the same to her brother. "Well done, Win. I'm very happy for both of you."

There was complete sincerity in her voice. Josephine immediately knew they were going to become dear friends. She was exceedingly different from her mother.

"Oh, my, I believe I heard a rap at the door. Of course, Radcliffe will take care of it, but we probably ought to be present to welcome our guests. What a wonderful, happy, cause for celebration. I had no idea we would be marking this date with an engagement. Do any of our other guests know about this?" Elisabeth asked.

"Only Josephine's uncle, Roderick Chambers, and her brother, Andrew. The others will be in for a surprise," answered Win.

"Well, let's greet them and make the reason for such festivity known," said Elisabeth.

Josephine was very taken with Elisabeth. She was a truly lovely girl. Her hair was not blonde, but neither was it dark. It probably would have been described as auburn but for the occasional lighter streaks of copper-penny red in it. It fell to her shoulders in beautiful, soft waves. She had a typical, English complexion, with cheeks the colour of peaches, like Josephine's, and a striking mouth with a full bottom lip, which she highlighted with lip rouge. She was a small girl. Her dress was white taffeta, and it had a large, scarlet sash at her tiny waistline. She must have inherited her warm personality from her father, Josephine pondered, just as her brother Win had.

Before they left the drawing room, Win told Josephine it was time to place the engagement ring on her finger. She had tucked it into her reticule, as he had instructed. He took it from her and slid it back onto her hand. Her eyes welled with tears. The three then left the drawing room, proceeding down the hallway to the great hall. It seemed everyone had arrived in a sort of mass grouping. Then, unexpectedly, the door opened once more. A sandy-haired man with a rather long face and high forehead drifted into the grand hallway, accompanied by an attractive young lady, somewhat over-dressed and wearing a definite expression of superiority.

"Well, by Jove," exclaimed Win. "Oliver. I had no idea you would be with us. Mother and Father said they thought you would be but weren't completely certain. I'm delighted to have your presence."

"It was a last-minute decision," Win's brother retorted. "Mother mentioned the dinner to me on the telephone last week. I didn't think I'd be able to make the trip from London, but I've bought a new La Gonda Coupe. What a beauty. She's royal blue and flies on the roadway." Then, as though he'd only just remembered her, he turned to his companion. "You must meet the stunning lady in my life. This is Lady Cynthia Wilkins-Young of Belgravia. Cynthia, this is my brother, Win."

Win took her hand and kissed it politely. "How nice that you could join us," he said. "You both need to meet all of the other guests. Most importantly, let me introduce the special lady in *my* life, Miss Josephine Chambers." Win placed his arm about her waist. Then he proceeded to introduce all of the others who were present.

"What, no title?" Oliver said to Josephine rather impertinently.

"Oliver. That's most unkind. Not everyone in the world has a title, or for that matter needs one to make them feel superior to others. Josephine does quite well without putting on airs. I can't remember a time in my life when I've met a lady with the charm and grace that Josephine possesses. As you're well aware, I've met debutante after debutante, Season after Season, so I feel very well-versed in giving my opinion on whether or not a lady needs a title to be desirable. Believe me, this lovely beauty on my arm needs no title before her name to make her a lady any man would be proud to call his own."

"I was only jesting, Win. You needn't take things so seriously," answered his brother.

Josephine brushed off the remark, hugging her uncle Roderick and her brother Andrew, while Win shook their hands. The physician who had been Win's classmate at Oxford, Thomas Drew, entered the foyer next, with Mrs. Lucy Kenslow, who looked to be in her early sixties and was the widowed lady who lived nearby. After introductions were made, Radcliffe took orders for drink preferences. The guests were led to the blue drawing room, where everyone made themselves comfortable.

Although it was the middle of summertime, Lord Winthrop had requested that fires be lit in both the drawing and dining rooms. They added to the ambiance of the evening. Drinks were served, and a large tray of *hors d'oeuvres* was set on the coffee table in front of the sofa. Before long, the lot of them were chatting and showing great affection towards one another. Lord and Lady Winthrop made the round of all guests, playing the perfect host and hostess.

Throughout it all, Win kept a surreptitious eye on Josephine. As far as he was concerned, she was the epitome of a lady, and there wasn't a person present who wasn't absolutely charmed by her, with the exception, perhaps, of his mother. Elisabeth seemed to be getting along nicely with Andrew, which pleased Win, since he would be most happy if his sister and Josephine's brother could be friends.

Lucy Kenslow was a quiet, rather small lady, who needed to be brought out of her shell. Josephine's uncle Roderick seemed to be the precise person to take on such a task. He paid a huge amount of attention to her, asking a multitude of questions concerning her life. She had lost her husband some seven years previously, and while the grieving phase was apparently behind her, it was quite obvious she assumed she would be spending the rest of her life as a widow. Yet, by the time the dinner gong rang, Roderick had her laughing at various remarks he'd made, and it looked as if he had done an excellent job charming her. For his part, Andrew was already on a first-name basis with nearly all of the guests.

When the dinner bell rang, Josephine placed her glass on a table and followed the others into the dining room. The Lord and Lady Winthrop sat at opposite ends of the table, which was set in a formal arrangement with gold-

and-white French Havilland china, fine sterling silver flatware, and exquisite crystal glassware. A footman stood behind each chair. Josephine felt somewhat out of her element, yet she didn't think anyone noticed. Nor did she believe anyone had noticed her lovely engagement ring, but she was actually rather glad, since she and Win planned on an announcement prior to the dinner.

Certainly, Josephine's family had not, by any means, been noble, but she was well-educated in the proper manner of dining in a formal setting. Nevertheless, footmen were a little much for her. Still, she was savvy enough to know that a lady removed her gloves and spread her serviette on her lap immediately upon being seated. The first course, consisting of court bouillon, was served, and a lovely Chardonnay was poured into one of the several wineglasses arranged above her charger and dinner plate. There were place cards by each guest's chair, and Josephine was delighted to see that she had been seated next to Win on one side and Elisabeth on the other. She wondered if Win had made the decision regarding the seating arrangements. The dinner proceeded, with a myriad of genuinely happy conversations and a growing feeling of cordiality among all guests.

During dinner, Win stood and announced that he and Josephine were engaged to be married. There were gasps, and smiles broke out on each person's face. Oliver's lady friend, Cynthia Wilkins-Young, looked somewhat stunned. It was obvious that she couldn't imagine a Winthrop marrying someone without a title. However, Oliver seemed genuinely happy for his brother. Everyone toasted them and began to ask questions about when the wedding would take place.

"Although I would marry her tomorrow, I believe we'll need to set a date for rougly a year from now. I believe that's probably sensible," replied Win. "From what I understand, it takes a young lady that long to arrange for a large, formal wedding." He chuckled.

"I suppose it will take place in the Winthrop Chapel?" remarked Oliver.

"Indeed," answered Win. "I'm not certain how many guests it will accommodate. I'll have to figure that. I'm sure it will be filled to capacity."

"The next year will be occupied with a plethora of engagement parties and the like," responded Elisabeth. "This is such exciting news. At last, I shall have a true sister."

She looked fondly at Josephine, and they both smiled warmly. After a considerable amount of time discussing the happy news, it finally came time for the gentlemen to gather in the library for brandy while the ladies returned to the drawing room. Conversation was light in both venues, with no controversial comments made. After they all joined together again, it was time for departure. There was no question as to whether all had enjoyed themselves, and new friendships had been formed.

David was summoned to bring the Rolls around, and Roderick, Andrew, Dr. Drew, and Lucy climbed inside. Roderick put his arm round Lucy's shoulders, holding her hand gently. Oliver and Cynthia departed in his stunning new automobile. While David was dispensing with the other guests, Elisabeth and Win took the opportunity to show Josephine a bit more of their splendid home. She couldn't help but admit to herself that it was so much more than she had anticipated.

When the threesome returned to the great hall, David was just entering after the task of delivering all guests to their respective abodes. Win summoned him, requesting that he now make ready to drive to Josephine's cottage, so Win might escort her home properly. Josephine was very relieved that the evening had ended, and her emotions gave way for a moment. She began to weep.

"I do hope I haven't caused irreparable damage to your relationship with your parents," she said to Win. "I understand your mother's point of view. Of course, I'm sure your parents have always dreamed of you marrying a spectacular member of the aristocracy. I have to be a letdown for both of them."

When the door closed, Win looked lovingly at Josephine and said, "Your ring looks stunning. The engagement will be announced in *The Times*, too. Stop your sniffling, darling. Everything will work out fine. I love you. I've made that clear. I intend to speak with my parents again when I return from delivering you to your uncle's cottage. We have announced our plans to everyone. Tomorrow by this time, the entire area surrounding Winthrop Manor will have heard the happy news."

"Oh, darling, I'm so terribly happy but a bit worried, too. It will be truly official, won't it? We need to have a long chat about preparations to be made and set a wedding date," said Josephine.

Win took her hand, and kissed it. "Josephine I'd wait forever for you, you know that," he said. "As I told our guests, I'd marry you tomorrow if I could, but I'd like to try to keep peace. I know we share the same feelings. I'm just relieved to know that my parents are being somewhat civil about this. The time will go fast—we'll be together every moment possible."

"I know, Win. I just so wish I could be your wife sooner than that, but I *do* understand."

"Yes, my precious, I know. I hate the thought of postponement for a year, but I do suppose you'll be making numerous trips back and forth to London, purchasing the paraphernalia that accompanies a wedding."

"No, I don't think many, really. Officially, I'm still in mourning. I believe Uncle Roderick has my mother's wedding gown, left to me, along with all of her other belongings. I plan to wear it if it can be altered to fit me. Mother was taller than I am, but that can be easily remedied. I've never seen the dress, but Mother had excellent fashion sense, so I should think I'll find it charming and certainly sentimental."

"I think that's a perfectly lovely idea, Josephine. I have to make a trip to London tomorrow to do some financial business for my father, which will give you a day to sort through clothing."

"Will you come to see me in the evening? We could dine at Uncle Roderick's, or perhaps we could go out to a restaurant."

"I vote for dining out. There's a charming, little bistro near Winthrop-on-Hart. I'll have David collect me at the station, and I'll come straight to you. Does that meet with your approval?"

"Of course, Win. You knew it would. Thank you again for a truly lovely evening. Now, let's allow David to finish his chores. Then you can complete your conversation with your parents, which, to be honest, I wouldn't be looking forward to if I were you."

Win helped her into the back seat of the Rolls Royce, and they vehicle began to move.

"You will never be seen as a letdown to anyone who cares about me," Win said, wrapping an arm around her shoulders and pulling her close. "I absolutely adore you, and there is no one on Earth I would rather have as my wife. So this conversation has ended."

He turned to her and kissed her passionately and for quite some time. When the kiss finally came to an end, both were breathing heavily. Josephine was keenly aware that David was sitting in the driver's seat in front of them, and he had to know exactly what was happening. She settled back against the cushioned seat, and a short time later, they reached her uncle's cottage.

"I think it's time I take leave," Win whispered. "I'll look for you tomorrow about seven o'clock in the evening if that suits you."

"Absolutely, Win. Seeing you always suits me," Josephine remarked as she smoothed her somewhat mussed hair and straightened her dress.

Win took hold of her hand, helping her to step out of the vehicle. They walked slowly toward the doorway and kissed once again.

"Until tomorrow evening," Win said, "and I'll be counting every minute. Sleep well, my pet. I love you."

"I needn't tell you how I feel. I'm amazed that my feet are touching the ground. I feel as though I'm floating."

They kissed once more, and then Win waited as she opened the door. Once inside, she turned and watched him walk away, broad-shouldered and slender, with his dark hair tousled by the slight breeze. Oh, what a lucky girl she was.

In the muddle and fuss of everything that had occurred during the evening, Win had completely forgotten about his conversation with his mother regarding Mrs. Whitaker's mental decline. He assumed his mother had sent Tom Drew to the kitchens, but nothing more had been mentioned about the situation. He would try to remember to ask about Tom's impressions when they next met.

When Win returned to Winthrop Manor, he nearly collided with Radcliffe, who was in his way out of the drawing room, carrying a tray to the kitchens.

"Oh, Radcliffe, you still have some work ahead, don't?"

"Yes, my lord, a bit," the butler answered.

"Do you know if my parents have retired, or are they still awake talking about the party?" Win asked.

"They're in the drawing room, my lord," Radcliffe responded.

12

❧

Win entered the drawing room to find his parents there, comfortably seated, obviously conversing about the dinner.

Win's mother looked startled and put her put her hand to her breast, exclaiming, "Oh, my goodness. Win, you frightened me. I thought you had left to escort Miss Chambers to her home."

"I have taken Josephine home. Now I want to speak with you and Father. We need to finish the conversation we started before the guests arrived."

"Yes, son, I think that's an excellent idea," answered the Lord Winthrop.

"Father, I intend to marry Josephine. I love her. Don't think I've been fooled by your seeming reasonableness."

"Win, I know what it means when boys your age talk about love. Believe me, son, if I was to give my approval to such a union, you wouldn't be the first son to wish his father hadn't been so agreeable. If this young lady in question belonged to your own class, or if she were even near it, that might make it a quite different matter. We aren't upset because you have, as you think, fallen in love, or that you wish to marry, although, you are very young. We're upset that you should even think of marrying a simple, rustic girl."

Win opened his mouth to protest, but his father raised his hand, making it clear he did not wish to hear any more arguments. "Win, this is so utterly ridiculous that it's impossible for me to treat the matter seriously."

"It's serious enough for me," Win answered. "If I don't marry Josephine Chambers, I shall never marry at all."

"Frankly, son, that would be better than making a supreme mistake."

"She is good and lovely, modest and graceful. Why would it be a mistake? I've never put any stock in the foolish laws of the class system. Why am I superior to her?"

"Win, most parents would refuse to even listen to such nonsense. I am listening and trying to convince you with common sense that the step you seem bent on taking is one that will cause you nothing but misery. I'm telling you simply that Josephine Chambers is not a fit wife for you, the heir to Winthrop Manor. I'm trying to be patient with you. I'm trying not to treat you as a young man whose head is turned by his first love, but as my son, who should be sensible with reason and thought. If you will promise to go abroad for a year, I guarantee you'll forget this foolish folly. Will you do that for me?"

"Father, I agreed to set a date for a year from now, knowing how you feel, because I did not wish to bring about a row. Nevertheless, no, I can't," Win answered. "I've promised Josephine to marry her. I'm not about to break my word. I have no intention of leaving her for a year. I'd be miserable, as would she."

"All right, Win. I'm not going to listen to any more of this nonsense. There's a limit to my patience. Once and for all, I am telling you I forbid any mention of such a marriage. I forbid it. If you choose to disobey me, you'll pay a very large penalty."

"What sort of penalty?" Win asked.

"A penalty I don't think you'll wish to pay," his father replied. "If you persist in this nonsense and actually marry the girl, I will never see you again. This will no longer be your home. Because of the laws of primogeniture, I can't disinherit you; but if you persist in this foolishness, I won't give you a penny while I'm living."

"Fine," answered Win. "I have thirty-thousand pounds a year that my Godfather left me."

His father's face grew white. "Yes," he answered. "You have that, and I can tell you it won't keep you in clothing and cigars, let alone all the grand things you've been accustomed to."

"Please, Father, give me your consent," Win begged passionately. "You know I love you, but I love Josephine, too. Don't make me give her up."

"You heard what I said. Do as I ask, and I'll make you a happy young man. Defy me and marry the girl, and I'll consider I'm no longer your father. You won't be worthy of the Winthrop name. You can make up your mind. That's my final word on the matter."

"Father, you have Oliver, as I said before. He brought what I'm certain you consider the perfect woman this evening. She's a phony, obviously narcissistic young lady. I'm sure you adore the fact that she carries a hyphenated surname. She'd make a fine countess."

"Win, I have no intention of making Oliver the heir to Winthrop Manor. You are our eldest son and our heir. I've told you before, and you already are well aware that I can do nothing about the law of primogeniture. I couldn't leave the estate and title to Oliver if I wanted to, and I don't want to. We're naturally shocked by your news. Nevertheless, I am the earl."

"If your attitude toward Josephine doesn't change rapidly, then she and I will immediately catch a train to Gretna Green and marry there. I'm sure that would cause untold embarrassment and uproar, but I don't care. I've made myself clear." Win was well aware of his parents' thoughts. Looking them in the eye, he said, "If I have to wait a decade for Josephine, I'll never change my mind. Get used to the idea that she will, indeed, be your daughter-in-law. We may agree to wait the year. Josephine hasn't said she wouldn't. I'm the one who wants to marry sooner than that. During the year, I suppose we might use the time to make plans for the most perfect wedding ever to take place in the Winthrop Manor chapel. Otherwise, we shall immediately elope to Gretna Green."

With that, he spun on his heel and left the room.

13

Very early the following morning, Josephine climbed up to the attic. It wasn't even seven o'clock. She was overwhelmed by the number of items stored in such minimal space. The attic did not cover the entire house but only stretched to halfway across the width of the structure. There were literally hundreds of boxes, most of them with her uncle's handwriting on them, marking them with specific items.

Then there were a number of old-fashioned trunks. They had no markings, which meant she would have to sort through each by hand in her quest to find her mother's wedding gown. He had informed her over morning tea and toast of his certainty that the wedding dress was packed away between layers of tissue paper and laid carefully in one of the trunks, along with the veil her mother had so gracefully worn, and even the bouquet of flowers, now dried into a nosegay of shriveled petals, wrapped in a separate, small box. Josephine was absolutely thrilled at the idea of being able to wed Win in the same gown her beloved mother had worn the day she married George Chambers.

She spent the majority of an hour in the dusty loft, pawing through literally hundreds of items. It was quite clear that her mother had been one who hated to part with treasures from her past. Finally, Josephine came upon a frock, tucked among several pieces of white tissue paper. The dress! There was simply nothing else it could be. She lifted the gown carefully from the truck, removing the tissue. Yes, there it was. Even after all the years it had been tucked away from the eyes of the world, the dress was in superb condition. Josephine instantly fell in love—with its design, its fabric, and with its simple example of excellent taste in fashion. She immediately shed the dress she was wearing and slipped the gorgeous gown over her head. Amid the myriad of old keepsakes that had been stored in the attic was a very old cheval mirror. She was dying to catch a glimpse of what she would look like in the gown. When she saw her reflection, it was truly beyond her wildest dreams.

Elegant, ivory-colored taffeta with a luscious, pearly sheen peeked out from beneath the loveliest coloured lace, which bore intricate embroidery on the sleeves and skirt hem. The one-piece gown was lightweight and incredibly feminine. Josephine couldn't imagine who wouldn't love the sensual whisper the taffeta made as she walked. A unique feature of the dress was the ivory-coloured panels that were gathered at the front waistline to fall gracefully 'round and down to the lower center back, held in place with a Guipure lace applique. It had center back snaps and hooks for closure.

Josephine was downright amazed that the delectable gown fit her so effortlessly. It might require a bit of alteration in the sleeves, since it appeared that they were a bit longer than her arms, and the same seemed true of the hemline. Josephine was a bit shorter than her mother had been. Though it would be a truly difficult task, she was confident a fine seamstress could accomplish whatever needed to be done. She believed she could have searched the world over and never found such a truly exquisite wedding gown. It meant the world to her to be able to wear the same frock in which her mother had spoken vows. Josephine firmly believed that her mother was able to see what a scrumptious bride she was going to be. She continued wearing the wedding dress, and beneath the layers of tissue paper, she found a slender box. It contained the lace veil, which obviously had been designed to be worn with the gown. It fell to the ground, covering the extensive train. There was absolutely no question in her mind that she would choose to wear her mother's magnificent dress.

Josephine very carefully made her way back down to the first level, where she excitedly searched for Roderick. Andrew was not at home, and apparently neither was Roderick. It was still so early; she couldn't imagine where they might be. Probably speaking with the workers in the fields. Josephine had a strong need to show off her discovery. Finally, she came upon their cook in the kitchen. It seemed a bit odd to see the enchanting wedding attire in that particular room, but Josephine simply had an overwhelming desire to display her find. The housekeeper's eyes filled with tears.

"Oh, Miss Josephine, I never dreamed I'd ever lay my eyes on that gorgeous gown again. It seems like yesterday I watched your mother walk slowly down the aisle to meet your father at the altar. They were such a beautiful couple and so young."

Josephine was thrilled with the reaction she had received from the treasured Chambers' cook. Josephine left the kitchen area and climbed the stairway to the first level with the intention of continuing on to her bedchamber to remove the gown. At that moment, Andrew and Roderick entered the house. They both stopped, looks of awe upon their faces.

"You look spectacular, Josephine. Is that Mother's wedding gown?" asked Andrew.

"Yes," she answered, twirling like a ballerina. "Do you think Win will like it?"

"He would have to be insane not to. I think it's splendid for you to be wearing your mother's gown. She would be so proud of you," said Uncle Roderick.

"Thank you. I simply adore it. Amazingly, it fits almost perfectly. It will require very few alterations."

"Mother was a little bit taller than you are," Andrew commented.

"Yes. We were very much alike. She was taller, however, so the dress will require shortening. I think Mother would be very happy to know I've chosen to wear her gown when I marry Win."

"She would be extraordinarily happy for you. Oh, my god, I wish both of your parents could be here to witness this happy event," added her uncle.

"I know. I was thinking the same thing. All mothers must long for the special day they see their daughters walk down the aisle on the arm of the man they love. Life seems so unfair at times."

"Well, I'll be there, sweet sister. Unless you want Uncle Roderick to do the honours."

"I think I'd rather it be you, Andrew. I love you, Uncle Roderick, immensely, but if it can't be father, I think I'd rather it be my brother."

"I understand, sweetheart. If you change your mind, I'll be there. However, I agree it should be Andrew. Just know I'll be here for you, no matter what," answered Uncle Roderick.

Josephine gave her brother and uncle giant hugs. "No girl has a more wonderful brother or uncle. I love you both so much. I do hope you find a spectacular lady to be your wife, Andrew. She's waiting for you somewhere."

"Yes. I'm certain of that, too. In fact, I'm beginning to think I just may have found her. Time will tell."

Josephine grabbed her brother's arm. "Andrew? Who? Please tell. You have never indicated more than a passing interest in any young lady. If you have an interest in someone, please share it with me. After all, if you marry, she'll become my sister, too."

"All in good time, my sweet sister. I've no idea if there's the slightest possibility that she has any interest in me."

"Not interested in you? She would have to be mad," cried Josephine. "You're perfect in every way."

"Ah, but you see, you and I share the same dilemma. I'm not of the aristocracy. You're fortunate that Win's parents have accepted you."

"Andrew, I'm not altogether certain they *have* accepted me. Especially not his mother. I don't want to lose him. He's threatened to allow Oliver to inherit Winthrop Manor if I don't meet with his mother's approval."

"Not many men would be willing to literally divorce his family and throw away his inheritance for the love of a woman," Andrew remarked.

"Yes, but you see, Win isn't like any other man I've ever known." Josephine smiled.

"No, I agree with that. He's a remarkable man. Perhaps I'll be as fortunate as you are."

"You won't tell me anymore about this mysterious young lady you have your eye upon?"

"Josephine, not yet. She has no idea of my feelings. I think it only fair that she be the first one to understand how I feel."

"Yes, I suppose so," Josephine answered with a smile. "Still, I'm your only sister. You will promise to tell me if something comes of it, won't you, Andrew?"

"Absolutely. Now change out of that gorgeous gown before it becomes soiled. I'm going to run into Winthrop-on-Hart. I have a few items I need to purchase. Nothing exciting. The field workers need some better tools. Do you want to accompany me?"

"Are the shops open? It's just a bit after eight," she said.

"Yes. Remember, this is a farm village. Shops open early and close early. We're not in London anymore." He laughed.

"Of course, I'd love the trip. It's beautiful outside. I won't be a tick." She smiled, turning and scampering up the stairway, holding the gown high above her ankles so as not to trip upon it.

A short while later, Andrew brought the small cart around to the front of the cottage. Josephine stood outside the door, ready to be collected. She wore a pale-blue muslin dress that had long sleeves and a pin-tucked bodice. She had no thought of doing any shopping, but it was always nice to accompany Andrew on an outing.

The team of horses trotted along the narrow road leading to the small village, and Josephine admired the lovely landscape as they moved along. Win had been correct back when they'd first met, when he'd spoken of how beautiful summertime was in this part of England. What a wonderful day that had been. She'd had no idea it was to be a watershed moment in her life.

Finally, they reached the outer limits of the village. Andrew parked the cart in a safe place. He lifted her to the ground, and they sauntered into the village of Winthrop-on-Hart. They strolled the pretty walkways and peered into shop windows. Winthrop-on-Hart was quite a small village, but Josephine thought it exceptionally quaint with its cobblestone streets and bowed-window storefronts. As they were standing in front of an exhibit of home furnishings, Oliver Winthrop and the same young woman who'd been with him at the dinner party came ambling down the walkway. They were not a handsome couple. While obviously of the aristocracy, as shown by their dress and the way they carried themselves, neither was particularly attractive. It was interesting how a title and money could overcome such disadvantages. Although Oliver had treated her kindly enough the previous evening, there had been an underlying tone of superiority, and the same thing could be said for Cynthia Wilkins-Young. Josephine was very thankful that she had Andrew with her. He was, and always had been, her protector. Whenever she was with him, she felt so much more secure. She and her brother continued their stroll, her arm through Andrew's. Andrew either hadn't noticed Oliver or was purposely ignoring the other couple. Josephine was glad that she had dressed in a becoming frock, and although she wasn't vain, she was aware that she was an attractive young lady. Though she carried no title, she *did* do her best to always look poised and impressive.

"Well, well. If it isn't my distinguished brother's intended wife," sneered Oliver, the moment they drew near. "Pardon me… Miss Chambers, is it? I'm still trying to recover from the shock that Win intends to marry beneath himself."

Josephine gasped. She was more than a little surprised at Oliver's rude behaviour. Had his decent behaviour the previous evening been nothing more than an act?

"One more word of that sort and I'll flatten you right here on the high street," retorted Andrew. "I am Josephine's brother, and I do not intend to stand here and listen to belittling remarks about my irreplaceable and lovely sister."

"Ah! I'm simply quivering in my boots, sir. I believe we met yesterday evening as well. Andrew is the name if I'm correct?"

"Yes, you're correct. And I believe Oliver is your name. If I recall, the lady by your side hyphenates her surname in an attempt to sound more upmarket."

"Cynthia happens to be the daughter of a baronet. She has been feted splendidly during this latest Season. I wouldn't expect you to know anything about the Season, since you're not of the aristocracy."

"No. We aren't. But I can assure you that my father undoubtedly paid more in taxes to Great Britain than your father takes into his coffers in a year's time."

"My dear fellow, people of good breeding never discuss financial matters," retorted Oliver.

"No. Not until the time to discuss a dowry. It's quite interesting how the aristocracy pays to marry off their daughters." Andrew laughed.

Oliver turned beet red. "What a cheeky, disgusting thing to say. Dowries are a treasured, age-old tradition. You're implying that gentlemen of the aristocracy sell their daughters to the highest bidder. No doubt, you expect your uncle will pay a dowry for the privilege of Win marrying your sister."

"Win is an extraordinary chap. Of course, he will do what's proper. But, I hope you aren't of the impression that Josephine wouldn't marry Win if he didn't have money. She'd marry him if he were a pauper. They are very much in love. Now, you—well, you're in a different category, aren't you?" Andrew laughed again. "Love never even enters the equation with unattractive chaps of the aristocracy. I graduated from Oxford. I know the way it works. After a so-called gentleman is wed, he takes a mistress. The wife generally takes a lover."

Apparently, Andrew had struck a nerve. Cynthia Wilkins-Young had turned scarlet.

"Why, you arsehole! I shan't stand here and listen to any more of this garbage. If you really believe your sister is going to be The Lady Winterdale, you'd better study up on the rules governing the proper guidelines for marriage among the gentry," Oliver nearly shouted.

"I know them well, Oliver. There is not one thing to stop your brother and Josephine from marrying. I intend to tell your brother every word you've spoken. You may live to regret them."

With that, Andrew and Josephine stepped around the astounded couple and continued their stroll along the high street.

"Andrew! That was the most abominable conversation I've ever been witness to. What a truly odious creature Oliver is. How will I cope with being his sister-in-law?"

"Don't let it be a bother, Josephine. He's a ridiculous fool. Win and he are nothing alike. I doubt there's much back and forth between them."

"I don't know. I only know I do intend to speak to Win about this encounter. Either his family stops persecuting me because I don't have a foolish title, or I may reconsider the entire thing. I love Win with all of my heart. Nonetheless, I have no intention of living my life around people with such a complete lack of character."

"Well, I must say, I can't blame you. I suspect Win will be outraged at his brother's arrogance. There is nothing whatsoever haughty about Win. I don't believe Oliver's behaviour will make Win very happy."

14

❧

After arriving back at the cottage, Josephine returned to her room. She had just removed her bonnet when she heard the sound of horse's hooves on the dusty road. She ran to the window and saw Win, already dismounting. It was still early in the day. He had never visited at such a time, and she hadn't been expecting him until seven that evening, when they were to go out to dinner. He seemed in a great hurry. She only took a moment to fasten a few curls that had fallen loose from her up-do, and then she scurried down the stairway. By the time she reached the foyer and placed her hand upon the doorknob, he'd already opened it. She was shocked at his appearance. Normally, Win was immaculate, in every sense of the word. Even if there was a hair out of place, he never looked unkempt. However, now he was breathing heavily and appeared all undone. He hadn't even bothered to change into his riding habit and was dressed in his usual daytime britches and a white shirt.

"Win," she cried. "Whatever is the matter? You seem terribly upset. Has something happened? I wasn't expecting you this early."

He put his arms around her, holding her closely. "Oh, my darling, Josephine. It's the worst possible news. Have you not heard?"

"Have I not heard what? Andrew and I just returned from a short jaunt to Winthrop-on-Hart. What am I supposed to have heard? Has something happened to one of your parents, to Oliver or Elisabeth?"

"No, no. Oh, damn. I forgot your uncle doesn't own a wireless or a telephone. Josephine, England has declared war on Germany."

"War? Why would England go to war with Germany? Do you think it's really true?"

"It's true, all right. The proclamation has been declared. There is general mobilisation taking place. Our troops are being sent to the Belgian border."

"How will this affect us?" she asked, stunned. "Of course, I love my country, but I also love you. You won't have to fight, will you?"

"Yes, sweetheart. I'm afraid I shall. The wireless announcer is making light of it for now, saying it will undoubtedly be over by Christmas. Still, I'm not so certain. I've never said anything, for fear of upsetting you. Nevertheless, trouble has been simmering abroad for a long time. It only took one seemingly unimportant event to ignite the flame."

"What event?" She frowned.

"It's complicated, Josephine. Too many occurrences for me to relate have taken place since then. It's all happened so quickly."

"I can't believe you haven't said anything to me, Win. You must have been concerned?"

"No, I can't say I have been. At least, not until very recently. I didn't learn about Russian involvement and Germany's invasion of Belgium right away. When I did hear, I was damn certain we would become involved. It's a bloody mess."

Win slammed his hand down on the hall table. His mouth was in a firm line, and there was no question about his anger and frustration.

"I hate to sound so unpatriotic, but what is going to happen to you and me?" Josephine asked miserably. She'd just stepped out of his arms.

Andrew came running down the stairway, stopped, and stared at Win.

"Ah, God. You've heard, too, haven't you?" he said.

"Yes, how did you receive the news?" queried Win.

"I took the horse and cart to the stables after Josephine and I went on a short errand to the village. Johnny, our stable boy, had been told by his parents. He related everything I needed to know. We're at war with Germany. I can't stop to talk now. I'll be back before too long."

"Where are you going, Andrew?" Josephine called as he ran out of the doorway.

"I have to see someone. Someone very important," he replied as he continued on his way.

Josephine turned to Win. She looked into his eyes. "I know, without you even saying anything, that you plan to enlist. I don't know if I can bear this, Win. What is going to happen to us?"

"Darling, throughout the entire ride over here, I've thought about it. There's been no call-up of troops in England yet. Of course, when that comes, I will have to go. Any man my age, including Andrew and my brother Oliver, will be conscripted. Nevertheless, I've made a decision. If you're in accord, then we must act quickly."

"What, Win? You know I'll agree to any suggestion you make."

"All right then. We're going to drive the Rolls Royce to Gretna Green today. We'll marry tonight. There will be no difficulty finding a vicar who'll do the honours. Gretna Green is known as a marriage haven. I realise it's in Scotland, so it will be quite a journey. I intend to tell my parents I'm going to London to make enquiries at the Department of Defense. You can say whatever you wish to your uncle. Either tell him the truth, or say you're spending the night with Elisabeth."

"I'll tell him the truth. There's no reason to lie. He'll agree with your plan. Nonetheless, darling, what about *your* parents? There will be a horrible row when they learn we've eloped."

"I can't be concerned about them. I only know I need you to be my wife before I leave to fight a war. With luck, the conflict will turn out to be short-lived."

She put her hand on his arm. "Win, are you absolutely certain about this? We're talking about the entire rest of our lives. It's the most important decision we'll ever make. They say people shouldn't make impulsive decisions in the midst of crisis."

"Josephine, I knew almost from the moment I saw you in front of your uncle's cottage that I was going to marry you someday. Well, that day has come. Please, sweetheart. We haven't a great deal of time. Tonight, you will be my wife. I never thought I'd be thanking the Germans for anything, but since they hold the key to our future, I am grateful. We're going to have a happy, wonderful life. I've never been so certain of anything. I've never known anyone like you. So, no more dithering. I shall never regret marrying you, Josephine. To be honest, it's the only good thing to come of this war. Now there will be no reason for us to wait a year."

"When do you plan on leaving?" she asked.

"As soon as possible. It's still early. I'm going to return to Winthrop Manor and pack a few items of clothing. Then I'll tell my parents the story about going to London. I'll come back here soon—probably within the hour."

15

Win hastily kissed her and rushed back out the door to mount Black Orchid. She watched him leave and stood absolutely still, trying at absorb everything that had happened in such an incredibly short period of time. Before he'd been gone only a few moments, she ran to the back of the house, where Uncle Roderick was sitting on the porch, reading the newspaper. She was certain he'd heard about what had taken place, but she had no idea if he would say anything about the war to her.

"Uncle Roderick, Win was here. He's just left. I haven't much time. I need to tell you our plans and pray you'll approve. I know you think the world of him, so please place your trust in him now. He'll be back in an hour or so to collect me in his auto. We're driving to Gretna Green and marrying. I'm sure you know about the war. Win says he feels obligated to enlist, but he definitely wants us to be married before that happens."

Her uncle sat in silence. He was clearly trying to gather his wits.

"I must be certain that you truly love Win with all your heart, Josephine. Marriage should be for a lifetime. Don't let the prospect of war muddle your thinking. Of course, you have my permission to do whatever you both have decided. I'd like to be present to see you wed, but it's a long trip for an old man. I believe it's best I stay here. You know I'll be with you in my heart."

"Uncle, you're so kind. So dear. I do adore Win. You know that. I want to be his wife. If the worst happens, and I lose him in the war, I'll always be glad I was his wife."

"Then you must begin to prepare for the journey. I imagine Win will return before you know it."

"Yes. Do you think it would be foolish if I were to take Mother's wedding gown? I know it won't be a proper wedding, as it would have been if we'd waited the year and married at Winthrop Manor. Still, I rather think Mother would want me to wear her dress."

"I don't think it would be foolish at all. Every bride deserves to wear whatever she chooses on her wedding day. I suspect Win would want you to bring it with you."

Josephine smiled broadly. "Then I shall, Uncle. All right then. I'm going to dash upstairs and prepare for the journey. Thank you so much. I love you."

With those words, Josephine turned and scurried to the front hall and up the stairway. She wasn't frightened in the least. It didn't matter where she married Win. She would be his wife. It was what she'd dreamt about from the moment she'd laid eyes upon him.

Dashing about her bedchamber, Josephine gathered everything she wished to bring with her on the journey. She left the wedding gown in the box it had been stored in, and added stockings, shoes, undergarments, and the veil. Then she placed two other day dresses in her valise, along with appropriate shoes. She was so glad she'd made the trip to London to shop for new clothing. Because of that shopping spree, she had no worries about a shortage of items for her wardrobe. She changed the frock she was wearing, slipping into a smart travelling suit of creme-coloured linen edged in black braid. The ensemble had a jaunty, little hat of the same colour, with a black feather. She slipped on a pair of black, leather gloves to complete the ensemble.

In a separate, small bag, she packed her cosmetics, perfume, and hair necessities. On the journey to London, she'd purchased feminine, lacy nightwear. She held those items to the light, dreaming about the night that lay ahead—her wedding night. What would it be like? Her mother was deceased and had never explained what her daughter should expect from the most intimate of all acts. She certainly knew, from schoolgirl chatter, essentially what would occur. However, no one she knew had actually been able to tell her what it was truly like. She simply knew she loved Win and believed with all her heart he would be the one to help her understand everything.

She'd nearly completed the packing when Andrew returned. She walked into the upstairs hall and watched him as he bounded up the stairs, taking them two at a time.

"Andrew. My goodness. What is causing you to be in such a frenzy?" she exclaimed.

"Well, my dear sister, I have wonderful news. You'll undoubtedly think I've gone mad, but I assure you, I'm quite sane."

"What on Earth…?"

"Elisabeth Winthrop has agreed to marry me. As soon as possible. Can you believe my good fortune? Elisabeth Winthrop. That special, elegant creature loves me and wants to be my wife. She doesn't want to wait until the war is over. We're eloping to Gretna Green."

Josephine was knocked-for-six. *Is this really happening?*

"Andrew. Slow down. We need to get everything straight. Are you telling me you've asked Elisabeth Winthrop, Win's sister, to marry you, and she's said yes? You've decided to elope to Gretna Green. Tonight?"

"Yes. Yes." He picked her up and spun her round, as he had when they were children. "Isn't it the happiest news imaginable? Naturally, we aren't telling her parents. I don't think they'd approve if I were the Prince of Wales. She says it doesn't matter to her. I have to prepare to leave. We'll be taking the train this evening."

"Andrew, wait," Josephine cried. "Wait." She pulled on his coattail until he stopped. "This doesn't make any sense. You two don't know each other well enough to be talking about marriage."

"Oh, but there's where you're wrong, dear sister. I've been seeing Elisabeth for over a year. My last year at Oxford, she was attending a fine school for young ladies not far from me. Actually, Dr. Drew introduced us. They're friends, and he had taken her to the theater one night when I ran into them. I thought she really cared about him, but it turned out that they are just good friends. We've been in love for a good time now, but the difficulty was her parents. We had the same problem you were worried about with Win. Nevertheless, she says she loves me and is willing to elope. Can you believe it?"

"No, actually, I can't. Why didn't you say anything when Win came calling on me?"

"I'd hoped things might work out. But, if you remember, I did have my doubts."

"Well, Andrew, you need to listen to me. You needn't take the train or any other method of transportation. Of course, you know how much Win and I love each other." Josephine paused and took a deep breath. "Andrew, Win and I decided earlier today to elope to Gretna Green and marry tonight. I imagine you told Elisabeth all about the war with Germany, just as Win did with me. We made up our minds very quickly. Win is picking me up within the hour. He's going to tell his parents that he wants to drive to London to check on military ranks and so forth. He's is going to borrow the Rolls. Elisabeth and you can come with us. I've already told Uncle our plans, and you must do the same thing. He was wonderful about everything. We need to get the word to Win, so he'll know to bring Elisabeth with him. How can we go about doing that?"

"I'll run out to speak with Johnny at the stable. I'll write a short note to Win. Johnny can handle it from there. He'll ride to Winthrop Manor and give the note to Radcliffe, asking him to pass it to Win."

"Wonderful. Oh, Andrew, how perfect. We can act as witnesses for each other. This is so exciting and romantic."

The driving time from Winthrop-on-Hart to Gretna Green was expected to take the foursome approximately four and a half hours. Win received the note from Andrew, told his sister of the change in plans, and at 2:00 p.m., they left Winthrop Manor to collect Josephine and Andrew. There was an air of exhilaration. Roderick bid them farewell and God Speed. Then they were off on their frenzied journey. Elisabeth and Win had no trouble with their parents, regarding the alleged trip to London. Their mother and father had told Win it made perfect sense for him to want every detail available about the prospects ahead for him as a member of the military.

Win *did* want such information and intended to search for it as soon as he had married Josephine. However, he had priorities, and marriage was the most significant. Actually, he felt strongly that his parents were rather glad about England's declaration of war. He was quite sure that this turn of events eased their stress regarding Win marrying Josephine. He also knew they would believe that when it came down to it, Win would never enlist. As heir to Winthrop Manor, he had ample reason to receive an exemption. Those engaged in agricultural pursuits would be entitled to such an immunity, since foodstuffs would be a necessary commodity for the country. Obviously, they scarcely knew their son and his strong sense of duty.

"Why are we going to Gretna Green?" Josephine asked, as the car began to head north. "Couldn't we have married closer to home?"

"Yes, undoubtedly," Win answered. "We're all of age. Gretna Green has always been known as the spot where young people elope because the marriage laws are different in Scotland, regarding eligibility to marry at a younger age without parental consent. Gretna Green is in Scotland, but only slightly across the UK border. Because it's so frequently visited by couples wishing to marry, all of the official components involved in the act are simplified, from start to finish. Time won't be wasted on obtaining a license and all of that rubbish."

"Isn't it incredible to have each other to witness our vows? Josephine, dear, may I ask what you plan to wear, or would you rather Win not know?" Elisabeth asked.

"He already knows," she answered, smiling as she turned to look at Win, as he sat to her right, driving the Rolls Royce. "I'm wearing my mother's wedding gown. Although it's to be an exceedingly simple ceremony, wearing that frock still carries so much meaning for me. What about you, Elisabeth?"

"Nothing so grand, although, I certainly wish I had something of that sort. Nonetheless, I am going to wear the dress I had on the other night. Do you remember it? It's white taffeta with a deep-crimson sash."

"Oh, yes, of course. It's breathtaking. I'm glad you'll be dressing formally. I would have felt a bit like a fish out of water if I'd worn a long, elaborate gown, and you'd worn a suit or day dress."

"Didn't your gown need alterations, Josephine?" her brother asked.

"Very few. I managed them myself today, while Win returned to Winthrop Manor. They didn't amount to much."

"Whether we're being married in the Winthrop Manor chapel with hundreds of guests, or at Gretna Green with just the four of us, I feel my gown should reflect the occasion," Elisabeth continued.

"Yes, exactly," agreed Josephine.

"Have you any idea exactly where the ceremony will be?" Elisabeth enquired.

"There are several venues in Gretna Green," answered Andrew. "It's quite traditional to marry in the Old Blacksmith's Shop, but many couples choose hotels, or there is the Gretna Old Parish Church. It's probably much too large, but if your preference is a religious ceremony, that would be most appropriate."

"Win, have you been to Gretna Green before?" Josephine asked.

"Yes. A chum from school married there. It was a proper wedding with some one hundred guests. I was a close friend of the groom, so, of course, I attended."

"What about you, Andrew?" asked Elisabeth.

"Rather the same situation as Win."

"Tell us more about the church," Josephine asked.

"Well, I know parts of Gretna Old Parish Church date as far back as the seventeenth century, and there are portions of the structure dating to medieval times. It's where the couple whose wedding I attended were married."

"I think it sounds divine," Elisabeth nearly whispered. "Who performs the ceremony?"

"The wedding I attended was officiated by a Church of Scotland minister. Quite similar to Church of England. If that's where we all agree upon being wed, arrangements can be made the moment we arrive. Since it isn't the weekend, I suspect there will be fewer weddings booked. If we're flexible as to the time of day, I foresee no difficulty," added Andrew.

"What do you think, Josephine?" asked Win. "Personally, I like the idea of a church wedding."

"Definitely," she replied. She looked back at Andrew and Elisabeth. "What about you two, Andrew?"

"Yes, of course," they both answered almost simultaneously.

"Well, that settles the primary decision," Win stated. "As soon as we arrive, we'll select a hotel and make arrangements for a church ceremony."

"I can't believe this is happening," Josephine murmured. "I never dreamed when I woke this morning that it would be my wedding day."

"I didn't, either." Elisabeth giggled. "I'm so happy you sent the note with Win. Wouldn't we have been surprised if we'd run into you at Gretna Green?"

"Apparently, great minds think alike." Win laughed. "Whose idea was it to run off to Gretna Green?"

"Mine," answered Andrew. "Since I'd attended the wedding I told you about, I immediately thought about Gretna."

"It was the first place to pop into my mind, too," Win chimed in.

On they rode, through the afternoon, in almost a straight line, south to north, from Hampshire to the Scottish border.

16

❦

Upon arrival at Gretna Greene, everyone agreed that Win would be the one to take charge of the planning. He was the eldest and had been there before. Of course, so had Andrew, but Win was a natural leader, so they all felt he would be the best of the four to make decisions. Win drove to the area where the foursome would be most likely to find suitable accommodations. Soon, they began to see numerous hotels and inns. One of the inns had a particularly quaint charm, and the girls squealed with delight at the idea of making it the headquarters for their stay. Therefore, Win parked the elegant automobile and excused himself, leaving Andrew, Elisabeth, and Josephine anxiously awaiting his return. At last, he came back to the car.

"I've booked two suites, each with a bedchamber, bath, and parlour. I think you young ladies should use one of them for the purpose of preparing yourselves for the wedding ceremony. Andrew and I shall settle in the other. After the wedding, we'll each take over a suite."

Everyone disengaged from the auto and entered the inn. They were shown to their respective rooms. Once an employee delivered their luggage, the girls were left to their own devices, while Andrew and Win went in search of a locale where they could learn the necessary requirements for marriage at the Old Church. They were fortunate, in that the church was available that very evening at 8:00 p.m.

The two men hurried back to the inn and presented the news to their brides-to-be. Josephine and Elisabeth were overjoyed. Not only had the men learned of the church's availability, but they also brought news that if the couple wished, they could be joined in wedlock in a joint ceremony, since witnesses were available upon request. The immediate response was a resounding *yes*. It was 6:00 p.m., which did not leave a great deal of time, but everyone retired to their assigned locations and promised to meet shortly before eight o'clock. Elisabeth and Josephine took a short lie-down, although both were much too overcome with joy to truly rest.

Preparations for the big event began about sixth-thirty. Baths were run, hair was freshly brushed and pinned into up-dos, and small amounts of lip rouge and other light cosmetics were applied. Finally, each girl helped the other negotiate buttons on the backs of their gowns. Their excitement was absolutely overwhelming. Elisabeth and Josephine giggled one moment and wept with happiness the next. They chatted as they dressed.

"Elisabeth, I'm so delighted you're going to be my sister-in-law. I never would have dreamed such a thing could happen. I didn't even know Andrew was seeing you. In fact, Win hinted about you having an interest in Dr. Drew. I thought that was why Win invited Tom to the dinner at Winthrop Manor the night I met you."

"Yes. To be honest, I *was* once rather intrigued by Tom. He's handsome, kind, and intelligent. Nonetheless, the moment I met Andrew, I was certain I'd met my soul mate. There was a definite feeling that our meeting was predestined. I can't really explain. Any other man I'd ever met flew completely out of my mind."

"You needn't explain to me. That's precisely the way I felt when Win came riding by our cottage. I was dumbstruck. I'm still dumbstruck. I'd never have believed in a thousand years I'd be his wife. I didn't even believe I wanted to be married. Isn't it amazing how love can turn one's life upside down?"

"Oh, Josephine. I didn't think I was ready for this step in my life, either. Now I can't imagine a life without Andrew."

"We're both very lucky, don't you think?" Josephine said.

At twenty minutes before eight o'clock, the two left their suite and descended the ornate staircase to the first-floor level of what had once been a lovely, old home.

Win and Andrew were waiting at the bottom of the stairs. When they first set eyes upon their intended brides, exclamations of awe filled the air.

"My dear, dear Josephine," Win said, in an emotion-filled voice. "You look so incredibly lovely. I want to always remember the way you look at this moment." He handed her a bouquet of white roses mixed with white violets. "Here, darling. You'll hand this off to one of the witnesses when the moment arrives." He also gave her a gold wedding band. "This, my love, is for you to place upon my finger. I have its companion in my pocket. I made certain it will fit splendidly with your engagement ring."

"Win, you've thought of everything. How wonderful. I shall always remember this moment."

Elisabeth and Andrew were engaged in a similar conversation. She'd had no engagement ring, but Andrew had purchased a complete set. He slipped the engagement ring on her finger and asked her properly to be his wife. The four of them broke into laughter.

"Since we're on our way to the church, I don't think there's any wonder about my answer." Elisabeth smiled.

The four then strolled out of the inn and to the automobile. Doors were held open while Josephine and Elisabeth entered its plush interior, settling their gowns about them.

Andrew slid into the back seat next to Elisabeth, and Win arranged himself behind the steering mechanism on the right, with Josephine to his left. It was a very short ride to the picturesque Old Parish Church. The ancient structure had borne witness to countless thousands of Gretna Green weddings over the centuries. A fragment of late-medieval window molding and what may have been two similar fragments were built into the west wall. The timbered roof and Gothic, stained glass windows, portions of which dated from the original medieval church, clearly set the old parish church apart from other Gretna wedding venues.

The lovely church's setting was very secluded, and there were private lawns as well as gardens. The environment brought tears to Josephine's eyes, since she had such a special love of the out-of-doors and enchanting gardens.

The vicar was awaiting their arrival at the entrance to the church. He was an elderly gentleman with steel-gray hair and penetrating blue eyes. He shook Win's and Andrew's hands and then greeted Josephine and Elisabeth.

"I welcome you to our historic wedding site. I'm looking forward to joining such bonny couples in matrimony," he exclaimed in a heavy, Scottish burr.

He brought them forward to the front of the altar and introduced them to the witnesses, who apparently performed such duties for a good many couples every day. He excused himself for a moment, and then returned in his vestments, carrying a black, theological book. He placed himself behind the altar and began to read the traditional marriage ceremony from the Book of Common Prayer. A pair of witnesses stood on either side of each couple. After vows were exchanged, each couple knelt, and a prayer was recited over them. Upon standing, bouquets were given back to each bride, and the vicar pronounced them husband and wife. Each couple kissed.

Because Josephine was wearing a true wedding ensemble, complete with a filmy, lace veil, Win lifted it and put his arms around her. The kiss wasn't the rapid, unromantic buss often seen at weddings. The two exchanged a true, deep, passionate meeting of their lips, holding each other tightly. All formalities were completed, including requirement of their signatures on a marriage license, and those of the witnesses and the vicar. They waited until Andrew and Elisabeth had followed the same procedure. Then the four shook hands with the vicar, accepting his congratulations. Once outside, they kissed fervently, laughing and shouting their happiness.

"Now we have reservations at a fine restaurant in Gretna Green, known as the Lion's Inn. It's one of the oldest spots around—one of the first houses built here," Win proclaimed.

The two couples were so filled with excitement. Dinner wasn't the primary thing on each of their minds, but tasks had to be completed in proper order. It was traditional to enjoy a lovely dinner after one's marriage. So they trooped to the quaint, very old restaurant and were shown to a nice table in a quiet, romantic corner. Win ordered a bottle of the finest champagne, as well as a fine tray of *hors d'oeuvres*. They each studied the menu and settled on selections for a gourmet dinner. When the champagne arrived, the wine steward uncorked the bottle, pouring a glass for Win, since he had placed the order. Win nodded his approval and pronounced it to be excellent, so the steward poured some into each person's glass. They performed a group toast, wishing each other happiness. The war, looming on the horizon, seemed very remote. Surely, it couldn't interfere with their happiness.

Following their truly wonderful dinner, the foursome strolled back to the inn. They climbed the staircase to the second level, where their suites were located. The girls hugged each other, and Win shook Andrew's hand.

"It's been quite a day," proclaimed Andrew.

"A wonderful, special day," added Elisabeth. "August the fourth. Most people will remember it because England declared war against Germany, but I'll tuck it into my memories as the happiest day of my life."

"Yes, I agree completely," exclaimed Josephine. "Whatever the future brings, I'll now be Win's wife. Imagine. This morning I was simply Miss Josephine Chambers. Now, I'm Mrs. Win Winthrop."

"No, no, darling. You are the Lady Winterdale, although most people will refer to you as Josephine Winterdale or simply 'my lady'."

"Oh, Lord. I don't care for the thought of being referred to as the Lady Winterdale. There must be millions of young ladies in this kingdom who would give an arm to become a viscountess. Here I am, complaining. I apologise, Win. Naturally, I'm proud to be your wife, and any title accompanying my marriage to you is an honour."

"It's all right, darling. I understand. It will take some getting used to. You needn't call me *sir*—except when we're in bed, sweetheart."

Josephine swatted at him. "Ha! I hope you don't hold your breath, waiting for that." She laughed.

Andrew then spoke. "Well, Elisabeth and I have just the reverse problem. She used to be Lady Elisabeth Bradley. Now she's simply Mrs. Andrew Chambers."

"Oh, no, not really, Andrew. According to the rules of the peerage, I have the right to keep the title of *Lady,* but it makes no difference to me, whatsoever. I've known many, many sons of earls, dukes, and baronets. None were the exceptional gentleman you are, my dear husband."

"Uh, oh." Win laughed. "Are you implying, as the son of an earl, I'm not the catch that Andrew is?"

"I think you're perfect for Josephine. However, I also know her feelings about titles. That isn't the reason she fell in love with you. I think we're all exactly where we belong, title or no title." Elisabeth smiled.

With that, the couples bid each other a good night and made plans to meet for breakfast at nine o'clock the next morning. Then the long drive back to Winthrop-on-Hart would loom ahead.

Win closed the door of the parlour behind him and Josephine. He then pulled his wife into his arms. Kissing her passionately, he planted little nibbles up and down her neck. Occasionally, he paused, telling her how happy he was and how much he loved her.

"You're my soul mate, darling. From tonight, onward, we'll always be one person, really."

She snuggled her head against his coat. "I love you so, Win. I don't want to think about ever being parted from you. This gruesome war has put a shadow on our union."

"Darling, nothing can ever cast a shadow over us. Certainly, I wish we didn't have to deal with this conflict with Germany. Nonetheless, we'll face whatever comes, and we'll face it together. Now, my pet. Wouldn't you like to be more comfortable out of your marvellous wedding gown? Why don't you change in the bath? I'll be waiting for you. Take your time. I won't be leaving." He smiled.

"Yes, darling. I think that's an excellent suggestion," she answered.

They embraced and kissed once again. Then she turned towards the door to the bath, disappearing across the threshold.

17

❧

Josephine emerged a half hour later, resembling a photo in a rather risque women's periodical. She was clad in a fine, ivory cotton batiste nightdress made of mixed laces and silk. The gown had a square neckline with lace trim. A slight bit of decolletage showed her lovely, well-endowed silhouette. Win was sitting on the sofa, sipping a glass of port. He'd been reading the newspaper. The most recent headlines announced a dire need for all men of fighting age to join the military. He was so relieved about having wed Josephine before having to leave her. He knew he would enlist as soon as they returned. He was certain Andrew would do the same. Neither planned on telling their brides until the actual time arrived.

When the door had opened, he'd put the newspaper aside and looked towards the doorway. He couldn't believe the ethereal beauty of the enchanting young lady who was now his wife. She had unpinned her lovely hair, and it fell in ringlets to her shoulders. Her skin looked creamy and soft. He too had changed into pyjamas with the Winthrop monogram on the cuffs. He stood and walked to her.

"Josephine, you are so beautiful. It's difficult to believe you're real, for you look like an angel. Would you like another glass of champagne or something else? There is a small bar in the room."

"Yes, I believe I would like that, Win. I might add that you look exceptionally handsome. Seeing the Winthrop monogram on your cuffs makes me realise that my own monogram has changed. Now, instead of JCE, for Josephine Elizabeth Chambers, it will be JBW, for Josephine Chambers Bradley. I like it."

Win finished pouring her a flute of champagne. "I like it, too, darling. It signifies that now you're genuinely my wife. Come, let's sit together on the sofa. I want you to relax. You aren't worried about our becoming intimate with each other, are you?"

"No, Win. I love you with all my heart. I'm quite innocent about such matters, but I trust you to know how to proceed."

"Is there anything you want to ask me? I do promise I'll make every effort not to cause you discomfort. You might feel a brief stab of pain, but it will only be momentary. Please tell me if anything upsets you."

She snuggled up next to him. "I don't expect anything to upset me, Win. I look forward to our becoming one."

He took the glass of champagne out of her hand, and together with his own glass of Port, placed them on the tea table. Then he put his arms round her and began kissing her tenderly as he ran his hands up and down her soft arms. As the kisses grew more intense, he managed to raise her to a standing position. He began to kiss her a bit below the square neckline of her gown. She leaned into him, and they kissed more fervently.

"Shall we move to the bedchamber?" he murmured.

"Yes, my love," she whispered in return.

He took her tiny hand and led her to the beautiful, canopied bed. The maid had turned the covers back, so the pristine, linen sheets awaited them. Bending her back against the comforter topping the sheets, Win continued to kiss her with even more desire. She returned his warmth. Soon, they were lying on top of the cool, smooth sheets. Win went further with his kisses, until he had exposed one breast and was able to discern her arousal. After a few more passionate moments, he helped her slip the nightdress over her head, exposing her silken body. Then he continued with kisses as far down as her lithe, tiny waistline. At the same time, he began to stroke her gently in the secret warmth between her legs.

"Oh, Win! I've never felt like this before," she whispered.

"I know, darling. Nor have I. You're my everything. My adorable, angelic wife."

Josephine wrapped her arms around her new husband, pulling him close. Soon, he lay on top of her, and the desire she felt was overwhelming. She had never experienced anything like it and could think of no words to explain the sensation. He continued kissing her breasts, and she could feel his manliness. Before she had a chance to utter another word, she magically welcomed him into her body. Suddenly, they truly were one. Josephine could never in a million years have described what she felt. There was a brief stab of pain, but it was completely obliterated by the incredible rapture encompassing her entire body. She literally felt as if she were flying. Without any thought, she cried out in wonder.

"Oh, my dearest Win. I love you so much. I don't want this to ever end. I could go on and on like this forever."

"Yes, Josephine. I'm exactly where you are, my adorable wife."

Together they reached the pinnacle of passion.

Afterwards, they lay in each other's arms as their breathing slowly returned to normal, and they revelled in the warmth of each other's body.

"Did I cause you discomfort, my pet?" Win whispered.

"Win, whatever slight discomfort lasted only a second. I'd endure ten times that much to experience the intensity that followed. Will it always be this way?"

"It will grow in intensity, darling. The first time usually isn't very pleasant for a woman. I'm so glad it was for you. I promise, it will grow more and more blissful as we become used to each other as lovers."

"I can't imagine anything more divine than what I've just experienced. I absolutely feel as if we are solely one person, and we always shall be."

"We shall be, my precious. For the rest of our lives."

Win, Josephine, Andrew, and Elisabeth all stepped out of the Rolls in front of the imposing facade of majestic Winthrop Manor. It wasn't quite cocktail hour, but 5:30 p.m. when they arrived. Both of the young newlywed brides peeked in the small, compact mirrors they carried, refreshing lip rouge and powdering their noses. Josephine tucked a few stray hairs under the fetching creme-coloured beret she wore, which matched her simple suit of the same colour. Elisabeth wore a sunny-yellow linen chemise with matching coat. They both looked extremely happy. On the left hand of each was an eye-catching wedding band. The same applied to the men. Win glanced at Josephine and saw she was nervously nibbling her bottom lip.

"Josephine, please *do* stop fussing. Everything will be all right. The deed has been done. We're legally married, and it can't be undone. Either my parents accept that as fact, or Oliver will be immensely happy to learn he's going to be an earl someday."

Andrew laughed. "I think old Oliver would be over-the-moon with happiness at that prospect," he said. "However, I don't think your father is going to allow things to get that far out-of-hand."

"No," commented Elisabeth. "He may be their son, but they certainly realise he's a terrible bore. Father would rather you married a cook or housemaid than see Oliver inherit the estate someday. Honestly. It's all so silly. What parents in the world wouldn't be overjoyed at having Josephine for a daughter-in-law?"

"Our mother, Elisabeth," Win replied. "The Lady Winthrop, better known as the indomitable Lady."

Elisabeth placed her hand over her mouth to stifle a giggle. "Oh, she's going to have the fit to end all fits. It's hard for me to picture the look on her face when she learns that not one but two of her children have married outside of the aristocracy."

"Well, come. Let's make the happy announcement," commented Win. "The sooner this scene is behind us, the sooner we can settle ourselves into married life."

He reached for Josephine's hand, and she willingly gave it to him. They entered the great hall. All was quiet. Perhaps his parents were having a lie-down before dinner? Just as that thought flitted through Win's mind, his parents appeared, descending the staircase. They were obviously dressed for dinner. Even when it was only to be the two of them, they never broke with tradition, always dressing formally.

"Why, you're back, Win," cried the Lady Winthrop, putting her hand over her heart, as if she'd stumbled upon a snake in the garden and suffered a terrible fright.

"Yes, Mother. I told you and father I wouldn't be gone more than the night. Although, I can tell you the absolute truth now. There was no journey to London. Instead, Josephine and I, and Andrew and Elisabeth took a jaunt to Gretna Green, where we enjoyed a lovely, double wedding in the Old Parish Church there. So then, congratulations are in order. Are you going to break out the top-of-the line champagne, Father?"

Both parents' faces paled. Win knew that they were having a hard time believing this was true.

"Oh, my Good Lord," exclaimed Mother. "You can't mean it. You've married without our permission? What would make you perform such an abominable act? Both of you? I would have thought one of you might have had some sense."

"Mother and Father, please remember your manners," Win said in a somber voice. "Josephine is now my wife. She has formally become Lady Winterdale, though she's not keen on titles, so you needn't worry about there being two Lady Winthrops on the premises in the future."

"No, I certainly won't worry about that," his mother nearly shouted. "She will not be residing at Winthrop Manor." His mother turned to his father and gave him a withering glare. "My lord, say something. This is absolute folly. Surely, it can't be legal?"

The Lord Winthrop moved to Win's side, his hand open, palm-up. "Have you a marriage certificate to prove that a legal ceremony took place? How old are you, Josephine?"

Win reached inside his jacket pocket and produced the paper the two had signed, along with the vicar and two witnesses, less than twenty-four hours before. He handed it to his father.

Josephine stood straight and decided she did not intend to be bullied.

"I am eighteen years. I have my record of birth in my reticule, since I knew it might be needed at Gretna Green." Opening the small, ivory-coloured purse, Josephine produced the document.

Win's father studied both legal affirmations carefully. Then he handed both papers back to his son. "Well, I can't see that anything can be done. Everything appears to be in order."

He turned toward his daughter. "Elisabeth, I have always credited you with good sense. I do hope you realise you've broken your mother's heart, as well as mine. Your mother has dreamt of a large, impressive wedding for you from the time you entered the world. It's beyond me why you would have done such a thing."

"Daddy, I knew, beyond any doubt, you would never have approved of my marriage to Andrew. I love him enormously. England has just declared war against Germany. The four of us know that Andrew and Win will be compelled to join the military. Neither Josephine nor I wished to wait."

"Oh, fiddle," interrupted her mother. "Everyone says the war will be over by Christmas. Neither of you young men need to rush to join-up immediately. What utter madness."

Andrew stepped forward. "Sir, I adore Elisabeth. I realise I don't have a title, but I'm far from penniless. She'll have the finest of everything. We'll live wherever she wishes. I have a degree in law from Oxford. We shall have a fine life. We're extremely happy to be married."

"I suppose both of these wretched unions have been consummated," cried Win's mother. "The mere thought of such a thing makes me sick. There is no way out. You're all going to be dreadfully sorry someday. You've done an exceptionally stupid thing."

"Be that as it may, Mother. If you'll excuse us, Josephine is going to accompany me to my bedchamber while I pack some clothing. Obviously, we aren't going to spend the night here."

"Yes. I intend to do the same thing," echoed Elisabeth.

"But where are you going to stay?" his mother asked, panic in her voice.

"We'll go to my uncle's cottage. He was exceedingly happy about our plans. There's no doubt he'll be thrilled to have us stay with him until we sort everything out," Josephine explained. "He has plenty of room. I have never in my life stayed where I was not welcome, and I have no intention of starting now. Nor does my brother."

"Naturally, Josephine is correct. As I said, I am very secure, financially. If Elisabeth wishes, we shall buy our own home. Josephine was also taken care of extremely well in our father's will," Andrew added.

"Although I'm completely aghast at what you have done, I do intend to act as a gentleman. Your uncle, Anthony, is entitled to a handsome dowry, and since Elisabeth has legally married you, I shall make arrangements to have a banque checque cut."

"There will be no need for that. Elisabeth will be well-provided for."

"I shall do the honourable thing," retorted the Lord Winthrop. "Then I assume there isn't any more to be said. I wish I could welcome the spouses of my children into our family. Unfortunately, I don't feel capable of doing so at the moment. Perhaps, in time, my lady and I will look at this abomination in a different way. At present, we are absolutely mortified. Please proceed with the necessary packing. David will drive you to your cottage home. Quite a come down, I should think, after Winthrop Manor."

"Not necessarily, Father," replied Win. "There is a lot to be said for feeling welcome and being in the company of a gentleman who is thrilled that we've taken this monumental step in our lives."

"Yes, yes," his mother responded. "I'm sure their uncle is quite happy. It isn't every day that one's niece and nephew marry into the aristocracy. I imagine he's delighted the two of you have managed such a coup."

"Oh, for the love of God, Mother. There are more important things in life besides one's class or title. Do you understand anything at all about love?"

"It's every bit as easy to fall in love with someone in your own social circle, than it is to move outside and marry into the family of a sheepherder."

"Josephine's uncle is not a sheepherder. He is a fine, educated gentleman. He holds a degree from Oxford. Her family are scarcely paupers. Andrew is an Oxford graduate, as was his father before him, and Josephine had the finest governess imaginable."

"Oh, yes, indeed. I'm certain she is terribly familiar with what constitutes the finest," his mother sneered. "At any rate, no matter what her education or who you managed to cosy up to in order to drop an aristocratic name or two along the way; ladies are bred, not manufactured."

"Enough is enough, Mother," exclaimed Win. "Come, Josephine. We need to assemble the few items I'll need for now and be on our way. Are you coming, Elisabeth?"

"Yes, of course." She had tears in her eyes. No doubt she had secretly hoped their parents might find a way to show a scintilla of understanding. That surely wasn't to be.

The two newly wed couples made their way to the third level of the house. Win and Elisabeth each went to their respective bedchambers, where they packed as much clothing as possible into one large trunk. When they finished, Win called David and asked him to have the trunk placed into the back of the horse-drawn carriage, adding that the four of them would be travelling by car to Roderick Chambers' cottage. Another of the workers on the estate would drive the trunk to their destination. The four of them marched back down the stairway, ready to begin their adventures as wives and husbands. The Lord and Lady Winthrop were sitting in the drawing room, no doubt lamenting the ingratitude and selfishness of their two offspring. Win waited until his sister,

Andrew, and Josephine had gone out the front doorway, and then he paused. He nodded to Josephine.

"I'll be right out, darling.

He turned and entered the drawing room, and silently glared at his parents. "I shall be joining the military quite soon. Because I'm of the aristocracy, I'll hold the rank of an officer, but since I haven't a bloody notion about anything to do with military procedure, like any other soldier, I'll be sent to a regular army post for basic training. I've no idea where that might be.

"Apparently, a new detail has been put into effect, known as the PALS Program, whereby men from the same locale are teamed with others from their area. Andrew and I hope to be allowed to participate in this scheme. While, as an officer, I shan't be expected to fight alongside members of my unit, I fully intend to do so. If there's one thing I cannot bear, it's the smugness of a chap who thinks because he carries a title, he is therefore exempt from the rigors of military life. I shall inform you as to where I'll be located. Otherwise, I intend no communication."

"Son, your actions are deplorable," answered his father. "Your mother and I _do_ wish you well. Since this is the path you've chosen to follow, you leave me little choice but to completely re-work my affairs and cut off any finances for you. There is nothing I can do about you eventually inheriting Winthrop Manor. You and your wife will not be permitted to live here until my death."

"And what, dear father, will be the case, if I should have the misfortune to lose my life in the war, and Josephine is left with my legitimate son? Things like that do occur."

"Then I would undoubtedly reconsider. A son of yours would take precedence over Oliver. That assumes, of course, that Josephine would allow the child to be raised here at Winthrop Manor."

"I can assure you with certainty that she definitely would not even consider such an arrangement, unless she, too, were allowed to live here with our son. In fact, I have no doubt that even under such circumstances, she would be most reluctant to take up residence with the two of you."

"I cannot promise such an arrangement. She does not have the proper background to competently oversee the rearing of a future earl."

"Then you may very well never see your grandson, if I'm fortunate enough to have her conceive a male child before I leave for military training. I wouldn't want you to, and I shall instruct Josephine accordingly before I leave Britain to fight the Huns. Naturally, there is no reason to think there will even be a son, but I intend to plan for any contingency."

"Win, I never dreamed you could be so cruel." His mother sniffed into her white lace handkerchief.

"It's ironic that you see my point of view as cruel, yet your own is viewed as absolutely without fault. I love my wife. To me, that is quite simple. Any children born of our union will be ours to nurture as we see fit. If, for some God-awful reason, I'm prevented from completing that task, I trust Josephine implicitly to rear our offspring in a proper manner." Win spoke firmly, and when he finished, he turned and hastened out of the house, destined for a new way of life. He had no idea where the journey would end, and he didn't care, as long as Josephine was always by his side, whether he was fighting in France or helping to fulfill her dream of planting a glorious English garden in front of their own cosy cottage.

The Lord and Lady Winthrop sat alone in their opulent drawing room. Both were stunned. How did everything go so wrong? the Lord Winthrop pondered. I can't think of the slightest thing we might have done to encourage such rebellious behaviour on the part of either Win or Elisabeth. They were, by far, favoured children. Nothing had been spared in bringing them up and seeing to it that they were given every advantage.

The Lady Winthrop continued to sniffle into her handkerchief. "Oliver was an unexpected child, and he delights in being able to boast about his fine, aristocratic family. He never considers an outing with a female who isn't of the aristocracy. He loathes the mere idea of association with those who aren't in line for a title and don't live in a grand, old manor house. Let's be honest, my lord. Oliver is a rather unpleasant chap. Win was, and always has been, our pride and joy. That we could see him marry a common girl who has never even been presented to the king and queen or participated in a Season is simply unthinkable.

"Then there's Elisabeth. Our lovely, refined Elisabeth. She would have been the *it* girl of the Season. She might have had her pick of any chap in the land. Yet she has chosen to become the wife of a construction worker's son. The fact that his father has a degree from Oxford, or that Andrew himself does, means nothing at all, because such accomplishments are of no value without the requisite titles. We've been living for the day when Win and Elisabeth were married to suitable mates, as well as to the joy of grandchildren. Now, it appears that the only grandchildren we're likely to know well will be Oliver's. It's difficult to imagine Oliver marrying a debutante from a distinguished family. He has the proper credentials, but he is not attractive—not in the least. It's not nice of me to say that, but unfortunately, it's true."

"My lord, I shall never understand why he inherited such terrible traits. When he was born with carrot-red hair and his face covered with freckles, I nearly died."

"Yes, well, I'm stunned that he grew into a man who is short and stocky, when Win is tall and slender. Oliver's nose is much too large for his face, and his teeth give him a rather "horsey" appearance. No amount of money, titles, or grand homes will make up for his many shortcomings," the Lord Winthrop lamented. "I suppose he'll marry a girl from a similar background with an equally unappealing appearance. In the course of two hours, our lives have gone to shambles. There will have to be some remedy found, but I haven't the slightest notion what it might be."

18

≈⋙≈

Win happily stepped out of the Rolls Royce in front of Roderick Chambers' cottage, along with Elisabeth, Josephine, and Andrew. Before they reached the front doorway, it flew open, and Roderick greeted them with outstretched arms.

"Ah, you've returned. I take it the journey was all you hoped it would be. Am I now welcoming a new son and daughter into the family?" he enquired.

"Indeed, you are, sir," answered Win. "We tied the knot in a charming double ceremony in the old Gretna Church. The vicar was a delightful gentleman. We stayed at a quaint inn and drove back today. We've already been to Winthrop Manor, and our reception was precisely what we expected it would be. It seems Elisabeth's and my actions have put a blight on the distinguished family name." He laughed heartily. "Frankly, I think some new blood is exactly what is needed on the family tree."

"Do come inside. I want to hear all about your adventure," said Roderick.

Everyone entered the cottage and made themselves comfortable in the parlour. Roderick served refreshments, and they began to converse.

"Oh, I am truly sorry to learn of your parents' reaction. I had hoped they would accept your choices and welcome you. Well, no matter. I happen to be delighted, and not because of your heritage," Roderick replied. "It's so obviously apparent that great love exists here. I have no doubt whatsoever that you'll all be extremely happy. Damn this wretched war. I'm afraid it may throw a wrench into the immediate future."

"Yes," Win replied. "Andrew and I must immediately look into what lies ahead for us."

"I know a recruitment office has been established in Winthrop-on-Hart," said Roderick. "I should think they can give you all the information you need."

"Yes. Absolutely. I'm glad we won't have to travel to London. We have many things to discuss. If Andrew and I have to go for military training immediately, appropriate arrangements need to be thought out for our wives."

"Win, you've no need for concern on that score. They can stay here with me for a long as necessary."

Win smiled. "That's good of you, Roderick. Nonetheless, I don't like the idea of their living with you for a long, long time. I know everyone is saying this conflict will be over by Christmas, but I'm not at all certain I believe that. I know Josephine has always dreamed of an English cottage in the country with a luscious garden adorning the front." He turned to his wife. "Darling, how would you like it if we put plans into motion to build your dream cottage?"

"Win, you know I'd adore such a thing. Uncle, you once said I might have a parcel of your land to build on. Would that really be possible?"

"Absolutely. We'll take a ride over the land tomorrow. I have a specific spot in mind."

"Elisabeth, how would you feel about sharing that sort of accommodation with me if Andrew and Win are gone a long time?" Josephine asked her sister-in-law.

"I would love it. I've always lived in the country. I don't want to leave this region. I know Andrew will need to live near London when he begins to read the law, but until then, I surely don't want to be alone," Elisabeth replied.

"Then we'll follow that plan for the immediate future," answered Win.

Josephine looked lovingly at her husband. "Still, Win, I suspect you haven't a great desire to spend the rest of your life in a modest cottage. Not after having grown up at Winthrop Manor," she remarked.

"No. I wouldn't want that forever. We'd keep the cottage as a nice place for a quiet get-a-way and probably buy an old country house in this region for our permanent home."

"I feel badly that because of me, you'll be losing your long-anticipated opportunity to marry and raise your own family at Winthrop Manor, at least until your father passes away, and you become the next earl. Perhaps your parents will stop this foolishness and allow us to move back to your true home."

"I'm not counting on that, darling. It's all right. You mean more to me than anything."

"Still, it seems so horribly unfair. I don't want to sound bitter, but I really am not very fond of Oliver, and it angers me to think he will enjoy the privileges, and you won't."

"Father can do whatever he chooses. We won't be destitute. In fact, in the long run, I have a suspicion I may enjoy my newfound freedom. We'll see what the military brings. If possible, I might even return to school to pursue a new career."

"I guess I'm fortunate not to have been tied up with a future pre-planned from the beginning of my life, simply because I'd been born into an aristocratic family." Andrew smiled. "I'll be doing what I've always dreamed—practicing law. So I guess there *are* advantages to being a simple man with no title."

"That's really true, Andrew. I've always disliked the fact that I didn't have the choice about choosing my own career."

Roderick had left the parlour and gone to the kitchen. He returned and announced that the cook had prepared a nice roast for dinner. It was ready to eat anytime they wished. They had not eaten since leaving Gretna Green, and everyone's eyes lit up at the sound of a beef roast. Roderick led the way to the dining room, where the table was set beautifully.

"How lovely, Uncle," said Josephine. "This was so thoughtful of you."

"Indeed, is certainly was," added Win.

Andrew and Elisabeth heartily agreed, as everyone took a place at the table. During the meal, the discussion moved back to all of the details of the wedding, and Roderick listened, obviously happy to hear about their trip.

Win covered his mouth and yawned. "Forgive me. I guess the drive back from Gretna Green tired me more than I realised. Dinner was marvellous. I'm filled to capacity and a bit tired."

"Yes, I think we probably all are. Would you understand if we excused ourselves and retired for the night, Uncle?" Josephine asked.

"Of course not. I'm sure you are all ready to go to your rooms. Come, let me show you where you'll be staying," he responded.

He led the way to the stairs and up, where he showed Win and Josephine to a very nicely arranged bedroom. Andrew and Elisabeth would be ensconced in the room across the hall. Win was surprised that each room even had its own bath. He and Josephine closed the door, after once again thanking Roderick for his hospitality and bidding everyone goodnight.

"This is truly lovely, darling," said Win. "I'm surprised we have a private bath. These older cottages generally aren't that well-equipped."

"Uncle Roderick had this one refurbished quite a while back. Don't forget, Andrew and I came to live with him."

"Yes, of course, that makes sense," answered Win.

Josephine found herself more relaxed and even eager for the wondrous desire she'd experienced on their wedding night. She was actually a bit impatient for the moment when her husband began to kiss her in what she would once have considered forbidden places. The routine she had followed the previous night was repeated, as she bathed, brushed her hair, and performed all of her regular nightly rituals. Then, Win repeated the routine he had followed on their wedding night. As they crawled into the lovely bed, she immediately snuggled into his arms.

"My little pet, you seem to want to be close to me even more than you did last night," Win murmured.

"Yes, I love you so, darling, and I realised this afternoon while we were at Winthrop Manor how much you have sacrificed for me."

"Sweetheart, I'd give up the world for you. You mean everything to me. Don't you dare ever forget that."

He began the familiar little nibbles on her neck she had already grown to love. His hand traveled down over her body again, and she knew what was going to happen next. He touched the soft fur between her legs, and she felt desire grow. Then he slipped her nightgown over her head and began to kiss her breasts. She was growing more and more passionate. She had mostly let him take charge the previous night, but now she felt a need to touch him in places she had never dreamed of, and it shocked her to discover what men were truly like when unclothed. She reached her hand between his legs, and he groaned in obvious pleasure.

"Does that make you happy, darling?" she whispered.

"Josephine, you'll never believe the ecstatic way you make me feel," he answered.

She was delighted that she was pleasing him as much as he had her.

"I hope I can always make you this happy, Win. I feel as though we are truly one person now." She wasn't uncomfortable with her desire to touch her husband, showing deep love for him in ways she would never have dreamed possible. He'd been correct. The act of making love *did* indeed grow more intense.

When they finally fell asleep, he lay with his back to her, and she spooned her body into his. It was so meaningful to feel utterly secure and loved by such a special man.

19

❧

Andrew and Win drove into Winthrop-on-Hart the next day to enquire about options available for them in the military. They came away knowing a great deal more. In a country defined by class, only "gentlemen" from the upper and middle classes could hope to become new officers in 1914 or 1915. Win knew with certainty he would qualify for such a rank, but since Andrew didn't have an aristocratic background, although he *had* attended Oxford, there had been some concern about whether he would be permitted to take part in Officer Training. They were told that Britain's public schools and universities were the main recruiting grounds for the new leaders needed, en masse, to manage the hundreds of thousands of new soldiers in the ranks. Both Andrew and Win had graduated Oxford, which meant they had superb educations. Thus, Win was very relieved to learn that he and Andrew would be able to train together.

Young officers were taught how to control and care for men and how to command their respect. Each had to lead a platoon of around thirty men, many older and from much tougher backgrounds than themselves. Training camps had cropped up all over England. Some of those were designated for officer training.

First, a young man needed to volunteer his services; then, immediately, he was sent to a camp for sixteen weeks of intense training. In just four months, a trainee would have to master the complexities of drill, the intricate etiquette of army life, and the strict rules of military discipline. An officer's prime concern was to set an example for his men and adhere to the duties of obedience, cleanliness, sobriety, and honesty. When training was complete, the young men would emerge as second lieutenants. It all sounded infinitely better than having to be an infantry soldier. Nothing about war appealed to either Win or Andrew, especially since they were newly married, but they made up their minds to enlist in officer training immediately.

They returned home from their visit to the recruiting office and passed the information on to Josephine and Elisabeth. Naturally, neither young lady was enthusiastic about losing their husband, even temporarily, to the war. Nevertheless, they both had pride in the men and admired their patriotism and courage.

While Andrew and Win had been in the village, Roderick had driven the ladies to the piece of land he'd recommended for the planned construction of Josephine's dream cottage. The spot was indeed perfect. If the cottage were situated properly, it would sit where the sun would shine nearly all day upon what would be the front-garden area, and there would be an enormous, old elm tree in back. A lovely, small stream ran through the property, and dozens of willow trees bent over the water, creating a quiet, serene setting. Both Josephine and Elisabeth adored the spot. As soon as their husbands returned, they were implored to accompany their wives back to the splendid building site. Josephine was already picturing her dream cottage. Win agreed that it truly was perfect land to build upon.

When they were back at Roderick's cottage, all sat at the old, round table in the dining area, sketching ideas for the home they imagined. Everyone made a suggestion. Before the evening ended, they had a good outline from which any architect could design a true blueprint. They all made a pact to never reveal the locale to Oliver. Neither Win nor Andrew wanted anyone at Winthrop Manor to know where their wives were living while the men were away, serving their country.

Germany had already invaded Belgium and parts of France. German troops were prevented from taking Paris and were defeated at the Battle of the Marne. Win and Andrew enlisted on September 10. There had never been any question as to whether they would take such a step. The only question had been when.

They called their wives and Roderick into the drawing room, sat them down, and broke the news as gently as possible. Josephine and Elisabeth had hoped and prayed they would never reach such a day, but as the streets had become more and more empty of young men, they knew their husbands would be leaving.

"When will you go?" asked Josephine, trying very hard not to break down.

"Quite soon, darling. Andrew and I visited the recruiting office again today. There is beginning to be a severe shortage of officers. We've both enlisted. Next Monday, we'll be sent to the Salisbury Plain for training. The time required for our introduction into the military will be sixteen weeks." Win smiled. "I don't think either of us is too anxious to become acquainted with machine guns, rifles, bayonets, or bombs. Nonetheless, those pieces of machinery will be our constant companions and may very well save our lives."

"My God, it's such a short time," cried Josephine. "You will be given at least a short furlough before you're sent abroad, won't you?"

"I would hope. Of course, you both know we'll write as often as possible. Your letters will be our lifeline home. Just knowing one from you is on its way will mean the world to both of us," said Win.

"Darling, do you intend to tell your parents about this?" asked Josephine.

"At first, I thought I wouldn't, but now, I think it's the only decent way to behave. No matter how narrow-minded they've been, I don't want to leave for battle without seeing them. I'll pop over to Winthrop Manor tomorrow for a quick chat."

"I'm proud of you. Just because they've acted like fools doesn't mean you're one, too. I know they love you with all their hearts. Going to see them to say goodbye only proves what a good person you are," Roderick said.

As the five of them had sat in the parlour, Roderick had listened quietly to the entire conversation. "Your parents should be proud to have raised such a fine young gentleman. I would have given anything to have been blessed with such a son. Unfortunately, my sweet wife, Thelma, was never able to conceive a child. That's probably one reason that Andrew and Josephine have always held such a very special place in my heart."

"Oh, Uncle, what a lovely thing for you to say," uttered Josephine.

"I want you to think of me as a son, Roderick. I know you're Josephine's uncle, but you're also a father figure. I wish I could have known her parents."

"You would have thought they were the creme of the crop. I know they would have thought you were."

"That's a fine compliment, Roderick. Thank you."

Josephine, Win, Andrew, Elisabeth, and Roderick sat up until quite late, discussing the eventuality of war. Win wanted the cottage to continue its construction, and Josephine was glad. It would provide something to keep her mind off of Win's absence. Elisabeth seemed every bit as excited, as well as downhearted to be saying goodbye to Andrew.

It was growing late, and the foursome knew there wouldn't be many more nights spent in each other's arms. It was already Thursday. Only four nights together. Andrew suggested it was time to turn in.

"I'll prepare a jolly, fine breakfast tomorrow and every day following, until we have to bid farewell for a time. From what I hear, the military food leaves a lot to be desired." Roderick laughed.

Win was in his wife's arms before the door was completely closed. It was rather cold in the room. After the warmth of the parlour with the lovely fire roaring, both Josephine and Win shivered. From the moment he'd learned he would be leaving for the Salisbury Plain, he'd wondered how long it would be before he held her again. The uncertainty of war also contributed to natural trembling. Win was terrified at the thought of losing his life or a limb in the war, but he wasn't about to admit it. The last thing Win wanted was for Josephine to know of the dreadful anxiety he harboured.

"Oh, my darling. How can I bear being separated from you? What if this war goes on and on and on?" Win whispered, tucking his head against her breast.

"Sweetheart, you'll be home soon," Josephine said. "Is there any chance the United States will join in this venture?"

"That's what we all hope. It hasn't gone on long enough yet, but I would think the Yanks will prove to be loyal allies. I'm sorry if I'm worrying you, Josephine. I don't mean to. For just a moment there, I felt a bit of anxiety. I'm sure everything will turn out for the best."

"But of course you're anxious. Do you know what sort of situation you'll be going into? Is there heavy fighting going on?"

"From what I read and hear, the Brits are about to find themselves in a wretched stalemate known as the war of attrition."

"What does that mean?" Josephine questioned.

"Basically, it marks the beginning of a nightmare called trench warfare. Right now, the Battle of Ypres is supposedly beginning. Trenches are starting to be built in France. At the conclusion of the battle, as I understand it, there will as be a line of trenches that run from The North Sea to the French-Swiss border."

What a mess, Josephine thought. In just a few days, her husband would leave, and neither of them had any idea when they might see each other again. Complicating matters even further, Josephine, although pitifully uneducated about such matters, suspected she was pregnant. She'd had no monthly curse since she and Win had married. She'd said nothing to Win, not wishing to put an extra burden on him, especially at a time when he was about to leave to fight a war. She suspected that her husband knew infinitely more than she did about women's cycles. She had a rudimentary knowledge of how the process worked, but no one had ever explained everything to her. She had gone back and forth in her head, trying to decide whether she should say anything to Win before he left, or wait and book an appointment with Dr. Drew, so she would know for certain before saying anything to her husband.

They kissed, passionately, but before their amorous activity progressed any further, Josephine made the decision to discuss her conundrum.

"Darling, I need to tell you something," she began.

"My pet, I have a hunch I know what you're about to say. Do you have a suspicion that you might be expecting a baby?" Win asked. "Be honest with me. I know there's been nothing to interrupt out lovemaking since we married."

"Aren't you the perceptive one?" She giggled. "That's exactly what I want to discuss with you. I haven't visited a physician, but I *do* suspect I'm pregnant. I wasn't trying to keep it from you. I just need to have it confirmed by a doctor."

"How far along do you think you are?" he asked.

"We were married August 4. It's now September 22. I suspect I conceived on our wedding night. So I'm probably just a bit over six weeks. It could be a false alarm, since my monthly isn't very late."

"Let me ask you a few questions. Perhaps I can help you to determine if you really *are* going to have a baby. Don't be frightened, Josephine. If you are expecting a child, it will be wonderful news."

"Yes, but we didn't plan on having a baby so soon. Especially with the war and all. It frightens me to think I might be expecting, and you won't be here with me."

"You wouldn't be all alone. There's your uncle and Elisabeth. Who knows? This foolish war could be all over by the time a child would be born."

"What were you meaning to ask me?" Josephine enquired, snuggling next to him.

"Have you noticed any other feelings that denote pregnancy?"

"I'm not certain what they'd be. I'm awfully naive when it comes to this topic, as you know."

"Yes." He laughed softly. "Have you experienced any nausea?" he asked. "Especially in the morning?"

"No. Not really. Perhaps for a few days, but nothing severe," she replied. "I assumed it was nerves about our wedding and such."

"Are your breasts tender?"

"Yes, they are. Is that a sign? I've wondered why they seem so uncomfortable."

"Have you gained any weight? Especially in the abdomen?"

"Not much. So perhaps it *is* only emotional. Do you think I *am* expecting a baby, Win?"

"I think it's a possibility. I don't mean to embarrass you, darling, but were you always quite regular with your monthly?"

"Yes. Very. Always. That's what alerted me. Oh, Win, I'm so ignorant about these things. I was too young for my mother to go into any detail with me. She *did* explain the rudimentary aspects about where babies come from and such, but she had no idea she wouldn't live to tell me everything. I feel rather ill-informed, to say the least. I just thought I haven't been because my body underwent changes—you know. Um, well, I'm not a virgin anymore. I thought that might make a difference."

"No, dear. It shouldn't." He stifled laughter. "We need to have Tom Drew over in Cloverdale have a look at you. I don't think there's much question, but he'll be able to tell us for certain."

"I'm a bit embarrassed to have Tom examine me since he's a chum of yours, but that's who I intended to see before I told you."

"Josephine, he's a professional. I know he's an excellent physician. I want to make certain you see someone I trust, and I *do* trust Tom implicitly." Win kissed her again. "I love you, darling. The thought of you carrying my baby is marvellous. I can't tell you how happy it makes me," he whispered.

Josephine began to weep.

"Sweetheart, what's the matter? Are you feeling poorly?"

"No. No. I'm crying because I'm so relieved and happy. I was frightened to tell you what I suspected. I thought you might be angry. Now here we are in a war, and you'll be leaving me. I'll have to go through having a baby by myself."

"Josephine, we have no idea how long this wretched war will last. It may all be over by then. If not, as I said, you won't be alone. You'll have Elisabeth, your uncle, and the doctor."

"But won't Dr. Drew have to join up and fight, too?"

"Not necessarily. He's a physician. Often, they're excluded from the military because their occupation is considered vital to the homeland. If Tom has to go into the military, I'll make certain you have an excellent doctor who is exempt. You will *not* be alone. For that matter, my mother may change her mind when she learns there's going to be a child. So it's very possible you'll have her to rely upon, too."

"Win, I don't trust your mother. I'm sorry. I don't mean to hurt you, but you know as well as I do that she dislikes me tremendously. I don't expect her to like my baby any more than she does me."

Win held her in his arms as she wept. "Hush, darling. There's nothing to cry about. Everything will be fine. If you don't want my mother near you, you needn't have her. Before I leave England, I'll make rock-solid plans. You'll be well taken care of."

"Do you promise?" Josephine sniffled.

"Absolutely. Now come snuggle next to me. This isn't a time for weeping. It's a time for joy. Because of our love a new life may very well enter this world. What could be more thrilling?"

"Nothing. No. Nothing at all. I *am* so happy. I never dreamed this would happen so soon. I just wish there wasn't a war."

"There's never a perfect time for a lot of things, Josephine. Nevertheless, as far as I'm concerned, we're the luckiest twosome alive. Now, come let me hold you in my arms and feel your lovely body next to mine. I'm going to miss that joy so much, my sweet. We don't have many nights before I leave. I'll call Tom in the morning, and we'll pay him a visit. I don't want you to be concerned. You are the most precious thing in the world to me, and so will a baby be. I *do* hope you're expecting. I can lay awake at nights when I'm away from you, thinking about the happy years we have to look forward to as a family. I love you so very much, my darling."

"Do you think it's safe for us to make love?" she asked.

"I don't think we need worry. Surely, you don't want to spend our last few nights together foregoing the joy of being as close together as possible," Win said.

"No, Win, I want to spend every moment we can in each other's arms. If I'm not expecting now, perhaps I will be soon."

20

_____

The following morning, Win telephoned Dr. Drew's office and made an appointment for Josephine to see him at one o'clock in the afternoon. Win asked Roderick if he might borrow his automobile, and, of course, the older man was only too happy to oblige. So Black Orchid remained in the stable, while Win and Josephine headed for the doctor's office. Josephine was chewing on her bottom lip.

"Darling, you've nothing to be frightened of. Tom is a wonderful chap. Believe me, you're not the first woman he's examined." He reached over and patted his wife's arm. "Everything will be fine. Won't you be relieved to know for certain if you truly are expecting a child? I certainly will be."

"Yes, of course, me, too. This is just very new to me, Win. I'll become accustomed to it. Actually, I'm rather happy to know the doctor is a chum of yours."

They arrived at Tom's office. Immediately upon entering, his nurse showed her to an examining room. Win made himself comfortable in the outer office. In about three-quarters of an hour, Josephine appeared, looking radiant. Win didn't have to ask what Tom's conclusion had been. Tom followed behind her, ready to speak to Win.

"Well, old chap, I'm happy to be the one to tell you that Josephine is going to have your child. What splendid news. I'm sure you're delighted. It's so nice to have cheerful news when we're surrounded each day by disgusting tales of the war."

"This *is* happy news." Win took hold of Josephine's hand. "When are we to expect the happy event?"

"She seems quite certain the baby was conceived August 4, your wedding night. Judging from that, I'd put the due date at about the middle of May. I want Josephine to see me every month from now on. Also, no strenuous lifting and a well-balanced diet. Absolutely no medication without checking with me first."

"What about, uh, well, you know, Tom? I'm leaving for military training very soon. I'd like to think I can make love to my wife before we part."

Tom laughed and patted Win on the back. "Yes. That's no problem. I'd put a moratorium on that at about three months, just as a precautionary measure. Not all physicians would agree with me, but that's the time when miscarriage is most prevalent."

"I'll probably be in France by then," Win murmured.

"I do wish you luck. I was given a deferment because of my occupation and the shortage of physicians in this area. On the one hand, I'm relieved not to have to fight the Huns, but I also feel a bit guilty. I hate anyone thinking I'm a slacker."

"No fear of that, Tom. Anyone who knows you is well aware you'd be ready to head for France in a heartbeat. As for myself, I'm delighted you'll be here to watch over my precious wife. It will make my time in France easier, knowing she's in the best hands and that I'll be returning to not just her, but a healthy son or daughter."

Win and Josephine left Dr. Drew's office, holding hands, broad smiles on their faces. They were both a bit stupefied, but their happiness far outweighed their shock. Win returned Josephine to her uncle's cottage and then announced he was going to make the trip to Winthrop Manor, which they had previously discussed.

Win mounted Black Orchid and rode to his former home. He'd not seen his parents since the unpleasant conversation he'd had with them after the return trip from Gretna Green. He didn't expect them to be overjoyed by his appearance. They would undoubtedly be under the impression their son had come to his senses and realised he'd made a dreadful mistake. They'd probably think he was about to initiate divorce proceedings. When they learned the true reason for his visit, Win expected another row.

He pulled up on the reins and came to a halt in front of the manor, tying Black Orchid to the hitching post. Normally, he would have ridden to the stables, but he had no intention of staying very long, so the stallion was left where Win could depart quickly. He rapped on the front door, although in the past he would merely have opened it and entered.

Radcliffe immediately answered the knock. "Why, how nice to see you my lord. It's been quite some time. You've been missed."

"Radcliffe, let's not pretend you don't know about the revolting row I had with my parents. I'm sure all the staff is aware of it. That's why I haven't been seen 'round here. I do hope you're aware of my marriage."

"Yes, sir, I did hear that. Your wife is lovely. Won't you come in?" the butler asked.

"Yes, I'd like to. Thank you. Are the Lord and Lady Winthrop at home?"

"Yes. I believe they're in the library, my lord."

Win walked swiftly down the long hallway, past the drawing room to the library. His parents were seated on one side of the massive desk, looking over some papers. It was probably a copy of the new will. As he entered the room, both his mother and his father looked up. It was clear that they were utterly surprised to see him.

"What are you doing here, Win?" asked his mother.

"While I'm well aware you have no desire to see me, I felt I needed to stop by and give you some news."

"What sort of news?" asked his father.

"May I sit down?" Win asked.

"Yes, certainly," answered his father.

"Thank you," Win responded. "I doubt either will please you much, but it seemed proper for me to tell you in person; although, I *did* consider writing a letter."

"Since you've obviously chosen to pay us a visit, may we hear whatever this news is?" his father queried in an irritated tone.

"Andrew and I have enlisted in officer training. We'll be sent to camp at Salisbury Plain for sixteen weeks of rigorous training and then on to France, I assume. I don't plan on writing to you, so if you want information about me, you'll have to speak with my wife. She may or may not choose to answer your inquiries."

"You didn't have to do such a foolish thing," the Lord Winthrop nearly shouted. "You are the eldest child in a very distinguished family, engaged in the care of thousands of acres of property. You would have been given an exemption."

"I didn't care to act like a weakling. At any rate, it was my understanding that I was persona non grata here. So if Oliver cares to use the exemption, allow him to do so. I see very little hope of his being of any value to our country."

"Have you finished with what you came to tell us?" asked his mother.

"No. The other news I've brought concerns my wife. Tom Drew, over in Cloverdale, confirmed this morning that Josephine is pregnant. I felt you should know, although I don't expect anything from you. Also, before you jump to conclusions and start ranting that Josephine was undoubtedly pregnant before we married, she was not. She conceived on our wedding night."

Win stood. Before either parent could utter another word, he headed for the hallway.

"Wait just a moment, son," the Lord Winthrop called.

Win came to a halt. "What else do we have to discuss?"

"This changes everything. It's exactly the scenario you painted when we first learned you had married Josephine. What if she has a male child? He would be the presumptive heir to Winthrop Manor. If something should happen to you in the war, God forbid, your son would inherit. He needs to be raised under our roof and not in some sheepherder's cottage by a mother with no experience in terms of etiquette required of an aristocratic child."

"I told you before, Josephine hasn't the slightest intention of moving in here or of seeing you take our child to raise. Don't even contemplate such a thing. I intend to have a new will drawn up. I'll make certain it's made abundantly clear that no offspring of mine will ever be taken from its mother."

"Are you insinuating that I would not raise a child properly?" his mother interjected.

"Yes, I suppose I am," answered Win. "In any case, whether you would or would not, my child will be raised by my lovely, sweet wife. Let's be honest, Mother. You didn't raise me. Nannies did. Why, our cook is more of a mother to me than you ever were." With that, Win turned abruptly and left the house.

Complete silence filled the library after Win's departure. Finally, the Lady Winthrop spoke.

"Damn you, my lord. If you hadn't threatened Win, telling him Josephine could never live in this house, we wouldn't be facing such a nightmare."

"I beg your pardon? If my memory serves me correctly, and it does, it was *you* who did the threatening. When he married Josephine, there was nothing we could do about it. It was completely legal. We should have accepted it. Oliver hasn't any business running this holding. He may be our son, but he's a fool. You know it, and so do I. Due to our own foolishness, we've lost the son who will be the next earl, and we've lost a potential grandchild. As well as a beautiful daughter."

Win picked up his travel bag and walked down the stairs. On this, his day of departure, in late September, 1914, his heart was heavy at the thought of leaving his beautiful wife. Josephine, Elisabeth, Andrew, and Roderick stood waiting for him in the downstairs front entry. The men kissed their wives goodbye, holding them tightly, promising over and over to come home safely, as if by making such a vow, it would definitely become reality.

Roderick drove the four of them to the rail station at Winthrop-on-Hart. It was a dreary day, with rain threatening. The weather conditions mirrored Win's mood, and Andrew didn't seem very chipper, either. When they reached the depot, Roderick shook the young men's hands but then remained in the car, leaving Win and Andrew alone to say good-bye. Both Josephine and Elisabeth had lost their composure and were weeping. Win fought back tears, as well, and Andrew kept blinking rapidly, and his eyes were suspiciously shiny. Win kept reminding Josephine to take care of herself and the baby and to write to him daily. He didn't know how often he would be able to write to her, but he vowed that it would be as often as possible.

"I'm going to miss you so much, darling. You'll be in my heart, no matter where I am," Win declared. "We'll get through this, and when it's over, nothing in life is ever going to part us again."

Over and over he kissed her tenderly and vowed his deep love. Finally, the conductor called for all passengers to board the train, and it was time to say their final goodbyes. Tears were streaming down Josephine's and Elisabeth's faces, and they were holding soggy handkerchiefs from all the crying they had done. But both took deep breaths and tried to smile. It started to rain as the trained pulled away, which seemed providential.

From their small village, Win and Andrew met up with other enlistees, and they all rode the train to Winchester, the primary city in Hampshire. Due to the army's desire to follow the new PALS plan, Win and Andrew would remain together throughout their training. A British general had suggested at the beginning of the war that men would be more willing to join up if they could serve with people they already knew. The idea was first tried in Liverpool, and its success prompted other towns and villages to form their own PALS units.

In Winchester, they all boarded another train, which carried them to the Salisbury Plain, where new training camps had been constructed. It had been a long, dismal day, and they were relieved to reach their destination. The camp was not only meant for officer training, but regular recruits from various areas were assigned there, as well. The regulars slept in tents, and officer trainees were accorded the luxury of a bunk in a corrugated hut. Andrew and Win, being the only officers who were new trainees, were able to share a hut.

Many rough weeks lay ahead of them. They left their old lives far behind and concentrated upon learning military discipline, drilling, and fighting with rifles and bayonets. The time spent in training created a spirit of camaraderie, as Win and Andrew became more familiar with each other's habits and lives. All the men learned to operate as a cohesive unit. Once the officers had been taught the rudiments of military training, they were put to work with the other soldiers, learning how to dig trenches. Practice trench systems provided more realistic training. Finally, it all ended, and they were issued the uniforms of second lieutenants. Then they received the happy news that they would be given a week's furlough before shipping out to France in January, 1915. They were assigned to the Eleventh Brigade, Fourth Division. Each carried a small book entitled: *Notes for Infantry Officers on Trench Infantry*.

21

❧❧

Upon their arrival at Winthrop-on-Hart, Win and Andrew were met by Josephine and Elisabeth, who were eagerly waiting at the station, hopping up and down with excitement. Both were weeping again, just as they had been when their husbands had departed for training, but these were tears of joy. Both were embraced so tightly, it was a wonder that each was able to breath. Tears and laughter mingled. There were endless exclamations regarding how handsome and debonair Win and Andrew looked in their officer uniforms. Roderick finally stepped from the car, having afforded the women an opportunity to be alone with their husbands. Then they all headed back to the cottage.

However, it wasn't the Chambers' cottage to which they returned. It was the *new* cottage—Josephine's dream cottage, complete and perfect in every way. Win and Andrew hadn't even given the project a thought during their sixteen-week absence. Now the sketches they'd made what seemed so long ago had come to life in the setting they'd chosen. In addition to the cottage, the beginnings of a lovely garden could be seen in the front area. Apparently, Josephine and Elisabeth had begun to actually live there shortly before their husbands were due to arrive.

Of course, many, many letters had been exchanged during that period, but the ladies had decided to surprise their husbands, and they'd kept mum about the construction project. At first, there had been uncertainty as to whether the project could continue, what with the shortage of men able to do the sort of work required. But men who were past the age for enlistment, and even a few who hadn't been accepted into the military due to poor eyesight or some other medical deterrent, had stepped forward to complete the job.

Win and Andrew were very impressed with the appearance of the new cottage. Inside, everything was organised and neat-as-a-pin. There were three bedchambers, each with an adjoining bath. The parlour and dining rooms were of a good size, and the kitchens sparkled with the latest in modern appliances. The cottage was completely furnished and looked extremely comfortable. There were chimney pieces in each bedchamber and in the parlour, as well as in the dining room. Josephine excitedly showed Win a diagram of the gardens, which she had planned for the coming summer. She'd already planted many perennial bulbs, which would germinate and poke their pretty heads above ground when spring arrived. Win silently hoped he would be there to see the beauty of the coming spring. Still, he had a sinking feeling that it would be a long while before he once again set eyes upon the pretty cottage.

The men's haversacks were placed on the floor inside the front entry. It was obvious they would be spending their leave with their wives in the new structure.

Josephine was clearly with child. It was amazing what four months had done to her lithe body. She told Win she could feel the baby kick, and that he or she was very active. She said Dr. Drew was most pleased with her progress, and the prediction was for a delivery date of May 5, 1915.

"Oh, God, I wish I knew I'd be here. However, progress is *not* being made in this wretched war. I suspect there is very little chance England will be anywhere near whipping the Huns by then."

"You mean the Brits aren't making any progress?" Josephine enquired.

"It's a stalemate, darling. The Germans fire from their trenches, and the British fire from theirs. Men are being slaughtered by the thousands, but nobody can say either side is winning. It almost looks as if the whole mess won't end until each side has wiped out the other. Whoever has the last men standing will have won."

"Then what in blazes is the point of the war?" she asked.

"That's an excellent question, Josephine. I'm not certain anyone really knows or has ever known. It's damned foolishness, but when so many men are being massacred, one can't simply shrug and say they want no part in it. It *is* a war. A brutal, bloody, ugly, disgusting war. They're calling it 'the war to end all wars'."

"Will it?" Josephine asked innocently.

"Sweetheart, as long as man has been on the Earth, there have been wars. I personally think it's naive to think this will be the last."

"So I shouldn't get my hopes up that you'll be home when the baby comes, nor even for quite some time after that?" Josephine replied sadly.

"I have to say you shouldn't. Just know I'll be praying for you and the baby. You'll be in my heart continually. I'll live for your letters. Naturally, I want you to send word the moment the baby is born. I'd give anything to be here. I hate the idea that you'll go through giving birth without me by your side to comfort you. Just always remember that I love you with all my heart, and I'll feel exactly the same way about our child."

By this time, the two had retired to their own bedchamber, under the auspices of having Win put his uniforms and other clothing away, and getting settled for the short time they would be home. Andrew and Elisabeth had done the same thing.

"Do you want to choose names, so if you're not here, we will have made that decision together? It's most important to me that you have just as much input regarding what we decide to call our child as I do. I'd feel dreadful if I made a mistake, and the poor baby was stuck with a moniker he or she despised, not to mention your feelings."

"Absolutely. Have you given the subject any thought? To be completely honest, I've had little time to devote to issues concerning the name of our forthcoming infant. However, I have time now, so the topic does need to be talked over. I assume you're in agreement with me that the baby should carry a tried and true name, befitting an old heritage, as opposed to some of the newer names I hear bantered about. I know how you feel about titles, but like it or not, the baby will someday be an earl or countess. I've always thought the use of family surnames can be nice. What do you think about using your maiden name as a second name for the baby?" asked Win. "It would be appropriate for either a boy or a girl."

"Oh, it would mean a lot to me if my maiden name were to be incorporated into our baby's name in some fashion. It would be a tribute to my parents."

"Yes, absolutely, darling. It's a fine, solid, English name. I should think it could be matched with a good many given names. But I definitely want your input. We must both agree on the name chosen. If it's a boy, what thoughts have you had?" he asked.

"I've considered George as a first name, after my father, but you might want to follow your own family line."

"No. I like George. It's a good, strong name. Have you any other family names that would go well with Chambers?"

"Well, my grandfather's name was Theodore. They called him Teddy. I like that."

"Oh, I love that. I'd rather turn it 'round and call him Theodore George Bradley. Then he'd be known as Teddy Bradley. I adore that. What do you think?"

"Why not Theodore Chambers Bradley?" Win suggested.

"I like it a lot, but I feel rather awful leaving your family out of a son's name."

"Don't be silly. I'm all for it. You know it doesn't really matter anyway. You understand that he'll rarely be called by his given name. Because of tradition and the aristocracy, as a child he'll be a viscount, like me, and later, of course, an earl. So things will progress as they always have, with most people referring to him as Winthrop, or Lord Winthrop—maybe he'll be lucky, and we can get by with Win again. If social restraints keep loosening, the lucky boy might even be able to use his actual birth name. Look at what's happened with the prince of Wales. He has a plethora of titles, yet everyone knows him as Edward or sometimes David. I'm sure some friends call him 'Wales', but the formal styling is becoming less rigid."

"Well, that would be fine with me, as you can imagine." Josephine laughed, as she hung a uniform in the cupboard. "But honestly, Win, I truly don't mean to leave your family out of consideration. They already don't look very favorably upon me. I don't want to be blamed for any more problems in your family."

"Josephine, you didn't do anything to cause the estrangement—they did. Let's leave it at that. So, we now have a boy's name. What about a little girl?"

"Oh, Win, I really don't know. There are so many pretty names for girls. Again, have you any family names?"

"None that I'm particularly fond of. My grandmothers were Edith and Lorene. I refuse to label a child with my mother's name, Beatrice. What was your mother's name?"

"Helen. I don't care for it, particularly, although I loved her dearly."

"I know. You love flowers so. Why don't we choose something like Jasmine or Violet?"

"I'm not very keen on either of those, but I *do* like something like Lillian, and we would call her Lilly."

"Yes, Yes. That's more like it. Since she would be born in May, it also goes with the season."

"And for a second name…? What about May? Lillian or Lilly Mae?"

"I love it," Win responded. "May would be spelled M-A-E, wouldn't it?"

"Yes, definitely. So, Win, we have the child's name, whether it be a boy or a girl. Whichever it turns out to be, we'll save the other name for our second child."

Win held Josephine in his arms. "So when you wire me, assuming I'm in France, just inform that either Lilly Mae or Teddy Chambers has arrived."

"Win, we're so very fortunate. I hate the war and you being away, but it's wonderful to have something so happy to look forward to. If only the Americans would join the fight. Between Britain and America, I think the Huns would be crushed in no time flat."

"Yes, I agree. I believe eventually they'll be in it. They're trying hard not to become involved, but they *are* equipping us with a lot of armaments. They're clearly on our side. Sooner or later, the Germans will get too big for their britches and make a gigantic mistake. They'll anger the Americans, and that will be that."

"Until that day comes, darling," said Josephine, "you must take every precaution to stay safe. You're going into a hell-hole, from what I've read in the newspapers."

"I know, my pet. Believe me. I fully intend to come back to you unharmed," Win declared.

Once again, Josephine stood with Win's arms wrapped around her at the Winthrop-on-Hart train station. Andrew and Elisabeth were close by, holding tightly to each other. The short furlough had come to an end all too quickly. It was sleeting and spitting snow on January 6, 1915, the day Andrew and Win had to once again board a train. They would be travelling to Charing Cross Station in London, where they would transfer to a railway line, which would carry them to Dover, the cross-channel ferry, and on to Calais, a French town on the eastern side of the English Channel.

From that locale, Win had information they'd be posted to the main base camp just outside the French village of Étaples. "My precious wife, don't be alarmed if you don't hear from me right away. We'll be travelling a good bit of the time, and there will be the usual time allotted for actually setting up our base. I'll contact you just as soon as possible. Please, though, write to me just as often as you can. Your letters will mean the world to me."

There were usually about one hundred thousand soldiers at a time housed at the camp. They'd be moved to whichever site they'd been assigned. It would definitely be someplace in either France or Belgium, wherever men were needed in the trenches.

Win wrote his first letter to Josephine upon arrival at Étaples.

March 1, 1915

My Dearest Love,

"We started for a camp in France at eleven in the morning. Upon our arrival at base camp, rifles, oil bottles, gas helmets, etc. were given to us. Base camp appears to be somewhat depressing. Reports are that we may not be here for more than three days before going "up the line." However, it could be anything from three days to three weeks. Every day, citizens from the village come with stalls into the camp and hold a sort of mart with chocolates, fruit, and postcards. It looks as if we'll be put through more training regarding the trenches. I guess they are trying to prepare us for life in those god-awful, narrow holes. We've also received training on how to deal with everything from lice, trench foot, and poison gas. Not very pleasant subjects. I long and long to see you, to clasp you in my arms, and I long with all my heart to see my baby when he or she arrives. Here I am, not but a week or so away from you, yet it seems a lifetime already. I haven't time to write more now but promise you will hear from me again soon. With all of my deepest love,

Win

Win was limited regarding exactly what he could write. All letters were censored, so recipients wouldn't be able to discern exactly where soldiers were located.

❧

Josephine received her second letter from Win more than three weeks after the first.

March 20, 1915
My Dearest Josephine,
Trench life is always one of considerable squalor, with so many men living in a very constrained space. Scraps of discarded food, empty tins, and other waste, and the nearby presence of the latrine, the general dirt of living half underground, unable to wash or change for days or weeks at a time, creates conditions of severe health risk—and that's not counting the military risks. Vermin, including rats and lice, are very numerous; disease is spread both by them and by the maggots and flies that thrive on the nearby remains of decomposing human and animal corpses. We troops in the trenches are also subjected to the weather: this winter in France is the coldest in living memory; the trenches flood, sometimes to waist height, whenever it rains. Men suffer from exposure, frostbite, trench foot—a wasting disease of the flesh caused by the foot being wet and cold, constrained into boots and puttees for days on end, that could cripple a man—and many diseases brought on or made worse by living in such a way. I apologise for being so graphic about the conditions under which I live. I could choose to billet with other officers in great, old houses, which the army has selected for officers, but I wouldn't even contemplate such a thing. How can I expect to command those of lower rank if I myself am not experiencing the same conditions they are? Andrew feels the same way.

The Western Front in Europe appears to have stabilised since the second battle of Ypres. The Germans have gone on the defensive. I don't think I'd better add more. I am hopeful they won't take any of our lads before this day is over. Both Andrew and I live in fright of being captured. I believe that would be worse than being killed.

I shall sign off for now. I love you with all my heart, darling. Take good care of yourself and our baby. In spite of this letter's tone, Andrew and I are getting along well. Please try not to worry.
All of my love,
Win

Josephine cried every time she received one of his letters. On the one hand, she was overjoyed to hear from him and to know he hadn't been injured, but he seemed to be living in such wretched conditions. Andrew's letters to Elisabeth sounded much the same. Often, both Josephine and Elisabeth wished their husbands had chosen not to fight with the men under their command. Josephine received another letter in early April. Both she and Elisabeth lamented about the sometimes-lengthy periods between letters.

April 14, 1915
Dear, Dear Josephine,
We are two miles from the trenches, and I shall face real battle on Sunday. A few shells have knocked us around, but we have taken no notice and surprisingly, sleep well. It is a glorious morning. We go over in two hours' time. It seems a long while to wait, and I think, whatever happens, we will all feel relieved once the line is launched.
No Man's Land is a tangled desert. Unless one can see it, one cannot imagine what a terrible state of disorder it is in. But we do not yet seem to have stopped the machine guns. These are popping off all along our parapet as I write. Please don't worry. The trenches don't seem too bad, really. My trench-mates are decent fellows, and we share bread, etc. Thank you so much, my pet, for the sweets and letters. We've now been paid, so I can buy a few more luxuries. I think of you every moment. You and the baby are always in the back of my mind. You must be over eight months along in pregnancy. Oh, to be there when the child comes. I pray for such a miracle every night. One never knows.
I must stop writing and rest, for I doubt there will be much sleep in the trenches tonight.
I love you, darling.
Win

Letters of that sort flew back and forth between France and England. Josephine wrote daily, and Win wrote whenever he could. His letters were more sporadic, and Josephine was always thrilled to see one with Win's handwriting. She lived in mortal terror of soldiers appearing at her doorway, announcing that he had been killed or severely injured. She had learned not to listen to rumours, which were rampant. If she believed everything she heard, she could not have endured the separation from her husband. She didn't allow her mind to travel to places where her darling Win might be lying dead with a bullet through his head. She'd heard stories about crows picking the eyes out of those soldiers whom the Germans had managed to hit with their dreaded bullets and grenades.

22

~

It was spring 1915. On April 22, the German army shocked the allied soldiers by firing more than one hundred and fifty tons of lethal chlorine gas against two divisions at Ypres in Belgium. Win and Andrew were both present during the horrendous attack. It absolutely devastated the Allied line. The deadly gas even permeated the trenches and was blown by the winds. Everywhere one looked, there were soldiers staggering about, unable to see or to breathe. Foam was coming out of their mouths. They fell to the ground and convulsed, dying horrific deaths. Many of the men were sobbing, calling for their mothers.

Why was it that men always called for their mothers at the end of their lives? Win wondered. He was certain that if ever faced with such a horrible situation, Josephine's would be the last name he uttered.

He'd never, in his wildest dreams, imagined anything remotely like what he witnessed. Shortly after the gas attack, Win realised that Andrew had inhaled what must have been a significant amount of the deadly poison. At first, he thought perhaps his dear chum and brother-in-law was only wounded. However, when Win reached his side, it was abundantly clear that Andrew, with whom he'd spent every hour of each day whenever possible and for so many months, was dying.

Many soldiers moved on, but others were writhing on the ground in agony, awaiting ambulances to collect them and take them to base hospitals. There was actually little that could be done for the wretched creatures. Win knelt with his arm about Andrew's shoulders, hoping against hope that something might help his friend. There was blood seeping from Andrew's mouth, and his skin had literally turned a greenish hue from him having breathed in the fatal gas. He was also convulsing, and mixed with blood there was froth. It was clear that Andrew had been called upon to pay the supreme sacrifice.

It was amazing Win hadn't also succumbed to the gas attack. He'd remembered from his training to cover his mouth. It was believed that the ammonia in urine counteracted the gas. So, after soaking a piece of torn shirt with his own bodily fluid, he had tied it round the lower half of his face. It must have contributed to saving his life.

Andrew died in Win's arms. There was almost a feeling of relief when Win saw that Andrew was no longer suffering. Win had seen many deaths during his military duty, but nothing had come close to the carnage he had just witnessed. Since he was the ranking officer, he buried his chum, calling upon three other men from his unit to dig graves for Andrew and four others. The ground was literally strewn with bodies—some dead and some still living, writhing on the ground in unimaginable agony. After the burial of Andrew, Win had no memory of how he'd managed to return to his base. He only knew he still had to face the nearly impossible task of writing to Elisabeth, Andrew's wife and Win's own sister. It was the end of a truly gruesome day.

Win had no idea what words he would choose. His wife was due to deliver their child in May. After seeing what had happened to his dearest friend, he wondered if he would be alive to learn whether he was the father of a boy or a girl.

Following the mournful task of writing to his sister, he trudged forward to join his regiment. The loss of Andrew had an enormous impact on Win. Prior to Andrew's death, the two would view going "over-the-top" as a great adventure. No matter how grim things had become, they always found something to joke about. All merriment was gone. Win slogged on and only hoped the beastly war would come to an end, so he could return to his beloved Josephine. His heart ached when he thought of the pain Elisabeth would be experiencing. He suspected that she would return to Winthrop Manor upon receipt of the news that she was a widow. Win didn't know how he felt about that. She should be with her parents, but he questioned whether they would do everything in their power to convince her she'd made an impulsive decision in marrying Andrew. Win was concerned about her.

Elisabeth received the letter from her brother a week later on April 27, 1915. Before she even opened it, she had a sick feeling in her stomach. The sight of Win's handwriting, addressed to her and not to his wife, gave her significant pause. Sure enough, when she opened the envelope and began to read, her head grew light. She was about to faint. Before she keeled over, she called for Josephine, who was immediately by her side. Elisabeth was lying on the front walk, having returned from the post box, the letter still clasped in her hand. Josephine cradled Elisabeth's head and smoothed back her hair. If she hadn't become conscious when she did, Josephine would have run back inside the cottage and called a physician. They had a telephone in their new home. Elisabeth's eyes fluttered and then opened.

"Oh, my God, Josephine. Read the letter. I can scarcely think," she whispered.

Josephine took the letter from her sister-in-law's hand and proceeded to read it. Andrew was dead. Dead and buried somewhere in France. It seemed impossible. Elisabeth had only yesterday received a letter from him, in which he'd said that over all, things weren't so terribly bad. Apparently, the disgusting Huns had used gas on their enemy. The letter was in Win's handwriting. Andrew had breathed the deadly toxicant, and the inexplicable effects had ended his life. Win had held Andrew as he died. Josephine's heart ached for Elisabeth. How on Earth could she possibly cope with such news?

Elisabeth fully opened her eyes. "He's dead, Josephine. My precious Andrew is dead. Oh, god. He's your only brother, too. I can't believe this has happened. I simply cannot imagine a future without Andrew."

Tears were streaming down Josephine's face, too. She had loved her brother from the moment she could first remember him. He'd always been there for her. It was impossible to think he would no longer be a part of her life. However, she quickly turned her thoughts to Elisabeth.

"Oh, you poor darling. What can I do to help? Shall I notify your parents? I know you've had a falling out, but at times like this, a girl needs her mother."

"No. No. She won't care," Elisabeth replied.

Then there was silence. Finally, Elisabeth pulled herself up into a sitting position.

"Yes. Yes. I *do* want my parents to know. My mother will undoubtedly be of no help, but my father has love in his heart. He'll understand how I feel."

"Certainly, I'll telephone them straightaway. Will you be all right if I leave you alone for just a minute? Do you need a glass of water or a cold cloth?"

"No, I'll be all right. Help me to my feet. I'll come into the house with you."

Josephine put her arm around her sister-in-law's waist and brought her to a standing position. Then the two entered the front door of the cottage. Josephine still held the crumpled letter in her hand. She helped Elisabeth to lie on the sofa in the parlour and quickly rang the Winthrop number. Radcliffe answered.

"Radcliffe, this is Josephine, Win's wife. I'm sorry to bother you, but is Win's father at home. Elisabeth has received some dreadful news. I must speak with him."

"Certainly, my lady. He's right here. Let me put him on," he replied.

The next voice she heard was that of the Lord Winthrop.

"Lord Winthrop here," he answered.

"My lord, this is Win's wife, Josephine. I am indeed sorry to bother you, but Elisabeth has just now learned that Andrew was killed by the wretched poisonous gas the Huns used on our troops on April 22. She's in a bad way. All undone. She needs her parents. Can you come?"

"Of course, Josephine. I'm grateful for your call. I'll have David bring me to your cottage in a tick."

"Wait. My lord, we no longer live with my uncle. Before Win left for the war, he commissioned a new cottage for Elisabeth and me on my Uncle Roderick's land. Let me give you the directions." She proceeded to do so while the Lord Winthrop wrote them down.

"Right," he responded. "I have it. I'll be there shortly."

Josephine replaced the receiver and went to Elisabeth's side. "I reached your father. He's on his way. He didn't mention your mother. I don't know if he's bringing her or not."

"God, I hope not. I'll be given some dreadful lecture about how I never should have married Andrew to begin with," cried Elisabeth.

"Oh, surely not. Your father sounds truly devastated. I feel certain your mother will share his feelings."

"Don't count on it, Josephine," Elisabeth managed to say between sobs. "Oh, dear God, what am I to do? I loved him so. I'll never love anyone like that again. I can't believe I'll never see him again."

"You *will* see him again. You were lawfully married in a Christian church. You'll be together again someday," Josephine responded. "I truly believe that."

"I know. I do, too. But it may be such an interminably long time. I wanted to have his children. I wanted to grow old with him. I wasn't ready to say goodbye."

"Darling girl, I know. That's the way I'd feel if Win were to die."

"Yes, but you're about to have his baby. You'll always have a part of him. I'm left with nothing."

"No. You have memories. Lovely memories. As long as you're alive, Andrew will be, too. The same is true of me. I remember when he was a youngster and was my older brother. He's still alive in my heart, just as he is in yours."

"That's a lovely way to think of it." She sniffled. "Still, I want his arms around me. I want to place my head on his shoulder. Oh, Josephine, how can I live without him?"

"Sweetheart, I wish I could tell you. I don't know. It's enough to send me over the cliff. I'd feel just as you do if I learned Win was never coming home to me. It's unbearable for me to imagine that I'll never see my brother again. I know they say time heals all wounds. There must be hundreds of thousands of women who've had to go through this, and think of how many more there will be. Take time to heal, Elisabeth. In time, I imagine the pain will ease. Think of what Andrew would want you to do."

Just then, there was a knock at their door. It had to be Elisabeth's father. Josephine opened it, and sure enough, there stood the Lord Winthrop.

"Hello, my lord," she said in a doleful voice. "Your daughter has suffered a devastating blow. She needs you. Please, come in."

He thanked her and entered the cottage, glancing about him in what Josephine clearly felt was a critical manner. Naturally, if her home was Winthrop Manor, she supposed she too might be critical of a small, thatched-roof cottage, but Elisabeth had chosen to make her home with Josephine when she might have stayed with her parents while Andrew was serving in the military. Josephine didn't care what his opinion was. She led him to the sofa, where his daughter was stretched out, a cloth on her head.

"Daddy," she murmured. "Daddy. My husband is dead. Gone. I'm heartbroken. I'll never see him again. I don't want to live."

"Now, now, Elisabeth. I truly *am* sorry for this horrible loss. I know you loved him, and I believe he loved you as much. Your mother and I were wrong not to have accepted your marriage. I apologise to you for that. However, we need to put those feeling into the past where they belong. Andrew's death changes everything. You belong back with us."

He turned to Josephine. "My dear, I know you've felt more secure having Elisabeth's company. Can I convince you to join us at Winthrop Manor, so the two of you won't be parted? Also, it's obvious your baby is due most any time. We'll make certain you have a nanny, and the child will have the best of everything. The house has a wonderful nursery, just waiting for another child to begin his or her life there. Please, say you'll come with Elisabeth. We'll all be a family.

"Absolutely not, my lord. I *do* believe it's probably best for Elisabeth to return to her parents. She has a long period of grief ahead of her. To see me have Win's baby would only remind her that she has nothing of Andrew left. I myself am crushed to have lost my only brother. I believe I belong right here in the cottage Win planned for me. I'll have my uncle Roderick if I feel lonely. I hate losing Elisabeth, but I want what's best for her." Josephine turned to her sister-in-law. "Elisabeth, if you prefer to stay with me, you know I adore being with you. However, I feel I must say that you probably belong with your own family, at least for a period. Should the time come when you want to return to me, you need only say the word."

"Oh, Josephine. You've been so good to me. I hate leaving you alone. I'm so undone. I don't know what the right thing to do is," she sobbed. "Daddy, is mother in agreement with you? I really cannot stand to listen to her berate me for marrying Andrew, or hear her make snide remarks about the fact that his pedigree wasn't as fine as mine. I loved him with all my heart. I always shall. Either both of you accept my feelings, or I'd prefer to stay with Josephine."

"We shall both accept it, Elisabeth. I've spoken with my lady. There will be no derogatory remarks made. She understands how deep your heartbreak must be. So please, agree to come home with me. It's where you belong, darling."

"All right. I *do* think it would be for the best right now. But if there is anything amiss, I'm returning to Josephine at once. I mean it."

"I realise you do. Now, David has the car waiting outside. Come with me, and we'll get you settled in your old bedchamber. Then I'll send him back to retrieve your clothing and whatever else you wish to bring home with you."

"All right," she answered, wiping her nose with a handkerchief. "Josephine, thank you so much for understanding. You've been such an incredible sister-in-law. Of course, I'll be your baby's aunt. You must bring him or her to see me the moment the birth occurs."

"I promise I shall," Josephine replied. "I think you're doing the proper thing. I believe it's what Andrew would have wanted. Don't worry. You're still my sister-in-law. Nothing will ever change that."

On May 12, 1915, Josephine went into labor. Elisabeth was no longer at the cottage. Josephine most definitely would have called Roderick, but he still had no telephone. She was completely alone. She was frightened and not certain what to do. She considered instructing the stable boy to run to her uncle's cottage and have him collect her in his automobile, but it was quite a distance from her cottage, and the pains seemed to be very close together. In a frantic moment, she telephoned Winthrop Manor. It truly was the only thing she might have done. Radcliffe answered, and she didn't ask for anyone else. Instead, she asked that the message of her labor be given to whoever was available.

Within half an hour, Josephine was at hospital in Winthrop-on-Hart. The Lord Winthrop had been given the word from Radcliffe, and he'd immediately jumped into the Rolls Royce, heading for Josephine's cottage. He hadn't even waited for David to drive him. As in any small village, word travelled quickly. Nearly everyone was aware that the Winthrop daughter-in-law was hospitalised and about to give birth to the first grandchild. There was a dilemma as to whether the Lady Winthrop should be present. After some discussion, she stayed at Winthrop Manor, knowing full well her husband would inform her when the baby arrived. Elisabeth rushed to Josephine's side. She'd been admitted at 10:15 a.m. It was the beginning of thirteen hours of very hard labor. Josephine was tiny, and finally, Dr. Morris made the decision to take the baby by Cesarean section. It was not what Josephine had wished, but she was so fatigued from endless hours of pain, she readily accepted his decision.

Thus, at eleven o'clock in the evening, Josephine gave birth to a splendid, healthy boy. She named him Andrew Chambers Winthrop. She hadn't forgotten the plans she and Win had made regarding choice of names, but after Andrew died, she'd decided to alter the first name from Theodore to Andrew. There was no doubt in her mind that Win would be in accord with that decision. The child looked like his father, though he had inherited Josephine's eyes. He had quite a sensational head of hair for a newborn—thick and black, like his father's. His features were perfect in every respect. The dark hair emphasized the true green of his eyes. All of the nurses on duty raved over what a beautiful baby he was.

Word was brought to the Lord Winthrop and Lady Elisabeth, who had waited those many hours at hospital. The Lord Winthrop immediately telephoned his wife, who longed to have a peek at this newest addition to the Winthrop family. However, she was well aware of the negative feelings still separating her from Josephine. Oliver Winthrop had been given an exemption from the military, on the grounds that he was the youngest son of an earl who owned thousands of acres of farmland in Hampshire, and he was indisputably needed to carry on the work of food production for the troops. He was greatly angered when word reached him about the birth of a nephew. The child's entrance into the world would have a great impact upon Oliver's future. Because Win now had a son, even if he didn't live through the ghastly war, where hundreds of thousands of men were losing their lives, his offspring would become heir to Winthrop Manor. Josephine instinctively knew Oliver's feelings when he paid a visit to hospital. He performed a lovely act of pretending to be a happy uncle, but Josephine knew where his true feelings lay.

Josephine immediately sent a wire to her husband, announcing the splendid news that they had a wonderful, little son and heir. In the last letter Josephine had received from Win, in late April,1915, he'd spoken of preparations for entrance into battle. He hadn't indicated his locale. There were so many battles occurring that he might have been anyplace. Of course, Josephine was always extremely concerned about extended lack of communication, but she was also aware that it was extremely difficult for soldiers to find time to write. When he wasn't in battle, he was trying to recuperate from the last one he'd endured. She continued to write to him daily. Having lived through the dreadful news of her brother's death, she was frightened every time any sort of information arrived. She couldn't help but wonder if each letter would be the last. She was discharged from hospital and returned to her cottage, where Uncle Roderick came to stay with her, along with a hired nurse to teach her how to care for the baby and allow her additional time to recuperate.

23

Josephine waited and waited for word from Win, knowing that he would write immediately when he learned he had a son. However, no letter arrived. Months and months went by, and it became obvious that something was terribly wrong. She grew more and more concerned as time went by. Then, in September, 1915, she received a letter from the military authorities, informing her that Win was missing in action and had been since the previous spring. That explained the incredibly long silence.

The wording could have meant anything from his having been taken prisoner, to desertion, which she firmly doubted, to German execution, or death on the battlefield and an inability to identify his corpse. She endured a substantial amount of agony, wondering what had become of her beloved husband. Because of her continued closeness with Elisabeth, they exchanged daily telephone calls. She felt certain Elisabeth would share the news of Win's disappearance with the Lord and Lady Winthrop and Oliver.

She wanted them to know. The Lord Winthrop had many contacts and was immensely well-equipped to obtain answers from the War Department. She sent a second copy of her original letter through the International Red Cross, praying that members of that group might come upon him when they toured German POW camps.

Once the Lord Winthrop learned of his son's disappearance, he began to make enquiries. Although there'd been no communication between Josephine and the Winthrop family, Win's father *did* immediately contact Josephine. She was most wary of his motives but was also aware that he could be of great help in locating Win. Regardless of the animosity between them, she felt Win would want her to be in contact with his father.

His father checked all British medical units in the area, through the Department of Defense and the Red Cross. Questions were asked of survivors of the action in which he'd gone missing. There had been scant hope of learning anything from fellow soldiers, since during the fog of war, few if any soldiers paid attention to which of their mates were killed or injured. Formal enquiries and an exchange of information between Britain and her enemies were made via neutral powers, but no evidence of significance was found. Josephine chose to believe he was in enemy hands, for then, at least, she could pray that when the Allies finally declared victory, he would come home to her. She was terribly anxious for such information to be confirmed.

She was told that British soldiers taken as prisoners in France were almost always moved to camps all over Europe. If that were the case, he was definitely incarcerated in a POW camp, but there was no indication as to where he was being held. It was a nightmare, but Josephine held on to that hope with all of her might that he was safe and alive.

Win was in the Netherlands. After his inhumane experience with the German use of poisonous gas, he'd been given a short rest behind the front lines, which was when he'd written his last letter to Josephine, in April, 1915. Then he'd been returned to the battlefield. He'd fought so many dangerous and brutal battles against the Germans, for such an extended period of time, that he'd nearly lost count. He'd come very close to injury and even death many times, but luck, or God, had always seemed to be by his side. However, on May 21, 2015, Win's luck ran out.

That night found Win on the left flank of a British attack at a small village in France. His division had met with stubbornness on the part of the enemy and resulted in heavy losses. He had started over-the-top under heavy fire and had reached the first German trench, jumping in. There had been seven Allied soldiers there, and Win was the highest-ranking, incapacitating and killing the Germans who were in his sight. He had led the way along the trench. Suddenly, a Hun came 'round the corner, but for some reason, he had chosen not to shoot Win, for he surely could have. Instead, he'd lowered his rifle. Win felt enormous relief, when out of the blue, the German soldier thrust his bayonet into Win's foot. The pain had been nearly unbearable, and Win had fleetingly wondered if he was about to be killed with the bayonet instead of a gun. Apparently, the answer was no, for he had then been told, in broken but understandable English, that he was being taken prisoner.

In less than one minute, his freedom was lost. It was the last thing he'd considered. He'd assumed he would either be killed or would retain his freedom until the beastly war had reached its conclusion. At that moment, he wished he might have died alongside Andrew. Win knew that intelligence gathered by capture was the reason behind such an act, but he had no intelligence to share and would not have done so, anyway.

Blood was seeping from his foot. It throbbed like the devil. Under no circumstances would it have been possible for Win to walk any distance. The Hun reached inside of his tunic. Removing a roll of gauze, along with adhesive tape, he wrapped Win's foot, taping the medical dressing into place. Win was surprised that an enemy would do such a thing. It was apparent that Win was going to be marched to a POW destination. Perhaps the German didn't want to waste valuable time while Win stumbled along as a wounded prisoner. It confused him as to why he had been bayoneted at all if there had been no intention to finish him off. The only rational explanation was that the German soldier had wanted his superiors to believe he had made an attempt to kill him but chose not to when capture was so readily at hand. After all, Win was a British officer. Officers were much more likely to have important information for the enemy. Win's instructions had always been to try to capture enemy officers, rather than kill them. Apparently, the enemy had received similar instructions.

Captured soldiers from both sides were interred all over Europe. The Netherlands, one of the few countries which remained neutral during the war, was filled with prisoner-of-war camps, which were scattered all over the countryside. That is where Win found himself after his dreadful capture. While men interred in his particular camp were supposed to be only those who'd been picked up while crossing the border into Holland, the Germans were known to take men they seized to the Dutch camp, too. Internment camps were becoming so terribly crowded with prisoners that it mattered little which destination the Germans chose for incarceration.

Win was not allowed to send or receive letters, so he had no way to convey his whereabouts to Josephine. The regulations regarding such a practice varied from camp to camp. Prisoners were supposed to be able to receive and send letters, but the practice was not allowed during the time Win was in the Dutch camp. Dutch officials opened and inspected every large parcel received through the Red Cross, but they did ignore small packages. The Red Cross *did* inspect the camp, but because it was in Holland, it tended to be forgotten much of the time. Had they remembered Win's camp on a regular basis, he might have been able to communicate with Josephine, but such a miracle never occurred. There was even one Red Cross nurse who refused to accept letters, if an English prisoner requested one to be sent to a loved one, because she was German. If an English prisoner asked her to send such a letter, she would answer, "Nein," and that was the end of any hope for a link to a loved one.

A fellow British prisoner, William Shore, had become quite friendly with a local girl, who visited the camp on a regular basis. Naturally, she wasn't able to actually enter the premises, but she stood on one side of the fence while William stood on the inside. The top of the barricade was strung with barbed wire, so there was no possibility of escape. William and Win had struck up quite a good friendship. As time passed, the two began to devise a scheme, which, if it was successful, would free them from the confines of the internment camp. The chances of being set free by the Germans were just about impossible, so they would have to improvise their own means of escape.

They were undoubtedly fortunate to be in a Dutch camp, for a variety of reason. In some of the other camps, rigid rules would have been adhered to, and the possibility of escape was truly non-existent.

One of the good things about being interred at the Dutch camp was the fact that prisoners had money to buy various things. The captured men were paid a certain amount by the Dutch authorities for tasks they performed. Local tradesmen brought goods to the camp in barrows. They sold fruit, cigarettes, chocolate, and other items, of which few prison camps had access. Of course, it was still a prisoner-of-war camp, and hoards of local people would come on Sundays to visit, as though they were visiting a zoo. The men behind the wire felt like caged animals. The men in the Dutch camp had to admit, however, that the treatment they received was undoubtedly somewhat better than what they would be subjected to at other camps within Germany.

Win longed to be free. Every officer had been instructed, during training in England, that his first and foremost objective, if captured, was to make an attempt to escape. It was a frightening goal. If a prisoner was captured, while trying to flee, the chances were great that he would be shot or hanged. Nonetheless, nothing on Earth could have stopped Win from making an effort to see Josephine. He was well aware that he was undoubtedly a father. The wish to see his child was overwhelming. He decided to bide his time, allow his foot some time to heal, and wait for the right opportunity, and then he and his new friend would make their move...

24

❧

Josephine and her son Andrew were still in her beloved cottage, awaiting news about her precious husband. It was December, 1915. Josephine had not heard from Win since before Andrew's birth. Andrew was now nearly seven months old. Christmas was approaching, but Josephine had no intention of celebrating the holiday without her husband. Uncle Roderick had suggested a nice dinner, but she had said she didn't feel like doing anything without Win. It seemed as though he had vanished into thin air. Everyone who could possibly be of assistance had been contacted, but there hadn't been one iota of positive news. Josephine refused to give up hope until she had definitive proof that Win was dead. Something deep inside her stubbornly believed that he was still alive. She was absolutely certain, beyond a shadow of a doubt, that she would know if her husband had died. Elisabeth continued to stay with her parents. As a result, Josephine saw little of her dear sister-in-law, but they did speak frequently by telephone, and Elisabeth came to play with her nephew now and then.

Baby Andrew kept Josephine exceptionally busy, but there were still many lonely hours. He was as active as one would expect him to be at his age. He was able to crawl well on his hands and knees and was even attempting to creep up the stairway; he sat confidently and walked while holding on to furniture. He was no longer a helpless infant and had even begun to imitate words. As a result, if Josephine hoped to accomplish anything without having to worry about her son hurting himself, she sometimes placed him in a playpen, sometimes referred to as a play-box, which was simply a wooden-slatted enclosure that protected him from harm yet allowed him to be nearby wherever she happened to be.

Josephine found that she needed some sort of hobby to pass the hours—something to take her mind off missing Win so desperately. Long ago, a governess had complimented Josephine on her skill as an artist. She'd never seen herself as talented, but she truly did enjoy painting. The memory popped into her head one day while the baby was napping. *Why not buy the essentials needed to try her hand at painting?* She asked Uncle Roderick to buy the necessary items for her to give it a go. The next time he was in Winthrop-on-Hart, he bought an easel, some blank canvases, and a complete set of oil paints. He also added a sketch book and grease pencils. She'd found pleasure in dabbing the paint on canvas and was surprised that the finished products weren't horrendous. She didn't expect to become a Monet or Da Vinci. Her primary goal was to keep busy, rather than continuing her unrelenting concentration upon Win's disappearance.

On a warm day in December, Josephine placed baby Andrew in his playpen under the large elm tree in the back of her cottage and began working on a painting. The weather was unusually warm, and Josephine was so weary of endless days, during which she and Andrew were confined to the cottage. A day outside in the fresh air and sunshine sounded like heaven. She'd brought her easel from the interior of the house and set it up a few yards from Andrew's pen. She'd already completed a sketch of the pretty stream flowing a few yards from the house, alongside the old elm tree. The remains of flowers could still be seen, where she'd planted a garden nearby. The next step involved transferring the sketch to canvas. It would be the most intricate painting she'd attempted thus far. Up until that time, she'd focused upon still-life scenes of vases filled with flowers spilling over the sides.

When everything was properly prepared, she suddenly realised she'd left her artist's smock in the cottage. Glancing 'round to make certain there was no one to be seen for miles, she decided it would be safe to leave Andrew for a tick. She ran into the cottage, searched about in various locales, and finally spotted it, hanging on a hook inside the pantry door.

Upon her return, she covered the day-dress she was wearing with the smock and began to mix paint colours. Her plan was to begin by painting the stream with the willow trees bending over it. Working carefully, Josephine was pleased with the result. After nearly an hour had hour passed, she put her brush down and stretched her back.

Then she strolled to Andrew's playpen, just to make certain he was still sleeping soundly, as he had been the last time she'd checked on him. When she peeked at the structure, it was empty. *Empty. Vacant. Void.* Her beloved son was nowhere to be seen. He was far too young to have crawled out of the play-pen. The only possible way it could be empty was if someone had stealthily crept up and stolen the baby while she was immersed in her painting, or maybe even when she'd run into the house to retrieve her smock, though she doubted it. In any event, her adored son was gone. Precious Andrew was missing. For a moment, Josephine stood stock still, in shock. She *had* placed him into the pen, *hadn't* she? Her memory was blank. She turned, ran into the cottage, and up the stairway. Perhaps he was still in his cot. That had to be the explanation. How could she have been so foolish as to leave him alone in the nursery? She berated herself for being so utterly stupid. She would never paint again. Obviously, her obsession with painting had caused her to focus too intemperately upon the senseless hobby.

When she entered his nursery, which Uncle Roderick had painted a lovely pale blue, she ran to his cot, which sat underneath a window. It, too, was unoccupied. She began hysterically screaming and crying. Where was Andrew? Someone had taken her baby. She dissolved into a panic. Running back down the stairs to the telephone, she lifted the receiver, terribly agitated. The operator enquired about the number with which she wished to be connected. Josephine screamed, saying she needed the police authorities immediately. The operator must have realised that the situation was serious, because she connected Josephine at once with the Winthrop-on-Hart constable's station. A man's voice came on the line. She was still sobbing and shrieking uncontrollably.

"Calm down, madam. I'm unable to understand what you're saying," the man implored.

Josephine took a deep breath. There were still tears flowing from her eyes. "Please—please send someone immediately. My infant has been stolen."

"Your child has been stolen? Tell me, where was the child?"

"He was in his playpen, outside, under a large elm tree, while I was working on an oil painting. He wasn't five feet from me. I'd been painting for about an hour. I stopped to check on him. The playpen I had him in was empty. It's empty."

"Have you searched the house? Are you certain the child was put into his playpen?"

"Yes, yes. Please, hurry. I'm telling you, my little son is gone. I live in the country. There are no other houses for miles. I see no possible way anyone could have taken him, but he is gone. Gone. If anything has happened to him, I shall die.

"His father is an officer in the army, and he's missing. I've not heard from him for over six months. God Almighty, please come."

"Give me your name and directions to your home," the constable requested.

"My name is Josephine Winthrop. My husband is Lord Win—Winterdale, the Lord Winthrop's son. But we don't make our home at Winthrop Manor." Josephine rattled off the fastest route to the cottage from the village.

The constable promised that he and his partner would be there as quickly as possible. He added that he wanted her to try to remain as calm as manageable.

"My God, I cannot be calm until my baby is found," she shouted.

"We're on our way, Lady Winterdale," he answered.

She hung up the telephone. She wanted to call her uncle, but he still had no telephone. Should she call Elisabeth at Winthrop Manor? She hated to alert Win's parents, but she needed all the help she could garner. So, she picked the telephone back up and told the operator to connect her with Winthrop Manor. Radcliffe answered the ring.

"Radcliffe, this is Josephine. Something horrible has happened."

Before she could explain her dilemma, Radcliffe interrupted and asked if Lord Win was dead.

"No, no. Not that, thank God. But nearly that bad. Andrew—baby Andrew is missing. Can you please let me speak to the Lord Winthrop?"

She hadn't meant to ask for Win's father, but since he was an older gentleman, she thought perhaps he might be the person who could help. It was only a few moments before his voice came on the line.

"Josephine? What's this I hear about Andrew missing? Have you contacted the authorities?"

"Yes. They're on their way. I was outside painting. I'd placed him in his playpen and set it under the elm tree in the back of the cottage. He was tucked in safely, not more than five feet from me. He was only left alone for a tick, when I ran back into the house because I'd forgotten my painting smock. It was just inside the door. Then I worked with the oils for approximately an hour. I stopped to stretch my back and flex my fingers, and also to check on the baby. When I looked into the playpen, he wasn't there."

"How could he possibly not have been there? That doesn't make a whit of sense."

"I'm telling you, my lord, he was *not* there, and he *is not* there. I've searched the house. I never heard an auto or a horse approach my property. There are no cottages nearby—not for miles. Yet, he is gone. *Gone.* Oh, God. What am I to do?"

"You say the authorities are on their way? They'll find him. Still, I'm going to have David drive me over to your cottage immediately."

"Will you please bring Elisabeth, too?" Josephine asked.

"Elisabeth isn't here. She's gone with Oliver to run a few errands. They've been gone quite some time. You don't want me to wait until she returns, do you?"

"No. Of course not. However, I *would* like you to stop and collect my uncle. He has no telephone line. I want him with me."

"I shall do so. I'm leaving here right now. It shouldn't take me a long time. Don't worry. We'll find him. Perhaps someone is playing a game."

"This is no game, my lord. There is nothing amusing about it. My precious son is gone. Please hurry."

After speaking to the Lord Winthrop, Josephine went back out to the playpen. She looked carefully at the toys and coverlet, which she'd tucked on the bottom. He'd been clad in a small, one-piece baby suit with feet. It was light blue with white stripes. She had also put a bonnet on his head, since, though it was a warm day, she didn't want him to become cold, should a wind pop up. She'd given him his bottle before he'd fallen asleep in the playpen. The bottle was still there. *Who would do such a thing? What sort of person would steal a mother's baby?* She stood by the playpen, alone and helpless, crying her heart out. In between sobs, she whispered his name over and over. *"Andrew. Andrew. My darling baby. Where are you? What's happened to you?"*

Josephine was beyond frantic. It seemed as though the authorities would never arrive. Finally, she heard a police siren in the distance. She looked up and saw the constable's auto come to a stop in front of the cottage. She ran to the car, shouting for the officers to come 'round the back, where the empty playpen sat. The men followed her lead, and moments later, everyone was gathered under the old elm.

The detectives immediately blocked the area with yellow crime scene tape. They took what seemed like hundreds of photographs of the empty carriage. With their hands covered with rubber gloves, they carefully crawled around the area to determine whether there were any footprints to be seen. One of the officers called to the other to bring a torch over. He thought he'd discovered some prints. Sure enough, there *was* the outline of shoes next to the side of the playpen where Josephine had not stood. They were rather large shoe prints but might have been worn by a man or a woman. Josephine stood outside the yellow tape, observing the men's every move. When the shoe prints were discovered, she screamed.

"How on God's green Earth could someone have sneaked up and stolen my baby without my hearing him? That's impossible. I wasn't that far away. Wouldn't a kidnapper have had an automobile? Wouldn't I have heard it?"

"Not necessarily, madam. The car may have been parked some distance away. It would only take a moment to snatch a child from a playpen." The chief detective began to crawl along the ground where the prints had been discovered. It was quite soft, as there'd been rain on and off over the past few days. In fact, this was the first truly warm, dry day in over a week. The footprints became farther apart, leading away from the playpen. The chief detective explained that the primary reason for such a find would have been that whomever took the child was running, once he or she had the infant.

"It's interesting that the babe didn't cry," muttered the inspector. He turned to Josephine. "Do you believe your child would have screamed or cried if a stranger approached him?"

"Yes, I think he would have. Unless whoever took him was someone he was familiar with. That would rule out most everybody. We're isolated here in the country. I have very few visitors."

"Can you name people with whom your son would be comfortable?"

"Not many. Of course, my uncle," she answered. "He can be ruled out. I'd trust Roderick with Andrew's life."

"Who else, Lady Winterdale?"

"Let me think. My sister-in-law, Elisabeth Chambers. She's my husband Win's sister. She is now a widow. We used to share this cottage until her husband was killed in the war. Then she moved back to Winthrop Manor to be with her family. It could never be Elisabeth. I suppose Andrew might not cry if his grandfather, the Lord Winthrop were to approach him. He's on his way here. He should arrive any moment. We aren't on friendly terms. He and the Lady Winthrop were most upset when they learned their eldest son, Win, had married me, since I have no title. Actually, I'm on better terms with the Lord Winthrop than I am with the Lady Winthrop. She's never even seen my son. There is another Winthrop—Oliver. He is my husband's younger brother. To my knowledge, he's never seen Andrew, either. My baby is a very loving child. It *is* possible that he wouldn't cry out if a stranger picked him up. He also may have been sleeping—you don't suppose it's possible somebody might have used some sort of substance to make him sleep more soundly?"

"Yes. Kidnappers have been known to use something like chloroform to make a child unconscious," the inspector murmured, more to himself than to the others.

Josephine heard his words. "Oh, good heavens, no," she cried. "Something like that could kill Andrew."

"I'm sorry, my lady, I was just thinking aloud. I highly doubt that was done. How long do you think the boy has been missing?" he went on to ask.

"At most, an hour. That's how long I was painting. Surely, I would have heard someone. Wouldn't I?" she asked pitifully.

"One would think so, but you never know. Anyone who would do something like this could be very well-rehearsed. If you were deeply absorbed in your painting, you might not have heard anything."

"Do you suppose it *is* a kidnapping?" asked Josephine. "Wouldn't the person leave a note or contact me?"

"In a kidnapping, we always expect contact with the perpetrator. You obviously have a telephone since you were able to get in touch with us. You need to stay close to that phone."

"Then I'm going back into the cottage. If you need to speak with me further, you're welcome to come inside."

Josephine was trembling from head to toe. If she'd lost Andrew, her entire world had collapsed. She needed Win's strong arms and wise thinking.

Who would do such a wicked thing? What would the motive be? Money? She would give everything she owned to hold her baby son. Did someone know she was the daughter-in-law of the Winthrops? Of course, many people did. However, if that were the motive, the person who had done such a dastardly deed also had to know that she had almost no contact with her in-laws. Still, they would know that the Lord Winthrop would never want anything dire to happen to his grandson. All these thoughts and more raced through Josephine's mind.

There was nothing to do but wait. The constables told her they were calling in Scotland Yard. Winthrop-on-Hart scarcely had the resources to deal with a high- profile kidnapping. Josephine threw herself down on the sofa in the parlour and sobbed.

"Oh, Win. I need you so," she cried.

25

❧❧❧

At nine o'clock in the morning, the telephone rang in Josephine's cottage. Her uncle had stayed with her the night before, and the pretty, little abode was well-covered surreptitiously with men from the constable's office in Winthrop-on-Hart. Josephine raised her brows and looked at the chief detective, silently asking whether he wanted her to answer the call. The detective gave a nod, indicating his preference that she pick up the receiver.

She quickly grabbed for it. "Hello," she said, trying to keep her voice from quivering.

An obviously camouflaged voice spoke. "I'm calling about your missing boy."

What the caller didn't know was that the detectives had already made certain the operator was listening to all calls placed to Josephine's cottage. Therefore, the means existed for the operator to report the number from which the call originated.

"Yes," answered Josephine, sounding calm, though her heart was racing a mile a second. "What about my baby? Is Andrew all right?"

"He's in fine fettle. You needn't worry about that. He wasn't taken because anyone wants money."

"Then why? Why?" Josephine could not hold back the tears. It was impossible to tell if the caller was a man or a woman. There must have been some sort of filter placed over the speaker because the voice was clearly camouflaged. "He's my baby—not even a year old. He needs his mummy. Please, please, why would you do something so cruel?"

"I shouldn't even be making this call," the person answered. "It could cause me no end of trouble. But I got to feeling sorry for you, being a mother with a husband who probably isn't coming home. So at least I wanted to let you know the baby is all right. He will be cared for by lovely people—not like the Winthrops, of course—but he'll have a very good life."

"Are you saying you have no intention of bringing him back at all?" Josephine asked. By then, she was trembling from head to toe.

"I'm afraid I have to give you that sad news."

"Think of how his father will feel when he returns from this dreadful war to find that he hasn't a son," Josephine pleaded.

"Jay… James—um, Win… He won't be coming back. He's been gone so long now, there isn't any hope that's he's alive. You have to understand that you aren't fit to raise him. He's much more highborn than you are. It's really better for him, you see. He'll be raised by someone who knows much more about the highborn."

"Please, tell me who I'm speaking with. Is this Win's mother?" Josephine pleaded.

"No. This isn't her. You don't know me. I have to go now. I just want you to know that little Andrew will be all right. No harm is going to come to him. You must forget him, and go on with your life."

The call disconnected, and all Josephine heard was dial tone.

She threw herself down onto the sofa and sobbed. "Oh, God! What am I to do? Please, someone help me," she cried.

"Tell us what you can about the call, Lady Winterdale," asked the constable. "Was it a man or a woman?"

"I really don't know. It might have been either, but if I had to guess, I would say a woman. The person sounded a bit um…down-market. Uneducated. The word 'fettle' was substituted for condition. When I asked if Andrew was all right, the person said he was in 'fine fettle'. But that could have been a ruse to throw me off. The voice was definitely altered. I'd say there was a handkerchief or some such thing placed over the receiver. I just don't understand anything. The person said money wasn't the motive for the kidnapping. Whoever it was indicated that I wasn't highborn enough to be raising a child who would someday be an earl's son. But they also said Win was undoubtedly dead and wouldn't be coming home."

"Madam, go over with me again the rules of inheritance in families like the Winthrops," the chief detective said.

"It's quite simple, really. If Win should die, which I don't even want to contemplate, his son would be the successor. Of course, someone would be named as a guardian in his place, to handle his affairs until he reached his majority. I suppose, as his mother, that would be me."

"And if Andrew should die, as well as your husband?" the inspector continued.

"Oh God. The next in line would be that disgusting Oliver."

"Do you believe Oliver capable of carrying out such a horrendous deed? Actually killing his own nephew?"

Josephine raised her head, eyes swollen and tears still falling. "I've never thought of it. I don't know him terribly well, to tell the truth. He and Win have never been close. I *do* know he is envious of Win because Win is the first-born son and will inherit everything. Well—not everything. Oliver would receive a share of the estate, but as far as the holding itself, it would go to Win, and he would naturally be the next earl."

"So, theoretically, there would be motive for Oliver to contemplate such an act?" replied the inspector. "Especially if he thinks that his brother is not going to return from the war."

"I suppose," answered Josephine. "I just have a hard time conceiving of Oliver doing away with his own nephew."

"Was anything else said during the conversation that might be a clue?" the chief detective continued.

"The only other thing I thought a bit odd was that the caller stumbled a little when referring to my husband. His Christian name is James, but most everyone has always called him Win, which, of course, would be derived from the title name—Winthrop. The person on the telephone first called him James. Then there was a pause, and they called him Jay. Finally, they referred to him as Win."

"Do you know of anyone who refers to him as Jay?"

"No. I've never heard him called that. I suppose it wouldn't be unusual. It's not an unheard of by-name for James."

"I'm beginning to think more and more that the culprit here is the uncle—Oliver. Whomever has taken your baby appears to have an interest in never seeing your husband become the next earl at Winthrop Manor. It would seem likely this individual hopes to see Oliver inherit. The Lord Winterdale has been missing for what? Over eight months, right? To my way of thinking, the telephone call points to Oliver more than anyone. If the Lord Winterdale doesn't return from the war, and Andrew is never found, Oliver will be the one who profits. You said the caller assured you the child was all right."

"Yes. But is he? Was that only said to ease my suffering? The caller said he or she would get into trouble if it was known that the call was placed. So getting in touch with me wasn't part of the plan," said Josephine. "Can't we call the operator who handled the call, and see if we can determine where it was placed from?"

"Yes. That's exactly my intention," he replied. Walking over to the telephone, he waited just a moment before the operator came on the line.

Josephine listened carefully to the detective's portion of the conversation.

"Yes, is this the operator who was present when a call was received at the Lady Winterdale's home?" the detective stated. He proceeded by giving her the exchange number. "Yes, That's good news. Can you give me the number from which the call originated?"

He motioned to Josephine that he needed a pen or pencil to write with. She quickly handed him a pad of paper and a pen. He listened as the operator spoke and scribbled on the paper.

"Are you able to give me the location of that number? All right, yes, I understand. I certainly appreciate your help. Please continue to monitor all calls to this number," he added.

The moment he placed the receiver back into its cradle, Josephine fired off a rapid series of questions.

"Where did the call originate? Was it local? Did she listen to the voice? Was it familiar to her?"

"Please allow me to answer, my lady. Yes, she listened to the call; no, she did not recognise the voice; it was not familiar to her; the number was local; unfortunately for us, it was placed from a telephone box in Winthrop-on-Hart."

"So we've learned nothing more," cried Josephine.

"Not quite true. We've learned that whomever has taken your child is still in this vicinity. There has been adequate time for the perpetrator to be far away by now. My hunch is that the individual lives in this area then."

"My god. What if it's Oliver? He could be telling me Andrew is all right in order to calm my fears. His motive could be to harm him—to do away with him, so if Win doesn't return from the war, Oliver will definitely inherit someday."

"That is a possibility. Not one I care to speculate upon. You know your brother-in-law. Do you honestly believe him capable of harming a small child?"

"Not really. He's very arrogant and rather immature. I do know he would do most anything to be able to inherit Winthrop Manor. To my knowledge, he has no skills of any sort. I've heard the Lord Winthrop refer to him as a fool. Frankly, I think it would be more likely for him to place Andrew with a kind, Christian family and pay them to raise him. I'm sure we're all aware that there are many needy families who make extra funds by acting as surrogates for women who give birth to children out of wedlock. Oh, Lord. If that *is* the case, we might never find my child. He could be anywhere in England."

"Let's not take our thoughts in that direction. I'm still more inclined to believe the infant is close by."

"What shall we do? I'm terrified. Uncle Roderick, will you please stay here with me tonight? I don't want to be alone."

"Of course, my dear. I also believe the authorities have indicated their intention to have a man posted here at all times."

"That does make me feel better," she responded. "Nevertheless, I still want you by my side. We *must* make a list of every possible person who could be the culprit."

"I definitely agree," Uncle Roderick answered. "There are only so many people who have an interest in who will become the next earl at Winthrop Manor."

"Yes," interjected the detective inspector. "I believe that would be an enormous help. Tomorrow, the men from Scotland Yard will arrive. You're well aware of their expertise. They seldom fail to resolve a case, and I scarcely believe this will be one of the few they don't solve. I'm going to take leave now, but if you should have any more calls—any at all—notify me immediately. I don't care if it's three o'clock in the morning. I'll want to know. My wife is well used to knocks at our door and midnight calls. Please, try to get some rest. I know it's difficult, but the last thing we need is Andrew's mum becoming fatigued and ill."

Josephine rose from the sofa and walked him to the door. "Thank you for everything you've done. I do feel better, just knowing expert authorities are involved. I would never have believed when I woke this morning and bathed and fed my precious son, that tonight, I wouldn't know his whereabouts or who is caring for him." Tears welled again in her eyes.

"God bless you, Lady Winterdale. I definitely feel at this juncture we'll find the little chap, and he'll be back in your arms very soon."

No matter how positive the detectives felt, another day and night passed with no further progress on the case. Josephine and Roderick had completed their list, which included Oliver, the Lord and Lady Winthrop, Oliver's lady friend, Cynthia Wilkins-Young, and even Elisabeth, whose name Josephine had been loath to add.

The Scotland Yard detectives arrived, and both Josephine and Roderick were most impressed with them. After listening to the entire story, they agreed with the local authorities regarding the belief that Andrew was still in the vicinity of Winthrop-on-Hart. That gave Josephine a bit of hope. One by one, the world-renowned detectives followed every possible lead. Every person on Josephine and Roderick's list was interrogated. And one by one, a checkmark was placed by their names, which didn't in any way clear them of distrust but helped keep track of who had and hadn't been interviewed. Even those with solid alibis were not released from suspicion. The action of primary importance was the news that Scotland Yard was going to pay Oliver a visit at Winthrop Manor. Josephine felt certain he had some part in this nightmare they were living in. She was somewhat confused about why people who had alibis were being questioned, but she also understood that Scotland Yard knew much more about solving crimes than she did.

When Josephine enquired as to why such persons were still regarded as possible suspects, she was told they had not ruled out the prospect that a member of the family had hired an unknown person to carry out the actual deed. The detectives instructed Josephine not to have any personal contact with any one of the possible suspects. She felt particularly sad not to be allowed to show a simple act of kindness toward Elisabeth. After all, they were still sisters-in-law, and Elisabeth was the widow of Josephine's brother. Josephine begged the authorities to make an exception regarding her dear friend, but they reiterated their command firmly, stating that she not converse with anyone in the family.

Besides her continual worry about her missing child, she was still consumed with anxiety about whether Win would ever be located. She had a definite belief that if he were to return home, the mystery of his son's disappearance would be solved. Every method utilised to locate Win had been met with disappointing results. Supposedly, the Red Cross was extremely efficient when it came to finding missing servicemen. Yet, the persons on the very top of the ladder hadn't been able to find a trace of him. Nonetheless, Josephine refused to give up hope. She harboured an inner feeling that he *was* alive and would eventually find his way back to her.

Uncle Roderick continually lamented that no lady should ever have had to face such a devastating and stressful time. It was horrific enough to have one's baby snatched. However, to live with that evil act while also being greatly troubled by the devastating possibility that she might never learn what had become of the man she adored was almost more than even a strong person should be forced to endure. Her uncle continuously said how impressed he was with Josephine's ability to carry on, and that he admired her strength and courage.

Still confined in the Netherlands, Win was well aware that he was certainly a father by then. If the child had been born on or near the due date, he or she would be somewhere near seven months of age. The wish to see his offspring was overwhelming. His injured foot had healed, but due to the lack of appropriate medical care, he had been left with constant pain and a permanent limp. Still, better that than the alternative—for a time, he'd feared the appendage might need to be amputated...

Now that he was as healthy as he ever would be, under the circumstances, he felt as though he had hit a wall. Nobody had the slightest notion of how long the wretched war would continue, and there didn't appear to be any end in sight. He would rather be dead than spend years and years not seeing the woman he adored or even knowing whether he was a father and if the child were a boy or a girl.

He would do whatever he had to do to be free again. Anything at all.

The chances were great that he would be shot or hanged if he attempted escape, but he and his fellow prisoner Will had spent months putting together a plan. The local woman Will had befriended their first week at the camp still came by nearly every other day to stand outside the fence and chat. With her help the men figured they had a better chance at making a clean getaway than most.

Although the prisoners were allowed to purchase cigarettes from the barrow men, there was nothing available to burn them. In order to light a cigarette, a prisoner would have to approach one of the guards and ask him to light it. The guards didn't want the prisoners setting something ablaze and causing an evacuation. However, with assistance from their Dutch girlfriend, Win and Will came up with a feasible scheme.

Win approached her one morning when she appeared outside the fence. She spoke some English, which facilitated matters. He was able to make it clear to her that he and William would be terribly happy if they could have their own source of heat to light cigarettes, instead of constantly needing to ask one of the guards. Later that same day, she reappeared and slipped an entire small box of wooden matches through the fence in a surreptitious manner. Win took them and quickly reached down, putting them into a shoe, since the prisoner uniforms had no pockets.

From that time forward, Win and William continued to put together their scheme, which wasn't really terribly difficult. Their primary need was waiting for the proper time to put their plan into action. The opportunity finally came on Christmas Eve, 1915. Win had not known that the camp authorities allowed prisoners to attend a concert of carols at the Dutch Reformed Church. Of course, several guards would accompany the prisoners, but because the camp was in an isolated area, the guards had taken advantage of their freedom from discipline and had enjoyed several bottles of alcoholic drinks in celebration of the holiday. Thus, the entire environment had a somewhat more relaxed feeling. Small Christmas packages had been allowed for the prisoners, and the prisoners were absolutely ecstatic about being able to attend the church service. The packages were opened shortly before the guard began to queue up the men for a march to the church.

Thus, when the time came to unlock the gates and escort prisoners to the church, there was a substantial heap of what had been wrapping paper stacked in a corner of the outdoor area. There was a queue of perhaps one hundred men in the line, and some twenty-five guards working escort. The majority of them were far from sober and were joking with one another while singing Christmas songs. Win was one of the first prisoners to leave his hut and join the group. When the locks were released, four guards began to lead the men toward the church, which was within sight of the camp. Will lagged behind and was one of the last in the queue.

"Fire!" he suddenly shouted.

There was a significant amount of commotion and turmoil. Smoke and flames rose from the place where the package paper had been piled. It had been a dry autumn, and it was also a quite windy day. The flames spread quickly. Before long, there was not one fire, but several. Stacks of debris scattered about caught fire, and then the guards' wooden barracks were ablaze. The far-from-sober guards were unorganised. Win thought several prisoners would use the opportunity to escape, but apparently, they were frightened of being shot or hanged, because most either stood stock still or tried to pitch in to put out the scattered fires Win and William acted in accordance with the plans they had made well in advance. They didn't run, which would no doubt call attention to them, but they walked rapidly through the gates. All the guards had turned their attention on the fire. Outside the camp, there was a one-lane road bordered by dense forests. Naturally, Win and William headed for that wooded area. There was shouting going on behind them in the camp, as the guards called for water.

Win and William reached the forest and then broke into a sprint, Win doing a kind of combination hop-run. His newly healed foot hurt like hell, but he kept moving. Apparently, the other prisoners chose to say nothing, for some of them surely had to have seen what took place, but no alarm was sounded.

As soon as Win and William felt they were far enough into the woods, they ripped off their uniforms, hiding them in the underbrush near some thick bushes. They had been issued long, winter underwear a few weeks earlier since the weather had turned cold. So, while not fully dressed, neither were they naked. As long as they stayed in the wooded area, they knew they would be safe, and their lack of outer clothing would not present a problem. According to the Dutch girl, small cabins were scattered throughout the woods, as this was a popular area for those who were nature-lovers or who hunted in the autumn. Their aim was to find one of these structures and pray there would be clothing inside.

Twenty minutes or so later, they came across a tiny, one-room building—more of a shack than a cabin—but their luck held out, and they found several sets of men's winter clothing in a dusty, cob-web covered cabinet. Whomever had left the clothes must have been very large, because Win and Will had to roll up the sleeves and pantlegs and use lengths of twine as belts to keep the trousers from falling down, but neither man complained. God must have been with them, because they each found a heavy, winter coat—over-sized but warm—as well as several sets of gloves, hats, and scarves.

Although they could no longer see or hear the prison camp, they dared not dally. Sooner or later, the guards would discover they'd escaped, and a search party would be organized. Before that happened, Win wanted to be far, far away.

They dressed quickly and headed back out into the forest, now better equipped to deal with their environment.

The Dutch girl had smuggled them in a map of the Netherlands, and they'd studied it very carefully. The nearest town looked to be Assen, some twenty miles west. Although they kept hidden in the trees, they made certain they followed the road and were surprised when they spotted a sign for Assen a short while later. Adrenaline must have been pouring through their bodies, since it didn't seem they'd made so much progress. They were starving but too terrified to stop at a café. If word of their escape had spread, the townsfolk might be watching for them. So they kept to the road. The next village on their route would be Zwolle, a very long way from their present locale. Yet, they had no choice but to keep moving. It wasn't late in the day. Neither man had a wristwatch, but they did know how to read the hours from the position of the sun. Win guessed it was nearly two o'clock. So, on they travelled toward Zwolle. Amazingly, they never saw another person on the roadway, nor did a vehicle drive by. After several more hours, the sun began to set lower in the western sky. Zwolle remained a considerable distance away. They'd seen signs with its name and the number of kilometers. The bottoms of their feet were covered with blisters from all the walking they'd done, even though they'd purposely worn two pairs of socks. Finally, they decided to go deeper into the woodland beside the road. There, they would bed down and get some rest.

From that day, forward, their plan was to travel at night, rather than during daylight hours. Both of their stomachs were past growling and were actually cramping with pain. They hadn't travelled far into the forest, when, surprisingly, they came upon another small cabin. This one was newer than the last, and at first, they were frightened, thinking it was surely inhabited. Still, it seemed to be a rather odd place for a home, since there was nothing of any consequence nearby—no place to buy foodstuffs or petrol, no close postal facility or physician's office. They sank down upon the ground and slowly crept nearer the unpretentious cabin. It was built from logs, probably cut from the surrounding forest. There was no automobile in sight and no lights in the structure. While it wasn't pitch dark outside, it was still quite dim. Nighttime was fast approaching. William reached one of the few windows. Silently, he rose and peeked inside. He was delighted to see that the place surely belonged to someone who undoubtedly used it for hunting purposes or perhaps as a summer get-away. There were deer antlers on the walls. It was clear that it was a sportsman's hideaway. It *was* a Sunday, but it looked as though the owner, if he'd been there at all, had left.

Win gathered his nerve and knocked on the door. Nobody answered. He and Will then walked around the cabin, looking into each window. It was not at all large, and the interior could easily be seen in its entirety. There was nobody inside. Will rammed his shoulder against the door, and it easily opened. Win and Will scurried inside, shutting and bolting the door, which amazingly hadn't shattered when Will had busted it open.

The cabin provided them with a cosy set-up. On one wall was a stone fireplace, with logs piled by its side. However, they were leery of starting a fire, for fear someone might see smoke rising from the chimney piece. A wooden sink and old-fashioned water pump sat next to the hearth, along with an icebox and a wooden cook stove. A sofa and some chairs were scattered about, and the ladder led to a loft, where they discovered two beds.

"You don't suppose there's food anywhere in here?" Win asked.

"Or more clothes?" added William.

"Only one way to find out," answered Win, as he came back down the ladder and quickly walked to the kitchen area, where cabinets hung on the walls.

Opening the doors, they discovered shelves filled with dozens and dozens of cans—carrots, beans, peas, spinach, sardines, tuna fish, and more… The men were so hungry, they were ready to rip them open with their bare hands, if such a thing had been remotely possible. Obviously, it wasn't, so they began to rummage through drawer after drawer.

Win shouted, "*Yes!*" There lay a can opener.

Next, thy began to rummage through the closets. One of them had children's clothing—hardly useful for them. But, in another, they discovered men's pants and shirts, and more heavy jackets. There were also gloves and socks, as well as more underclothing. Again, the clothes were larger than either one of them wore, but they would definitely suffice. They could change out of their dirty, wet clothing, so they'd look less conspicuous when the time came to start moving again.

After Win and William had eaten everything they could find that sounded the least bit palatable, they both lay down, one in each of the two beds, and slept for an entire day. After a good rest, they filled their haversacks with a great many of the remaining cans of food, including vegetables, fruits, sardines, crackers, and soup. They also took two bowls and some utensils for eating. Win had found some medical supplies in a cabinet. He used one of the thick bandages to wrap his foot and ankle, hoping to add more support and perhaps ease some of the pain. They still had miles to travel, and he hurt more with each step he took.

He and Will waited for nightfall and then once again entered the dark, forested countryside. They had studied their map and were quite certain they knew their locale. It appeared they were near the train station that would take them to Rotterdam. If they could make it to Rotterdam, they could change to another train and would eventually end up in England. There was also the hope that they would be able to find their regiment.

Sure enough, after tramping through the woods for several hours, Win heard the sound of a train whistle. It was the sign they'd been waiting for. Obviously, they were very near the tracks. They stayed in the woods, but soon they were able to actually see the railway line. They continued to follow it for a few more miles. Several trains roared by, as Win and Will struggled along. Finally, they spotted the station. They were in a very small village, and no one seemed to pay any particular attention to the two rather down-market chaps. Win had learned a bit of the Dutch language while incarcerated. He walked bravely to the ticket window.

"*Twee kartyes naar Rotterdam,*" he said, exactly as he had practiced.

He and Will bought newspapers, pretending to read them after they boarded the train. Will told Win he was going to close his eyes and pretend to be asleep. They were supposed to change trains at Utrecht, but they spotted Dutch policemen on the platform, so the dared not disembark. Eventually, they arrived…not in Rotterdam, but in Amsterdam. Their original idea had been to board a ship in Rotterdam. Having arrived in Amsterdam, they hadn't the faintest idea what to do next.

They began to walk around the town, and after a spell, Win spotted a shop with an English name—*Bell's Asbestos Company*.

"I don't think I can stay on my feet much longer," Win told Will. "I think we should take our chances and go in here. Someone might be able to help us."

Will nodded his agreement, and they went inside, assuming as casual an air as possible, considering their appearance and Win's physical condition.

A man came forward to assist them.

Win smiled. "Is Mr. Bell in?"

The man laughed. "This shop is part of a chain in Europe, and there is no 'Mr. Bell'." He looked them up and down. "What can I do for you…gentlemen?"

Win took a deep breath and spilled the beans, explaining who he and Shore were.

The gentleman was extremely nice. Not only that, but he was an Englishman. Because Holland was a neutral country, there were any number of English people living and working there, but the man told them that if he were caught helping escapees, he would be expelled from the country. However, after he phoned the British consul and the consul said that on no account were Win and William to go near that office, and they had no wish to know or hear anything about them, the kind shopkeeper decided to help them himself. Needless to say, Will and Win were immensely relieved.

26

❧❧

Win and Will reached Rotterdam without any other mishap, but they encountered another next problem when they tried to get onto the docks. There were police at the entrance, so Win and Will hung about until they saw a man pushing an overloaded barrow towards the docks. Win and William whipped off their straw hats and bent down, helping him push the barrow through the entrance. The man was very pleased to have had their help, and Win and Will were delighted. Nobody challenged them, and the police took no notice.

Their shopkeeper friend in Amsterdam had learned that the SS Cromer was sailing that night and had told them to make for it. They waited until no one was about then ran up the gang-plank to the ship, where they were met by the cook, who was lounging about the deck. Win greased the man's palm quite considerably, but the man seemed quite congenial, and Win felt certain the cook would have helped them anyway. The cook was the only man on board, and he hid them below until the captain and the crew came back from shore.

Win would have loved to think their troubles were over, and certainly, they were much safer than they had been. But they still had to reach Winthrop-on-Hart. When the cook introduced Win and Will to the captain, the man agreed to assist them, as well. He dressed them in greasy overalls and told them to look busy when the police came 'round to inspect the boat before she sailed. When the police came into the engine room, the captain followed, telling the officers to hurry up because he didn't want to miss the tide. What a night it was, for the cook had used the money Win gave him to send ashore for a *lot* of beer. The next morning, they were up on deck, feasting their eyes on dear old England as they approached Harwich.

When the ship docked at the Harwich Naval Port, Will and Win were two of the first to step onto the pier. The knowledge that they were once again standing on English soil nearly caused Win to become giddy. They were both totally prepared to tell the authorities of their miserable escape from the German POW camp in Holland. However, nobody asked them to show papers, and nothing was said to them. Their plan was to notify the military authorities, and then, as quickly as possible, return to their respective homes. William was from a small village in Southwest England. He and Win promised to stay in touch with each other. They boarded the train together at Harwich.

While travelling by train from Harwich to Liverpool Station in London, an elderly lady approached them. After taking note of their untidy civilian clothes, she glared at them.

"Why in the hell aren't you two young, healthy men out there with your British brothers, fighting those disgusting Huns?" she demanded in a loud voice.

Win and Will looked at each other and busted out laughing—this being the first time either of them had found any humor in their situation. The old woman, obviously angry at their response, huffed and strode away down the aisle, where she took up a seat in the rear of the train.

Win and Will arrived in London on a Wednesday. Win said his good-byes to Will and then immediately visited a men's clothing emporium, purchasing a new suit of clothing and everything he needed to accompany it. He was not about to meet his beloved Josephine looking like a pathetic vagrant. When he'd left Winthrop-on-Hart, Josephine did not have a telephone in their cottage. So he decided not to make an attempt to get word to her about his safe return. His primary goal was to travel to Winthrop-on-Hart by the fastest method possible and to hold his precious wife in his arms. Thoughts of their child occupied his mind incessantly. He had no idea if he had a son or daughter, and it didn't truly matter. As long as everything had gone well, Win would be a happy man.

He made his way to the railway station and checked the schedules. He hadn't expected to find a train that would take him directly to Winthrop-on-

Hart. The best he could do was to take a line to Winchester. From that point, there would be one more short ride on another train to his beloved wife. His foot hurt terribly. It throbbed, and pains shot up and down his leg. Before he continued on his way to Hampshire, he knew he had no choice but to see a physician. Therefore, he stopped a fellow about to cross the street and asked where the nearest hospital was located. He learned that there was a military hospital in Colchester, which was the city connected to Harwich. He immediately found his way there, and after what seemed an interminable wait, he was seen by an emergency physician.

He told his story to the doctor, who marvelled that Win and Will had successfully escaped, and he examined Win's foot. As Win had suspected, it had healed wrong. The physician discussed amputation, but Win refused to consider such a thing. He wanted to be seen by his friend Dr. Drew in Winthrop-on-Hart. If indeed amputation was necessary, he wanted it performed in a London hospital.

So the Colchester doctor used a bandage to rewrap the foot and ankle, much as Will had done. Will thanked the man for his assistance and hurried on his way. All he wanted was to return to the small cottage he had built for his beautiful wife.

Upon leaving the medical facility, he found his way to the train station again. He knew he needed to report to the military authorities but was willing to take the chance on returning to his home first. Surely, there would not be any harsh penalty if he chose that route. It was completely obvious that his wound was, at the very least, a blighty. Blighties were injuries that were considered serious enough to render a soldier incapable of performing any further military duties, thus calling for discharge, yet not serious to cause permanent disability. Win was not at all certain that his wound wasn't beyond a blighty and might very well cause permanent disability. Still, seeing his child and Josephine were more important to him than anything in the world—even the possibility of having his foot amputated.

The station in London was swarming with military men in uniform. He wished he could collect a new uniform, but he didn't have any desire to be detained by English authorities while questioned about his imprisonment. That could wait. He boarded the train for Winchester and slept during the entire journey. When the conductor announced that the train had reached Winchester, Win knew he wasn't far from home. He considered placing a call to Winthrop Manor, where the auto would have been dispatched immediately to collect him, but he had no idea what the situation was at his former home. Hopefully, due to his long absence, his parents had reconciled with Josephine, but he couldn't be certain. Thus, he boarded the train to Winthrop-on-Hart, knowing it was the last leg of his wretched journey.

At long last, the train pulled into the small station, with which he was so familiar. As he stepped from the car, he spotted the stationmaster. They were well-acquainted.

"By God," Walter Pitts shouted.

Win grinned and limped his way toward the man.

"I can't believe what my eyes are telling me. Is that really you, Lord Winterdale? Everyone in these parts has been well certain we'd lost you to the damn Huns. Yet, here you are. Limping, are you? Are you badly wounded? Where in blazes is your uniform?"

"I've been through it, Walt. Pretty badly," answered Win. "I was captured and incarcerated in a Dutch POW camp. I was bayoneted when I was taken prisoner. That's the reason for the limp. The damn Hun drove the thing right through my foot. I had it looked at in the hospital at Harwich, but I want to see Tom Drew, over in Cloverdale. Then I'll undoubtedly travel to London. The Harwich physician mentioned amputation. I hope it doesn't come to that. I could have stopped over in London, but I wanted to see Josephine so badly."

"How did you manage to get out of there?" asked Walter.

"Another chap and I managed to think up a foolproof scheme to escape, and we pulled it off. I just wanted to get home. Can you find me a ride to my wife's cottage?" he asked.

"You bet, Captain. I'll take you myself. There ain't another train coming through for three hours. Here, let me help you to my auto."

Win leaned on the older man and was delighted to slide onto the front seat of his car, which had definitely seen better days. The door closed, and Walt walked around to the right side, arranging himself behind the steering wheel.

"What is the news, Walt?" asked Win. "What do you hear of my wife and family?"

"Family, indeed," exclaimed Mr. Pitts. "You've a fine boy. I heard your wife is doing well. I haven't seen her, or any of your kin, for that matter. I'm sure she's busy with the baby and such."

My God, thought Win. *A boy. A son. What spectacular news.* "Have you heard what Josephine named our son?" he asked.

"Let me see—someone told me… I'm fairly certain it's Andrew. Named after her brother who died in France. I think she's calling him Andy. It's a right fine name."

"Yes, I like it," Win answered. "We had settled on George, but when her brother was killed, she obviously changed her mind. I imagine she stayed with the second name choice—her maiden name, Chambers. A good, solid, English name. Andrew Chambers Winthrop. God, I cannot wait to see him and, naturally, Josephine. I know she's probably been sick with worry. I wasn't able to get any letters out of the camp. I was in the Netherlands. If she wrote, it would have been through the Red Cross, and I never received any letters. She most likely thinks I'm dead."

"Well, she'll be a mighty happy woman to see you. I'd suggest you might think of shaving, though." Walt laughed. "I know me own wife don't like it when I grow a beard. They aren't allowed in the military, are they?"

"Oh, they've eased up on regulations a bit. But you're right. I have a razor in my haversack. I just need some soap and water."

"We can take care of that. I'll stop at the Wayside Inn. After that, we'll almost be to your cottage. They'll be pleased to assist you. You want to look your best for your beautiful wife and that new babe."

"Great idea, Walt."

Win disengaged from the auto and allowed Walt to help him as they walked inside together. The inn had a men's room and a ladies' room off their lobby. Win disappeared through the men's door with his kit under his arm, leaving Walt sitting in a club chair to wait.

When Win returned, he looked like a different man. He wished he had his uniform, but the suit he'd purchased in Harwich was a great improvement over the pitiful, oversized clothing he and William had worn throughout their journey. Win had even made an attempt at trimming his hair and hadn't done a terrible job. Clean-shaven and even wearing new men's cologne, he looked a lot more like the Win with whom Josephine had fallen in love.

Walt started for the doorway, but Win asked him to wait a moment. He'd decided to try to place a call to the cottage—the local operator would know if Josephine had a connection. If it was all right for him to tidy up before seeing his beloved, then it was only right for him to give her fair warning of his arrival. He walked to the front desk and asked the young man who stood there if he had a telephone Win might use.

The boy nodded cordially. "Aren't you Jim Winthrop?"

Win smiled. "I'm surprised anyone would know who I am. I'm a bit rough around the edges. A fellow military chap and I escaped a German prison camp in Holland over a week ago. I've got to report to the military authorities, but I have a beautiful wife and a new baby waiting for me at home, so the army can wait a bit longer."

"I'm Johnny Blair. My dad was David Blair. I live down the high street in Winthrop-on-Hart."

"Oh, certainly, I know David. We used to go hunting together when we were very young. How is he?"

"He was killed in France. He wasn't there long. They got him straightaway."

"Oh, God, I'm sorry, Johnny. Your dad was a fine chap. Is your mum holding up all right?"

"Yes. She's got the smaller ones to look after, so she keeps busy. They're five of us in all. I'm the oldest."

"It's lucky you aren't old enough to join up. Your mum needs you here, no doubt."

"Well, welcome home to you," the boy exclaimed. "I'll bet you could tell some stories."

"Yes. Pretty harrowing at that. Thanks for the welcome. Well, I want to try to reach Josephine—give her a warning that I'll be there shortly."

"Of course. I'll go in the back and sort mail, so you can have some privacy."

Win picked up the phone and was connected with the operator. After she'd identified herself, he enquired as to whether she had a listing for Josephine Winthrop. There was a pause, and then she replied.

"Indeed, I do. Would you like me to ring her number?"

"Yes…please." Win was as nervous as he could ever remember being. After so long, he was about to hear her lyrical voice.

He could hear the telephone ring, and then she said hello.

"Josephine? It's Win. Darling, I'm home."

"Win? My Win? How can you be home? Where are you? Oh, goodness, I'm all undone."

"Walt Pitts, the stationmaster, offered to drive me to the cottage. I'm only a few miles away."

"Oh, Win. I can't believe this. I've prayed and prayed for you."

"I understand we have a little son. Andrew Chambers Winthrop, is it?"

"Yes, darling. We did. But, Win, someone has kidnapped him. It happened several days ago. Scotland Yard is on the case. I'm frantic. Oh, I'm so terribly glad you're here. Please, just come home, and I'll tell you everything."

"Kidnapped. Oh, my god. Of course, I'll be there as fast as we can drive. I love you, my angel."

"I love you, too, Win. Please do hurry."

27

❧

Win and Walter returned to the auto, continuing on their route to the cottage Win had built for her before he'd joined the military. Win's mood had changed, going from anticipatory to anxious and uneasy. Who in the world would steal a tiny baby? What would their motive be? Money…? Had someone tried to demand a ransom for the safe return of his child?

A few minutes later, Walt pulled the car into the gravelled drive at the cottage. Before Win could extricate himself from the auto, Josephine came running out of the front doorway. He opened the automobile door, and she literally fell into his arms. He held her tightly. Closing his eyes, he drank in her fragrance—hyacinth with a touch of lavender, which she'd always worn since the beginning of their relationship. It was difficult for him to believe he was holding his precious angel. He had dreamed of this moment since leaving her at Winthrop-on-Hart.

"Oh, Win. I feel as if God has answered my prayers. Never in my life have I needed someone more. Darling, we have a beautiful baby boy. Andrew Chambers Winthrop. I sometimes call him Andy. Is that all right with you?"

"Of course, sweetheart. But what is this about a kidnapping? What the hell were you talking about? I've been frantic since you said he'd been taken. Who would kidnap a baby, especially here in the country? You need to tell me all of the details quickly. How long has he been gone? How could something like that happen? God, Josephine, he's our everything. Life has been a nightmare as it is, but this is the worst yet."

"You need to come inside, and I'll start at the beginning and tell you everything. I don't want to let you go and would give everything if I didn't have to tell you all of this. It truly is a nightmare."

"Yes, of course, darling. Let me just say goodbye to Walt and thank him." He climbed out of the vehicle and went around to the other side, where Walt was taking Win's haversack from the back seat.

Win picked up his bag. "Thanks so much for bringing me home. It would have taken me much longer if you hadn't offered to drive me. I'll tell you more about what happened to Andrew later, once I learn the whole story."

"You're most welcome, sir. It was a pleasure to be of service to you. I hope everything turns out all right. Should I keep my mouth shut about your son being taken, or is it all right if I mention it to anyone I run into? Seems to me, the more people who know about it, the better the chances of his being found. Nevertheless, I'm no detective."

"Tell anybody you want, Walt. You're right. The more people who know, the more likely it is he'll be found."

"Will do, my lord. I wish you well." Walt climbed back in behind the steering and turned the auto in a circle and headed out to the main road back toward the rail station.

Josephine and Win entered the cottage. Win was mad with concern, and before they discussed anything else, he needed Josephine to tell him what was going on as far as the investigation into his son's disappearance… Not to mention, how had the kidnapper gotten his hands on the child to begin with.

"Let's sit at the table," Win told her. "I can't be on my feet much longer."

Josephine hurried to pull out a chair for him. "Win! You're limping! What happened? Are you hurt?"

"I'll tell you everything later, darling." Win slumped into the chair, leaving his bag on the floor right inside the doorway. "Right now, I need to know what happened to little Andrew."

"Oh, Win, it's so strange. I wanted to do some oil painting down by the stream, so I took Andy outside with me. I put him in his playpen, which I'd placed under the large elm. I wasn't far from him at all. I lost myself in the beauty of the day, and I was preoccupied with the canvas I was working on. But the only time I wasn't within steps of Andy was when I realised I'd left my paint smock inside. He was sleeping soundly in the playpen, so I dashed inside the kitchen, and after running around the cottage like a mad woman, I found it hanging on the back of the pantry door. I wasn't gone three minutes, if that."

She went on, giving him every detail about what had happened, and when she'd nearly finished speaking she had reached the part of the story where she was telling Win about the strange telephone call she'd received.

"Darling, could you tell anything—anything at all—by the voice.? An accent, a manner of speaking of any kind, any particular words?" Win asked.

"The person went on to say that it was absolutely necessary Andy have an upbringing of the sort *Jay* had. Obviously, whoever it was, they were referring to you as *Jay*. I figured many people in Winthrop-on-Hart probably called you that when you were growing up. It's not an unusual by-name for James. Does that mean anything to you?" Josephine asked.

"My god! You bet it does. I have to get over to Winthrop Manor as quickly as I can," Win practically shouted.

"Oh, Win, what did I say that causes you want to go to Winthrop Manor?"

"My pet, I can't stop to tell you now. However, I'm just about one hundred percent certain I'm right. Please, come with me to the manor."

"Yes, of course, I will. Especially if you think you know where Andy might be. We can take Uncle Roderick's car. He's bought a new one since you left and gave me the old one, so I could get around, if need be."

"Yes. Come. There is no time to waste. I'll try to explain a bit more while we're driving over there," said Win, as he plucked the key to the automobile from a hook in the kitchen.

Josephine had to almost run to keep up with him. She jumped into the automobile beside her husband, still not quite believing he was home. "Win, where have you been? Where is your uniform?"

"Sweetheart, I've so much to tell you. I was in a POW camp in Holland. From what I heard, some internment camps allowed mail to be sent and received, but the one I was in didn't, so I couldn't contact you. I went crazy wanting to know if you were all right and wanting to tell you I was fine. The place I was in wasn't too terrible, compared to many I heard about. Anyway, another chap and I devised a scheme to escape, and it worked. We had a long slog before we finally reached a train. A damned Hun bayoneted me before I was taken prisoner. He threw the bayonet right into my ankle. Actually, he could have killed me, so I guess I should be thankful. The wound needs to be examined by a good doctor, and I probably need surgery. I'm certain it didn't heal properly, so I might have a permanent limp."

"Oh, my poor Win. Are you in terrible pain?"

"I have been in pain for so long now, it seems normal." He laughed ruefully.

"As for everything else, it will have to wait. My first priority is to find our son. My god, Josephine. You must have been insane with worry."

"I have been frightened out of my wits, afraid for both Andy and you. Thank goodness, you're home again. Oh, Win, I've missed you so much. We did get your letter about Andrew's death. Of course, you can imagine the state Elisabeth is in because of that. When she read your letter, her heart broke. She's back at Winthrop Manor now. I honestly don't know if she'll ever recover from the loss. I know I'd feel the same way if I'd lost you. Now you're all I have in the world. You and Uncle Roderick and, hopefully, Andy. My parents are gone and my older brother is dead. I loved him so."

"I understand, darling. How is your uncle. I'm sure he's been worried sick, too."

"Yes, he has. Of course, I thank God every day for Uncle's presence. He has been my rock, really. He has stayed with me since Andy was taken. He often leaves and returns to his cottage during the day, in order to make certain everything is taken care of there, but then he come back to me at night. He'll be so thrilled to know you're home."

Win turned the automobile into the gravelled driveway at Winthrop Manor. "I wondered if I'd ever see this place again," he murmured. "It *is* good to see nothing has changed."

He stopped the car in front of the house, and both he and Josephine immediately left the auto, climbing the few steps to the front entrance. Win no longer had a key, so he used the brass knocker.

Almost at once, Radcliffe opened the door. "Well, if this isn't the biggest shock I've ever had, I don't know what is," he remarked with surprise in his voice. "Lord Winterdale. I cannot believe you're back with us. Your parents aren't going to believe this. Please—please, come right in. Limping, are you? Have you been wounded? Come in and sit down."

"I'll explain it all later," answered Win. "I haven't time to sit down. Where is Mrs. Whitaker?"

"Mrs. Whitaker? Why, in the kitchen, I imagine, where she always is. I saw her very early when the staff had breakfast together. Why do you want Mrs. Whitaker?"

"I also want Oliver. Is he here?"

"My Lord, the Scotland Yard men are speaking with him, but I imagine they would be delighted to see you and to know you're alive. They're in the drawing room."

Win made his way straight to the drawing room, and Josephine hurried to keep up with him. There sat Oliver, on the white velvet sofa, with two men across from him. Josephine recognized them as being from Scotland Yard.

"What the hell is going on here?" Win shouted.

"Ah, are you Lord Winterdale?" asked one of the inspectors.

"Yes, I am. I've managed to escape a prisoner of war camp in the Netherlands and have been on the road for weeks. Now, I've arrived to learn that my son is missing. Josephine tells me that all of the authorities think my brother may have something to do with this?"

"Please, sit down, my lord," replied the chief inspector.

Win did so. Then he looked straight at Oliver and asked, "Are you involved in the disappearance of our son? You had better be honest, you damn rogue. If you are, I can promise you, we'll find out, so you would be better off telling the truth."

"Win, I'm delighted to see you home. I didn't think I'd ever see you alive again. Of course, I didn't have anything to do with Andrew's disappearance. Why would I do such a thing? He's my nephew. This is crazy."

Win turned to the inspector. "We need to send someone to find our cook, Vera Whitaker, and have her brought up here immediately."

"May I inquire why, sir?" the inspector asked.

"I think I know what's happened to my son. Don't let that brother of mine move. I'll go fetch Mrs. Whitaker myself."

Josephine watched Oliver closely. His face took on a sickly look. He said nothing, but the expression proved a definite uneasiness. Could Win be correct? Had his brother played a role in Andrew's disappearance?

"Never mind," Win said. "I'm going to speak with her alone in the kitchens. She's likely to be more honest with me if Oliver isn't present."

Win made his way down the stairs to the kitchen. *Damn this foot,* he thought. It kept him from moving as quickly as he wanted. Josephine followed directly behind him. He was nearly certain he knew what had transpired. Vera should have the answer if his hunch was correct. She definitely was a link to Andrew's disappearance.

They entered the kitchen to find Mrs. Whitaker standing at the counter with dough rolled out in front of her. Obviously, she was about to do some baking. She didn't even glance up as Josephine and Win entered the room.

"Mrs. Whitaker, I need to speak with you. Put down those utensils, and come here," Win instructed.

Vera looked up, and a shocked expression came over her face. "What in heaven's name? My Jay. You're home." She ran to Win, embracing him with all of her might. "How on Earth—the war hasn't ended—I'm shocked to see you here, but oh, so happy."

"Yes, it's good to be back. Nevertheless, you may not be so happy when I've finished speaking to you."

"What do you mean? Why wouldn't I be happy after I've spoken to you? I'm confused," Mrs. Whitaker answered. She paused. "Would you like some warm cookies? I'm just taking a batch from the oven."

It seemed an odd question to ask at such a time.

"No, I don't care for any cookies. I want an answer to one question, Vera, and I don't want any foolishness."

"What question?" she enquired. "You sound awfully stern. You've never spoken to me like that before." Tears welled in her eyes, and her bottom lip trembled.

"I've never had reason to, but I do now. What do you know about the kidnapping of my baby boy?" he asked her.

"Why, all I know is that he went missing from his playpen outside of your cottage. I learned that from your brother, Oliver. I've been worried sick. Have there been any new developments?"

"I suspect so. Someone telephoned Josephine the evening he was taken. Whoever the person was, they referred to me as Jay. Now, Mrs. Whitaker, do you know of anybody, besides you, who would use that name when referring to me?"

"Well, I suppose there could be a number of people. Jay is not an uncommon by-name for James. When I was coming up, there was a boy in my neighbourhood named James, and everyone knew him as Jay." She paused again. "Are you certain I can't tempt you with some cookies? They're my sugar cookies, Jay. You've always loved them so."

"Vera, stop it. Why do you persist with the subject of sugar cookies when my precious son is missing? The fact that your neighbour was called Jay is precisely why you slapped that label on me when I came into the world," Win said.

Josephine took a seat in the chair at the kitchen table. His poor wife looked rather ill. No doubt, she'd begun to put the facts together.

"What are you trying to say?" Vera said. "Do you think I had something to do with your boy's disappearance?" She had a very confused expression on her face.

Win recalled the night of the dinner at Winthrop Manor when he'd first introduced Josephine to his parents. At that time, he had been so consumed with obtaining his parents' approval for marriage to Josephine, he'd paid scant attention when his mother had told him of her concern regarding Mrs. Whitaker, and the possibility that her mind was deteriorating. Now the conversation came back to him.

"Vera, I don't want to frighten you with harsh words. You know how much I have loved you all my life. I think it's a distinct possibility, Vera, that perhaps you had something to do with Andrew's disappearance, but that you didn't mean to hurt me or Josephine. Scotland Yard is involved in this investigation. If you aren't going to be straight with me, I'll call the chief detective inspector immediately. He is right upstairs in the drawing room. Perhaps you might choose to be honest with him," Win threatened. He knew he was frightening her, but he had to have the truth. He was making every attempt to be kind.

"Oh, please, no. You wouldn't do that, would you? I've loved you all your life," Mrs. Whitaker pleaded. "My darling Jay. I'm so happy to see you. Won't you please help yourself to a cookie?"

Win was extremely distraught. It was clear to him that the beloved cook was having grave difficulties with her thinking.

"I would love to have some of your cookies, if doing so would bring back my son," Win replied. "But first, I must know where he is. You can help me so much by telling me why in blazes you would have anything to do with such a cruel action."

Vera was silent for a minute. Clearly, she was trying to decide what to do. Win had no doubt she was involved in Andrew's disappearance. Her features showed anxiety and confusion. Finally, she sank down in a chair by the table and began to speak.

"Jay— I would never have had anything to do with causing you pain. I thought what I was doing was right and proper," she began.

"Do continue, Mrs. Whitaker. I believe you," Win replied.

"Well, I overheard my lord and my lady talking about you and your wife. Both of them were saying how worried they were about something bad happening to you in the war. It was after Mr. Andrew was killed. The Lord Winthrop said he was happy to have a grandson to take over the estate if you died. He didn't want Oliver to be the one to run it. Then my lady said she didn't think Miss Josephine was the proper person to raise little Andrew since she didn't have a title and such. She said Miss Josephine refused to consider living at Winthrop Manor. They thought the boy should be raised in aristocratic surroundings—did I pronounce that right?"

"Did you pronounce what right?" Win asked.

"Aristocratic," replied the cook.

"Yes, yes. Go on, Mrs. Whitaker," Win answered impatiently.

"Well, after I heard all that, I worried and worried. If something happened to you—God forbid—my sister could raise the baby. She's married to a gentleman who has a very nice position. They're considered gentrified. I suppose you think it's strange that a cook in a great house could have a sister who is quite high on the social scale."

Win had always known that Mrs. Whitaker came from a better background than the average cook in a great house. "Go on, Vera," he pressed her.

"Well, my sister Emily—you know who I mean; the one who has a very nice house in London. She can't have children. They've tried and tried, but there's something not right. She's cried so about it. They would like to adopt a baby, but it's not easy.

"Then your brother Oliver got to talking to me one day while he was in the kitchen. I'd made him one of my special sandwiches. He said he didn't think you would survive the war. Nobody in the family had heard anything about you since the letter from the military people arrived, saying you was missing in action. So many months had gone by and still no word. Oliver said he hoped your Andrew grew up to be a seemly member of the gentry. Otherwise, Oliver said, he'd have to take over Winthrop Manor, and he wasn't keen on that."

Win was well aware that Oliver hoped to become the next earl. *He must have been manipulating Mrs. Whitaker.* "Where did Oliver think the child would be raised in the manner befitting an earl?"

"He didn't know, really. It was me who told him about my sister. Emily wanted a child but couldn't ever have one. I said I thought it was very mean for anyone to think about not allowing the babe's mother to care for him until the age of majority. He told me Miss Josephine simply wasn't fit to raise a viscount. I couldn't understand why he thought that, and I even said she'd never agree to let another person raise Andrew. He said she would, because she was very young and comely and would want to re-marry, but she hadn't even been presented to the king and queen, so there was scant chance she'd marry a man of the sort Andrew's father was, meaning you, Jay. That's when he asked if I knew any lady who wished for a child."

Win put his head in his hands. *What a wicked, scoundrel of a brother I have.* "What in blazes made him think you would know someone worthy of raising my son?" Win asked.

"Oliver knew I come from a nice background. I'd told him about Emily before. Well, we talked some more about it. He said he'd take care of getting the baby from Miss Josephine, and that they would give him to Emily. All Oliver wanted me to do was take the babe to Emily in London. Well, of course, he wanted me to tell Emily I'd learned of a baby who needed a good home. I was to tell her that the boy's father was killed in the war, and the mother and father hadn't been married, so the mother wanted to have the babe adopted out and raised proper. I argued some, because I didn't want to tell a lie. He said it wasn't really a bad lie. He was sure you'd been killed, and he knew I'd heard your parents saying your wife wasn't fit to raise the babe, and he needs two parents.

"After a lot of talking, he started to make sense to me. It would solve a lot of problems. Emily would be able to have the baby she wanted so dearly, and Andrew would have a mother and father who could give him the sort of life you would want for him.

"I couldn't figure how he would take the baby. I wasn't sure Josephine would give him away, but he told me he knew her much better than I did.

Well, that was true. I wanted what was best for your son, so I agreed to help in any way I could.

"The next thing I knew, Oliver brought the child here, to Winthrop Manor, and instructed me to immediately take the train to London, where Emily lives. He said he'd tell my lord and my lady that he'd sent me on a journey to London to buy some truffles from Harrods for a special dish he wished to have me prepare. I did what he told me to do. Emily was so happy. She just loved that baby the moment she laid eyes on him. She had a beautiful nursery all prepared and everything. Emily asked about papers and the like. She wanted to make sure everything was legal. Oliver had sent along a document—did I pronounce that right?"

"Yes, yes, go on, Vera."

"Well, the document was signed with him as the baby's guardian. It said you was killed in the war, and your wife felt it better to have Andrew raised right and proper. Oliver signed it, and so did Emily. I got to be the witness. Only, Oliver didn't use his proper name. He wrote Oscar Littleton. I remember that, because it seemed strange, but he said that's how things were done.

"When I returned, Oliver said it was all finished and done. He went off somewhere, and I started to do some baking. The more I thought about it, I got to feeling bad. I felt sorry for your wife. I thought she should at least know that her little baby wasn't hurt or dead. So early the next morning, I put a cloth over the receiver and dialed her number. Oliver didn't know I was doing that, and I knew he'd be mad if he found out. But there didn't seem any harm in it, and if it made your wife feel a little better, then I couldn't see why I shouldn't call.

"To tell the truth, I felt even worse after I made the call. She sounded so upset. I wanted to be honest, but it was too late for that. I knew Andrew would be fine, and your Josephine would recover in time. Win had heard all he needed to hear. He sat absolutely still for a moment.

28

He now had the entire story, or at least the portion that would lead him to his precious son. Now, he needed to consider what the next course of action should be. The Scotland Yard detectives were still interviewing Oliver in the drawing room, and Win was well-aware that they would immediately make their way to London and retrieve the child. But he was also concerned that Mrs. Whitaker would be treated very roughly, and Oliver would be only too happy to place all the blame on her. He was also frightened that the police would take the infant and place him in some sort of government care until everything was sorted out. He wanted to hold his son for the first time. He wanted to sleep in his own home with his wife and child. Thus, as far as Win was concerned, he would take charge of the situation, and if there was a penalty to pay later, he would be glad to do so. Hadn't poor Josephine been through enough? Hadn't he? He decisively knew what his actions must be.

"Mrs. Whitaker, you have been a tremendous help. Please, just continue with your baking, unless you are summoned to speak to the inspectors upstairs. Josephine and I are going to London to bring our baby home. I'm not placing any of this on you. Oliver is not a good person, and, unfortunately, he used you as a means to accomplish what he set out to do. I don't want you to worry. Once we have Andrew home, we'll all be in a much better position to decide exactly what will happen going forward."

She nodded, although it was quite clear she did not completely understand all of the intricacies involved. Win kissed her on the cheek and told her he and his wife would see her upon their return.

This was not her fault, he thought. *There was definitely something amiss in the way her brain was working. She hadn't been using common sense. Mrs. Whitaker might not be uncommonly bright, but Win was certain she would never, ever have considered doing anything to harm him or his child.*

He glanced across the table at the face of the woman he loved more than anyone else on Earth. Perhaps because he had been in such a rush when he'd reached the cottage and learned of the kidnapping, he hadn't taken time to notice how totally different Josephine looked. She was pale and wan and looked to be several stones thinner than she'd been when he'd left for the war. Her nails had been bitten to the quick; her lips were chapped, and her skin looked dry. *What horrors has she endured? Worry about losing her husband, the kidnapping of her beloved baby, no parents to console her—not even her brother.* Oliver would pay for this, he vowed to himself. That thought kept running through his head.

Mrs. Whitaker was still sitting at the table with them. Once again, she offered cookies, and Win agreed to take a couple of them. She seemed pleased and not at all aware of the unmitigated harm she had caused.

Josephine had spent the entire time during Vera's recitation of the events leading to the baby's disappearance with her head on the table, buried into folded arms. She was exhausted and terribly relieved to have her husband home to take charge. He had managed to do just that, and it appeared that baby Andrew would be returning to his mommy and daddy. She raised her head. Tears of relief created snail's tracks on her cheeks. She reached across the table, taking Win's hand in hers.

"I love you so much, darling. Thank God you're home, and we're going to be a family after all this time."

"Everything will be fine, sweetheart. You can finally relax. I can't imagine the heartache you've experienced. I'm so terribly sorry. I so wish I could have been here, so you didn't have to face all this alone."

"The important thing is that you're here now, Win," she answered.

"Miss Josephine," said Vera. "I'm truly sorry if I caused you hurt. I thought I was doing the right thing. I should have known better. I hope you won't be mad at me forever."

"It's all right, Vera. I'm not angry with you. Thank you for being honest with us. None of this was your fault. There are evil people in the world, and Oliver is one of them. I know you didn't have any idea that he was just using you to get what he wanted."

"What did he want out of this, Miss Josephine?" Vera asked.

"He wanted to assume the title of earl someday. He thought my husband wouldn't come home from the war, and without the baby, Oliver would be the next in line to inherit. Do you understand?"

"Yes. I do, indeed, my lady. What a wretched, beastly thing to do. I hope Scotland Yard makes him pay for what he did."

"They will, Vera. Don't worry about that," answered Win.

"Mrs. Whitaker," Win asked, "where does your sister Emily live?"

"Why, in Kensington, of course, Jay. Where so many up-market families live. Would you like her address?"

"Yes. Yes, I would. Did you take our son, Andrew, to your sister's house? If so, how did you reach London?"

"Yes, Jay, I took him. He was right well taken care of, too. I wrapped him in his soft blanket, and he wore a little knit cap on his head. I knitted it for him," she pronounced with pride. "Oliver met me down the road from the cottage where your wife been living. He took me to the station in the next village over. Cloverhill. I boarded a train there, and before I knew it, there I was at Charing Cross Station. Aren't railroads wonderful?"

"So, then you went directly to your sister's home?"

"Yes, Jay. Oliver even gave me money to take a taxicab, so I didn't have to ride the tube. At the time, I figured it was right nice of him to do that. Now I don't think so though. He's a very bad person."

"Very bad, indeed," Win replied. "So, you took Andrew to Emily's home. Was that all there was to the journey?"

"Well, yes, Jay. I stayed a while to make sure everything was right and proper ready for little Andrew. Emily was very excited. I told you, she'd fixed up a very pretty nursery for him. But then it was time for me to catch the return train, so I told them goodbye. I even had money to take a taxicab back to the station."

"And you returned to Winthrop Manor and never said a word to anyone?"

"No, Jay. Except for Oliver, of course. I reported to him, and he told me he was very proud of me. 'I'm very, very proud of you, Mrs. Whitaker'. Those were his exact words." She seemed thrilled to have received praise from him.

"Well, I do thank you, Mrs. Whitaker. Josephine and I shall take it from here. You have been a great help."

"Am I in trouble, Jay? Are the Scotland police going to come to take me away?"

"No, Vera, I don't believe so. They may speak to you, but I don't think you should have fear of being in trouble," he said kindly.

With that, Win took his wife's hand, and they left the kitchen area and hurried up the stairway to the first level. Thankfully, he ran into his father almost immediately.

"Win! My God! I can't believe my eyes. We thought for certain we'd lost you," cried the Lord Winthrop.

"No, I'm safe. I was a POW, but I escaped. More about that later. Right now, I've got to retrieve my son."

"Your son? Nobody knows where he is," the Lord Winthrop said, looking confused.

"Yes. We do now. Mrs. Whitaker had the details we needed. Oliver was behind all of this. Where the hell is he?"

"Still in the drawing room, I believe. Talking with the chap from Scotland Yard."

"Just don't let him near Mrs. Whitaker. Summon the inspector, and speak to him alone. Tell him I know everything. Give them this address in London." Win handed the scrap of paper to his father. He had the address for Emily's sister memorised. "This is where my son should be. We're on our way there now."

The Lord Winthrop looked terribly confused but agreed to follow Win's instructions.

"We'll be back just as soon as we've retrieved Andrew. I don't want Oliver to have time to think up some sort of excuse, so whatever you do, keep the information from him. Also, don't let he and Mrs. Whitaker speak to each other."

Win took hold of his wife's hand, and together, they rushed from the house.

"Wait, Win," his father called. "Are you heading to London?"

"Yes, Father, of course. I'm going to bring my son home."

Late that night, Win and Josephine returned to Winthrop Manor. Josephine held baby Andrew in her arms. It had been a mad dash to London, but Mrs. Whitaker's sister, Emily Dawson, proved to be easy to deal with and extremely understanding. Win had explained the wretched scheme that Oliver had planned. Naturally, Mrs. Dawson had been under the impression the baby was a result of a young, unwed girl and a man who'd refused to marry her. It came as a frightening revelation that the baby was actually the offspring of a viscount and his viscountess. While she'd grown exceptionally fond of the child already, Win gave his solemn promise she would be allowed to see Andrew whenever she chose, although such a reunion would have to take place at the Winthrop home.

Emily understood the situation and felt remorse for the heartache she had unwillingly been a part of, due to her agreement to take custody of the child. Thus, there was no delay in the return of the infant.

When they reached Winthrop Manor, Win assisted his wife and child from the vehicle, and they went inside. As luck would have it, Oliver and the detectives from Scotland Yard were still there. Win strode ahead, into the drawing room.

"We've just returned from London and are aware of the evil you've committed. What sort of a person could let his own nephew be adopted by other people, in order to assure that he could become the next earl?" Win shouted when he saw his brother.

Josephine handed Andrew to Win and ran over to Oliver, beating him on the chest as hard as her tiny hands could move. The Lord Winthrop gently pulled her away and then turned toward the inspectors. He made it clear he did not want them to go light on Oliver. He hoped Oliver was about to pay a severe penalty. What he had done had been vicious and cruel.

The physician, Dr. Drew, had also been summoned to the residence. The Lady Winthrop requested that he evaluate Mrs. Whitaker and give some sort of rationale behind her odd behaviour. After spending over an hour speaking with her, he came away certain she suffered from some sort of brain malady. Whether it was due to her age or something more serious, such as a brain growth or some another disease, he wasn't able to determine.

"All I'm able to tell you with certainty, madam, is that the poor woman is definitely not able to think clearly. We don't have ways of determining exactly what the problem is or the extent to which she suffers from dementia, but I highly recommend she be removed from further duties."

"Oh, but, Dr. Drew, she has been like a member of our family for decades. She isn't going to understand why we're taking her away from her beloved kitchen duties," Win's mother replied.

"Simply be kind, milady. You needn't try to explain that she shows signs of mental decline. Tell her she needs rest. She's worked long and hard and performed excellently. Don't send her away from Winthrop Manor."

"I would never think of sending her away from us. She'll be given a comfortable room here, and if a companion is needn't for further care, she shall have one."

❧❧

Josephine and Win, along with little Andrew, were standing in the great hall, as Mrs. Whitaker ascended the stairway from the kitchen to kiss and cuddle the child. She seemed completely unaware of the part she had played in causing heartache to Win and Josephine. Win's mother planned to kindly take her to the drawing room, give her a nice cup of tea, and explain that she was going to be retiring to a life of comfort. Most importantly, she would know that Winthrop Manor would always be her home.

While standing in the great hall, the Lord Winthrop asked Win and Josephine whether they would please consider returning to the live at the estate permanently. "This will be your home someday. Let your son grow up here, please. Your mother and I will move to the dower house. Let us try to be a family, Win. That's the way it always should have been. We were very, very remiss in our reaction to your marriage. We know that now. Let us try to make it up to you. We won't interfere with your life. Please, do think carefully about such a move."

"Not at present. I'm not certain what our plans will be," Win replied. "It's possible. We need to be alone for a spell. I must spend time with my son.

He's nearing a year old. Josephine has to recover from the ordeal she's been through. We'll discuss the possibility of returning to live here at a later date."

As Josephine and Win prepared to return to their cottage, each grandparent kissed Andrew. Mrs. Whitaker watched them as they left Winthrop Manor through the front entry. Oliver was being escorted through the front entry, as well, with handcuffs clasped firmly on his wrists, his arms secured behind his back. They had arrested him on the charge of kidnapping. The Lord Winthrop said he would not even contact a barrister on his son's behalf. Oliver was basically on his own.

Win and Josephine left Winthrop Manor and walked toward the automobile. Josephine cuddled her precious son in her arms.

"Jay," Mrs. Whitaker called from the front doorway. "Would you like me to send some cookies home with you? The baby might like them. You did at that age."

THE END

About The Author

Mary Christian Payne was highly successful in several management positions in Fortune 500 Companies, in New York City, St. Louis, Missouri, Orlando Florida, and Tulsa, Oklahoma. Her work included Grant writing, and designing and writing Training Manuals for Executive Training Programs.

She left the corporate world, and became Director of Career Development at the Women' Resource Center at the University of Tulsa, where she designed a program that enabled hundreds of adult women to return to college and better their lives. She received the Mayor's Pinnacle Award in 1993 for this achievement. Mary left that position when the Center closed, and then opened her own Career Counseling Center. She retired in 2008.

Mary Christian Payne became a successful, best-selling author at the age of 71, with the help of her publisher, Tom Corson-Knowles. All of her life, she had wanted to write, and had received accolades for her unpublished work. She was encouraged in college, and writing was a significant part of the various jobs she held.

In 2013, she read Tom Corson-Knowles' book about publishing on Kindle. She wrote to him and he telephoned her. The rest is history. Since that time, she has published nine books, with more on the way.

Mary lost her husband in June 2015, after 33 years of marriage. The grief process brought a lull to her writing, but she found that putting words on paper helped immensely. She is now in the process of writing her second novel since his death. She lives in Tulsa, Oklahoma, with her two beloved Maltese dogs.

Sign up for the newsletter to get news, updates and new release info from Mary Christian Payne: **www.TCKPublishing.com/mary**

Get Book Deals
and Discounts

Get discounts and special deals on books at

www.tckpublishing.com/bookdeals

Other Books by
Mary Christian Payne

❧❧

THE SOMERVILLE TRILOGY
Willow Grove Abbey: Book 1 of the Somerville Trilogy
St. James Road: Book 2 of the Somerville Trilogy
Serendipity: Book 3 of the Somerville Trilogy

THE CLAYBOURNE TRILOGY
The White Feather: Book 1 of the Claybourne Trilogy
The White Butterfly: Book 2 of the Claybourne Trilogy
White Cliffs of Dover: Book 3 of the Claybourne Trilogy

THE THORNTON TRILOGY
No Regrets: Book 1 of The Thornton Trilogy
No Gentleman: Book 2 of the Thornton Trilogy
No Secrets: Book 3 of the Thornton Trilogy

THE HERRINGTON TRILOGY
Picture of Innocence: Book 1 of The Herrington Trilogy
Picture of Intrigue: Book 2 of the Herrington Trilogy
Picture of a Dream: Book 3 of the Herrington Trilogy

Printed in Great Britain
by Amazon

46269292R00116